Created by
WARREN MURPHY
and RICHARD SAPIR

THE Destroyer ™

AMERICAN OBSESSION

#109

The Destroyer fights the battle of the bulge...

GOLD EAGLE·63224
$5.50 U.S./$6.50 CAN.

ISBN 0-373-63224-X

9 780373 632244

50550

THE RICH AND THE BEAUTIFUL

Puma Lee lifted her leg, marveling at the swell of her own thigh muscles, the glorious definition. Her tanned, oiled skin shone like silk. On her face was an expression of perfect delight.

"Where's Chiz?" she asked her attorney, Jimmy Koch-Roche.

"He still doesn't answer his car phone. I hope he didn't have an accident on the way...."

A rap on the outside of the driver window interrupted him. The attorney turned to face a uniformed officer, then hit the power button to lower the window.

"Today is definitely your lucky day, Jimmy," the cop said. "Ms. Lee's husband was picked up a few minutes ago at a convenience store in Hollywood."

"On what charge?"

"Nine counts of first-degree murder. And they got the whole thing on the store's closed-circuit video. Major ugly. He gave up without a struggle, though."

The officer looked past the attorney, around the Jag's headrest, into the back seat. "Sorry to bring you such bad news, ma'am," he said to the screen goddess.

Created by
WARREN MURPHY
and RICHARD SAPIR

THE

Destroyer™

AMERICAN OBSESSION

A GOLD EAGLE BOOK FROM

WORLDWIDE®

TORONTO • NEW YORK • LONDON
AMSTERDAM • PARIS • SYDNEY • HAMBURG
STOCKHOLM • ATHENS • TOKYO • MILAN
MADRID • WARSAW • BUDAPEST • AUCKLAND

First edition October 1997
ISBN 0-373-63224-X

Special thanks and acknowledgment to
Alan Philipson for his contribution to this work.

AMERICAN OBSESSION

Printed in U.S.A.

To the greater glory of the
illustrious House of Sinanju

PROLOGUE

From the top of the white granite campanile, a great bell tolled twice. The quavery tones echoed around the wide brick quadrangle that formed the core of the Purblind University campus. With its lecture halls' stately parapets, steeply sloping roofs, tall windows and ivy-covered walls, as well as its broad, curving walkways, Purblind seemed an idealized vision of an American institution of higher learning. Under the whistle of the winter wind, one could almost hear a sweater-clad glee club humming a rousing drinking song.

But appearances could be deceptive.

There was no glee club at Purblind University.

Nor was there a tower bell. The peals came from a digital recording of a sixteenth-century church clock in Bruges, Belgium, and the recording was amplified and played through huge audio speakers concealed in the top of the campanile.

Likewise, Purblind had no athletic teams.

No school paper.

No school colors.

Purblind University was a research institution. A knowledge factory. Which meant it was devoted to the study of one subject: the making of money. Students, and particularly undergraduate students, were considered a regrettable annoyance by professors and administrators because they drained away time and energy that might have been more profitably spent on the development of patentable products and processes. Products and processes that could be licensed to commercial interests. The name of the game at Purblind was royalties.

Most of the university's funding came from faceless corporate donors or research partners. The Agro-Chemical Information Council. The National Cybertronics Consortium. The American Meat Board. The Dairy Consumption Task Force. The International Society for Pharmaceutical Advancement.

In its ten years of existence, P.U.'s basic-research successes had produced a parade of well-known consumer products: One Million Flushes Toilet Bowl Cleaner; Perpetu-Wrap, an infinitely reusable synthetic gift-wrap material; Your New Face, a noninvasive, do-it-yourself home-plastic-surgery kit based on Perpetu-Wrap technology; All-White Chicken, genetically engineered to have vestigial legs and thighs; and PG-5, widely used as a freshness stabilizer for processed food, as a UV protectant for outdoor house paint and, in high concentrations, as a chemical-warfare nerve agent. The school's individual triumphs could have easily stocked the shelves of a gas-station minimart.

As the recorded bell tones faded into the distance, professors and their graduate-student assistants single-filed, like so many families of white ducks, out of the cafeteria in their lab coats and into the chill, dark February afternoon. Inside the steamy warmth of the cafeteria, a few undergraduates lingered over the dregs of their café mochas. As they commiserated over the trials of life at old P.U., a scrawny, balding scarecrow of a man entered via a side door and passed through the turnstile into the food-service area. His skin was pale as milk and liberally dotted with brown moles of various sizes. The skinny scientist carried with him a truly awesome odor. Not quite as meaty as skunk. Not quite as fecal as civet cat. It crept through the cafeteria like a noxious fog.

"Jee-zus!" one of the students gasped as he clamped a hand defensively over his nose and mouth. "How can that dweeb stand himself?"

"Why don't you go over and ask him?" suggested the undergrad sitting on the other side of the table.

"Uh-uh," the first student replied, sweeping his notebooks into his day pack and scraping back his chair. "If I don't get out of here quick, I'm gonna hurl."

The sentiment was universal.

Breathing through their mouths, the lunchtime stragglers rushed past the cash register for the exits.

The hapless cashier remained trapped at her post. Her face flushed deep red as she watched the scarecrow man mull over the day's hot selections. The cafeteria servers, plump middle-aged women in disposable plastic hair caps and gloves, had already made themselves scarce, as they always did whenever "Professor Polecat" appeared.

The scientist's campus nickname was, in fact, doubly erroneous. Carlos Sternovsky was a research assistant, not a professor, and he didn't work with *Mephitis mephitis*, the striped skunk, but rather with *Gulo gulo*, the wolverine. Same taxonomic family, Mustelidae, but different subfamily and species.

Sternovsky helped himself from the stainless-steel tray of simmering pork goulash, then to steamed brussels sprouts, to a whole-wheat dinner roll and a dish of Jell-O fruit salad. For him, the food had no aroma and virtually no taste. A childhood virus had destroyed his sense of smell, and with it, the ability to distinguish complex flavors. Despite the loss, he still felt hunger, and he appeased it every five or six hours in as rational a way as possible, based on the prevailing theory of proper diet composition: the food pyramid.

The cashier grimaced as he took the time to count out exact change. Her expression said, *God, don't you ever wash?* She was a simple, ignorant undergrad. Of course he washed. And he changed his lab coats daily. But washing and changing never did any good because of the chemical nature of the odor. The oil-based, superconcentrated musk spray had to wear off his skin, like layers of paint—and because he was constantly reexposed to it, that never happened.

She took the money from him but didn't put it in the register. It went first into one airtight bag. Then that sealed bag went into another. As he turned away with his tray, she was looking frantically under the counter for something to wipe off her hands with.

Though he could have sat down anywhere, Sternovsky took his usual seat at his usual table. He felt no anticipatory pleasure as he stared down at the paprika-seasoned meat stew. He got no enjoyment from chewing and swallowing the meat, either, but he did feel relief as the gnawing pains in his belly gradually subsided. The only sound in the cavernous hall was the scraping of a cheap metal knife and fork against a thick, institutional-ceramic plate. He finished the last spoonful of lime Jell-O and wiped his mouth with a paper napkin. When he looked around, the place was deserted. The cashier had slipped away while his back was turned. That didn't surprise him. He was used to being shunned. For the year and a half he'd been employed by Purblind, he'd endured official and unofficial scorn on a daily basis.

Six more months remained on his contract with the school's biochemistry department. According to the fine print in that eight-page, single-spaced document, for the princely sum of $16,500 a year the university held title to every thought in his head. Never mind the fact that his research supervisor had undermined his work from day one, and through funding cutbacks had tried to force him to abandon his chosen line of inquiry and move on to something more "promising."

Sternovsky had swum alone and against the current for more than a year before achieving the initial breakthrough in his research. Despite the encouraging results, despite his monumental solo effort, on the recommendation of his supervisor the biochem department had flatly refused to underwrite the cost of a primate testing program. For Sternovsky, it was a teeth-rattling slap in the mouth.

In the end, he had paid for Arnold, his pygmy chimpanzee, out of his own pocket, this by downgrading his transportation, by spending the last of a small inheritance and by maxing out all his credit cards. When the primate study began to bear fruit, the embittered scientist had kept the news from his supervisor. He knew if the department got interested in his research at this late stage, Purblind U. would steal all credit for the discovery. His doubting Thomas overseer would claim the Nobel. The university would suck up the commercial royalties, which could, over time, run into billions of dollars. And for all his trouble and pain, he would be put onto the street without so much as a thank-you when his employment contract ran out. Or even before, if they could prove he'd misappropriated so much as a rusty paper clip.

Sternovsky bussed his tray and tossed his napkin into the recycle bin.

It was his last lunch at good old P.U.

As THE BIOCHEMIST TREKKED back to his lab, an icy wind flapped his khaki slacks against a pair of calves as thin as flagpoles. On either side of him, columns of steam billowed like Yellowstone geysers from grated vents set in the sprawling lawns. Beneath the soggy sod and the winding brick walkway was an anthill of underground levels that housed the university's main laboratories.

Because of the oppressive stench of his research animals, Sternovsky had been consigned to a temporary trailer on the outermost fringe of the campus, in the farthest corner of Parking Lot ZZ. Following the recent winter storm, the university's snowplow had scraped the asphalt clean, leaving piles of dirty snow heaped in the shade around the base of the trailer, blocking access to the wooden steps. Days had passed since the plow operator's little joke, but the compacted snow had yet to melt. To reach the trailer's door, Sternovsky had to follow the path he'd beaten through the waist-high slush.

Though he normally kept his laboratory scrupulously neat and as sterile as an operating room, today the long, narrow room looked as though a whirlwind had swept through it. A tricolor of gore, excrement and yellow-green musk splattered the walls and tracked the aisles between worktables. Steel cage doors stood ajar, and already-sacrificed wolverines lay sprawled on countertops or in heaps on the sheet vinyl floor.

The dead animals were roughly three and a half feet long, counting their short, thickly furred tails. Their coats were blackish brown, with light brown bands along both sides of the body from shoulder to rump; the light-colored bands joined each other across the base of the tail. The creatures had short, massive legs and wide feet tipped with huge claws. With their bony skulls, small, rounded ears and stubby muzzles, their heads looked almost bearlike. Native Americans referred to them as ''skunk bears,'' for reasons obvious to anyone with a functioning nose.

Before his lunch break, Sternovsky had harvested all but three of his lab subjects. Now it was time to finish the job. He donned a gray rubber smock and knee boots, a plastic face shield and leather gauntlets. From the steel sink, he retrieved an enameled tray that held a half-dozen loaded syringes. The fluid in the disposable hypodermics was the palest of pale blues.

Blue as a cloudless summer sky.

Heart-stopping blue.

He moved gingerly down the slick aisle toward the last two cages in the row. Excited by the smell of blood and the sound of his approach, the surviving animals growled and screeched. The sixty-five-pound male wolverine he'd named Donny was well into his second hour of mating with the much smaller Marie. It sometimes took as long as two hours for the animals to complete the reproductive act. Prolonged and vigorous mating caused female wolverines to ovulate; as it turned out, the accompanying changes in levels of hormone production were the key to Sternovsky's breakthrough. To pin and hold the knotted wolverines hard against the inside of the bars, he pulled the lever on the cage's built-in trap, which provided safe access for superficial examinations—and injections.

Donny kept humping even as Sternovsky slid the needle into his shoulder. When the scientist pushed in the plunger, the wolverine let out a scream, arched his matted tail and sprayed yellow-green gunk from his anal gland. Donny's wickedly curved fangs and four-inch claws scored the steel bars with fresh, bright scars. Like a wind-up doll ticking down, his frantic hip movements slowed, and his tongue lolled out of the side of his mouth. Then he began to quiver all over; not in ecstasy, but in the convulsive throes of death. Sternovsky made a luckier hit on Marie, injecting her in a vein, and she gave up the ghost at once.

After moving their limp forms from the cage to the nearby countertop, Sternovsky quickly shaved their heads with an electric razor, doused the bare white skin with orange disinfectant, then sliced their skulls open with a battery-powered autopsy saw, leaving the cap of bone to hang back by an attached flap of scalp. The treasure he sought lay at the base of their brains, a bit of differentiated tissue called the hypothalamus. He deftly scooped out the tissue with a sterilized melon-baller and plopped the pair of warm, bloody gobbets into prelabeled plastic jars. He would trim away the unnecessary tissue later, at his leisure.

The scientist paused in front of the last cage. He was breathing so hard he fogged up the inside of his face shield. He had to flip it out of the way in order to see the huddled, hairy form of Arnold at the back of the steel pen. Though *Gulo gulo* were powerful and fearsome creatures—on a whim, evolution had made dachshunds out of grizzly bears—the pygmy chimpanzee was the test animal that really scared him; in fact, he had recurring, wake-up-screaming nightmares about Arnold getting loose in the grad-student dormitory.

Barely three feet tall, the chimp currently weighed in at 160 pounds—twice the normal size for his species. Arnold was neither cute nor cuddly. He was a nearly perfect cube of densely corded, evil-tempered muscle. With Arnold, there was none of the sign language, sensitive-fellow-primate, Discovery Channel doo-dah. The glint in his squinty, root-beer brown eyes said only one thing: *I want to hurt you.*

Sternovsky didn't reach for the cage's lever. Compressing the chimp with the built-in trap was no longer possible, as he'd learned to resist such efforts with his tree-trunk legs. Sternovsky didn't attempt to use a prod to administer the lethal injection. No hypodermic needle could penetrate Arnold's thick muscles without breaking off.

And yet the job had to be done.

The scientist put the tray of syringes down on the countertop and picked up a yard-long piece of Parkerized steel pipe he'd borrowed from the university's marine-sciences department. It was a bang-stick—a bare-bones, stockless 12-gauge designed to serve as an underwater defense against attacking sharks. The weapon had no visible trigger; instead, it fired one high-brass shotgun shell when the muzzle was rammed against its intended target. Holding the bang-stick by its Hypalon grip, Sternovsky pulled the cotter-pin safety and let it dangle by its thong. From the back of the cage, Arnold glared at him.

The scientist felt suddenly queasy. This chimp was no dim-witted shark. When you stuck something into his cage, he grabbed for it. And he was quick. His forearms were easily as big as Sternovsky's thighs; with hand strength alone, he had bowed the cage's braced, 440A stainless-steel bars. If he decided to, the chimp could easily pull the offending bang-stick away—or worse, use it to jerk his keeper within reach. The scientist didn't doubt that Arnold had the power to tear a human arm from its socket, and that he would do so with relish, if given the opportunity.

From the side pocket of his rubber apron, Sternovsky took a large, misshapen fast-food sandwich. The grease on Arnold's favorite treat, long since congealed, had melted the bun to mush and turned the wrapping paper translucent. As Sternovsky waved the three-quarter-pound, triple-bacon-and-cheese burger back and forth, the chimp sniffed the air with keen interest.

When Arnold stirred himself from the back of the cage, eyes on the prize, the scientist thrust the bang-stick through the bars. Before the chimp could seize the barrel and bend it into a pretzel, Sternovsky rammed the muzzle between his burly pectorals. A rocking blast lifted the huge ape, bounced him off the bars at the rear of the cage and sent him crashing face first to the mesh floor. Amazingly, even though it was a contact wound, there was no through-and-through, no grisly splatter across the trailer's wall. Arnold's massive back muscles contained all the double-aught buckshot.

With profound relief, Sternovsky watched the blood drain from the motionless body. He didn't open the cage door until he was certain that the beast was dead and his own hands had stopped shaking. Dragging the corpse from the cage, he quickly shaved and sawed open the skull, then used the power tool to make a Y-shaped incision below the powder-blackened entry wound. Working quickly, he took minute samples of various organs and tissues for later analysis.

The lab seemed eerily quiet as he emptied the refrigerator, transferring small racks of glass vials of wolverine hormones—extracted for certain targeted neuropeptides—and the chimp-tissue sampler into a six-pack cooler marked Biological Specimens. After packing the cooler with dry ice, he sealed the lid with duct tape and affixed the necessary prestamped export documentation from the U.S. Department of the Interior.

After stuffing his backpack with a six-inch-thick stack of floppy disks that held all his experimental data and research notes, he began erasing his laboratory computer's hard drive. While the autodestruct program was running, he stripped down to his jockey shorts in front of the sink and, using a gallon of tomato juice, scrubbed himself raw. Washing with tomato juice supposedly countered the stench of musk spray. Because he couldn't tell if it had worked or not, he doused himself liberally with Old Spice before putting on baggy tan corduroy pants, a rumpled brown cord sports jacket, a blue polyester dress shirt and a skinny red knit tie. Before Sternovsky left the trailer, to make extrasure that no one at Purblind could recover his research data, he reloaded the bangstick and blasted the drive tower into a thousand pieces.

His Toyota was the only car in Parking Lot ZZ.

Rust spots on hood, roof and fenders bled through the silver blue paint of the 1978 Celica two-door, which had replaced the three-year-old Saturn he'd sold in order to fund his primate study. Opening the driver's door, he leaned in and put the cooler and backpack on the rear bench seat, beside a small canvas suitcase. As he carefully folded himself into the blue-faux-fur-covered bucket seat, the top of his skull brushed the headliner, disarranging his thready comb-over. The Celica was a tight fit for him—even with the front seat as far back as it would go, his knees bracketed the steering wheel. The windshield resembled the view slit of a World War II artillery bunker.

After an uncomfortable forty-minute drive, Sternovsky arrived at the Philadelphia airport. He parked the Toyota by the curb, in the passenger-unloading tow-away zone. As he entered the terminal, he dropped the car keys into a trash can. Once inside, Sternovsky followed the overhead signs to the Pan Asian Airlines ticket counter. There was no one ahead of him in the roped-off queue.

On the other side of the service counter a button-cute Oriental female in a blue blazer chirped a sneeze into a Kleenex before asking for his travel documents. She displayed efficient two-handed work at the computer keyboard, cheerily confirming his seat assignment and checking through his small suitcase. Sternovsky, the smell-leper, was not used to such cordial treatment from strangers. It made him feel a bit giddy.

The ticket clerk handed him his passport, export papers and boarding pass. Despite her heavy head cold, she smiled brightly and said, ''Enjoy your visit to Taiwan.''

1

Naked but for a gargantuan jockstrap, Bradley "the Fighting Vehicle" Boomtower stood in front of his spanking-new locker. Its hooks and shelves held the tools of his trade: shoulder pads, knee pads, elbow pads, a selection of size-18 cleated athletic shoes, a pumpkin orange helmet and matching uniform shirt with the number 96, front and back, and ninja black uniform pants.

The garish team colors, also evident in the locker room's paint and carpet, were no mere accident of bad taste. The owners of the L.A. Riots, professional football's most recent expansion franchise, had shelled out big bucks in order to develop an organizational image that was marketable right out of the box. The Halloween theme was further underscored by the team's official motto, Trick Or Treat.

With two hours until kickoff, Boomtower's fellow Riots were obsessively focused on "Trick." As harried trainers taped up their ankles, wrists and hands, they bellowed dire threats against the opposing players. This while Boomtower drifted, alone and oarless, in 'Treat.'' On the floor at his feet lay a pile of crumpled plastic wrappers and a litter of green-and-white waxed-paper boxes. The sides of the boxes read Manteca, a Spanish word that sounded much classier, and more dietetically correct, than the English equivalent. Boomtower's eyes slitted with pleasure as he sucked at the nub end of what had once been a one-pound block of white lard.

Between muttered mantras and reciprocal helmet-to-helmet head-bangs, the other Riots stole furtive looks at Number 96. Over the course of a week, Bradley Boomtower had undergone a most startling physical transformation. The six-foot-five-inch, 370-pound nose tackle, whose midsection-circling, jiggling mass of blubber had been a personal trademark since his college days, had gained more than a hundred pounds.

Strange, yes.

Unheard-of, yes.

But stranger still was the fact that in just seven days his more than thirty percent body fat had all but disappeared. With his skin suddenly shrink-wrapped over layers of bulging muscles, Boomtower had acquired the ''cut'' look of a world-champion bodybuilder. Only he was bigger. Hugely bigger.

Beyond Mr. Universe.

Beyond Animal.

During the week's final practice, there had been no stopping his pass rush. It didn't matter if he was triple- or even quadruple-teamed. Like a man playing with small boys, he mowed down the offensive line. He did it so many times that the head coach had to yank him from the scrimmage for fear someone might be seriously hurt. Since then, for the very same reason, the L.A. Riots had given their nose tackle an extrawide berth.

As gametime approached, only Boomtower's locker neighbor, a high-draft-pick, rookie running back, had the nerve—or lack of good sense—to directly address the changed man. Unable to restrain his curiosity about all the green-and-white boxes, Regional Parks said, "Hey, F.V., what's that nasty-looking stuff you're eating?"

By way of answer, Boomtower toed one of the empty cartons toward the running back. Parks picked it up. When he read the label, his jaw dropped.

"Man, have you lost your mind?" the star running back exclaimed. "This crap is nothing but sweepings. It's the hog fat that falls on the butcher-shop floor."

"What's your point?" Boomtower said as he inside-outed the plastic wrapper so he could lick it clean.

"Jeez, everybody knows it's artery-clogging poison. It's heart-attack city."

"Nah, it's energy food."

Number 96 mopped his grease-ringed mouth with an orange-and-black towel, then pulled his L.A. Riots jersey over his head. Since high school, his XXXL uniform shirt had always been stretched as tight as a sausage casing. It still was, only now it conformed to a different shape. Instead of hanging like a half-inflated truck tire around his waist, the main mass of his torso had taken a two-and-a-half-foot jump to his chest and shoulders. Under the tortured Lycra-blend orange fabric, the topography of monstrous lats, delts, abs and pecs was clearly visible.

With the ice broken by the rookie, other players in various stages of battle dress began to gather around the nose tackle's locker, admiration and awe on their faces. At five hundred pounds—stripped weight—Bradley Boomtower was easily the heaviest man ever to play professional football. And in football, heavy was good, if not God. The more you weighed, the harder you were to move or deflect—by the fourth quarter of a game, a ten percent weight advantage could reduce opponents to quivering lumps of jelly.

One of the linebackers pointed at the gear still hanging in Boomtower's locker. Half-laughing, he said, "Say, F.V., didn't you forget something?"

All eyes shifted from the locker to Boomtower's shoulders. Given his grossly overdeveloped deltoid muscles, it was difficult to tell whether he was wearing any protection under the jersey.

"Fuck the pads, you know what I'm sayin'?" Boomtower replied.

The L.A. Riots exchanged uncomfortable glances. The physical transformation they'd witnessed was not natural. Boomtower had to be taking *something*. As professional athletes, they knew all about performance-enhancing drugs and their side effects, which included irrational behavior.

As Boomtower reached for his uniform pants, the fearless running back pointed at his backside and said, "What's that stuck on your butt? It looks like a time-release patch. Are you on some new kind of steroid? Human growth hormones?"

Boomtower patted the two-by-two-inch square of pink adhesive bandage. "It's magic, you know what I'm sayin'?"

"What kind of magic is that?" Parks asked.

The players edged in closer, straining to hear.

"Cutting edge. I eat nothin' but fat and I get thin. The more fat I eat, the thinner I get. Thinner and bigger. And I got my mind on the game, you know what I'm sayin'?"

"Uh, not exactly," the rookie admitted.

Moving quick as a cat, Boomtower provided a demonstration. He snatched hold of a 275-pound defensive end by the back of his trouser waistband. Then, with one hand and a seemingly effortless upward thrust, like he was hoisting nothing more substantial than a broomstick, he bashed the man's unhelmeted head through the gridwork of orange acoustic ceiling tiles. With nightcrawler-sized veins popping out on his massive right arm, Boomtower held the guy trapped there while he helplessly thrashed and kicked. "Now, do you know what I'm sayin'?" he asked his teammates.

There was a stunned silence in the locker room.

Boomtower carefully set down the defensive end. Flecks of orange paint stuck to the man's face, and a trickle of blood from a cut on his forehead ran down and off the tip of his nose.

"Who'd you score it off?" the Riots' center asked.

The Fighting Vehicle shook his head. "That's a secret."

"You got any more?" demanded the confetti-speckled, bloody-faced defensive end.

"Yeah, I got more, but this stuff ain't cheap, you know what I'm sayin'?"

"How much?"

"Twenty-five hundred a pop. One pop a day. Run you around one mill a year to stay on the program."

The players made a mad dash for their respective lockers. In a matter of seconds, thick wads of cash appeared from all sides; Boomtower's teammates fanned him with greenbacks like an Oriental emperor.

"Fuck that shit!" said Regional Parks as he removed both of his diamond ear studs. He slapped the pea-sized gems into Bradley Boomtower's open palm and said, "I'll take all the extra magic you got."

2

His name was Remo, and he knew he was being stalked.

A late-model, four-door gray sedan crept along the city street thirty yards behind him. Relying on his years of training in Sinanju, the oldest of the martial arts, Remo crossed with the traffic light, taking the briefest of sideways looks as he passed the car. There were four heads inside, and beneath the heads were four extremely large bodies. In that same blink of an eye, his mind registered the car's proximity to the pavement, a function of overloaded shocks and springs.

Under similar circumstances, a normal person would have been alarmed, if not panicked. What with its indigenous ethnic gangs and freelance psychopaths, Los Angeles had a well-deserved reputation for violence, senseless and otherwise. Yet this Remo, this wiry man in a faded black T-shirt and baggy tan chinos, strolled through Koreatown as if he didn't have a care in the world. With his whole being, he sucked in the beautiful, mild October evening and admired its smog-created, fire-orange-and-turquoise sunset. Along the parking strip to his left, 50-foot-tall palm trees jutted up from rectangular openings in the sidewalk, like widely spaced hairs on a concrete scalp.

Remo turned into a small strip mall that divided the block of two-story apartments and cut through the small parking lot. From the accumulation of stains on its asphalt, the mall was, by mall standards, ancient. No amount of scrubbing by the shopping center's current owners could remove the rainbow residue of decades of illicit midnight oil changes. The signs above the freshly repainted, chain-link-fenced storefronts were all written in Korean ideograms. The minimall housed a dry cleaner, a discount-jewelry-and-electronics store, the Kimchi Noodle Palace and Mr. Yi's fish market.

"Ah, the venerable pupil of the venerated Master of Asian cooking," said Yi as the second-greatest assassin on earth entered his narrow, spotlessly clean shop. The fishmonger had decided that these two customers were master chefs, and neither of them bothered to correct this misconception. He was short and squat, with a perpetual smile on his face. Yi smiled even when he was angry. His thick black hair was stuffed under a white golf cap; his uniform and apron were likewise white. A totally assimilated resident of central Los Angeles, he wore a belt holster clipped to the small of his wide back, and in the holster was a compact, 8-shot pistol. Like ninety-five percent of his fellow citizens, Yi had no aspirations to assassinhood; he just wanted to survive to see the weekend.

It was always cool inside Yi's shop, thanks to the white tile floor and the open beds of heavily iced seafood along the walls. The smell was of salt, bleach and iodine. Behind the glass of the refrigerated display case sat heaps of whole and filleted tuna, bonito, mackerel, sole and sea bass. Stuck in each pile of fish was a little plastic sign with Korean characters on it. In addition to the standard fare, Yi stocked some of the oddities of the Asian table. Sea cucumber. Urchin. Bloodworm. A selection of chichi bottom-crawlers for the *quesadillas* and *frittatas* of discerning, jaded Los Angelinos.

In the reflection of the refrigerator case's glass, Remo saw the gray sedan pull into the mall's lot and stop, parking sideways across the painted stripes on the asphalt. All the car doors opened, and its occupants piled out, on the run.

"I put aside for you something special," Yi told him, opening a stainless-steel cooler behind the display case. As he turned back with the prize, he said, "Today fresh from Yellow Sea."

The pewter-colored sea creature the fishmonger held up so proudly was more than three feet in length and weighed less than two pounds. But for the greenish fin that ran from behind its head to the tip of its pointed tail, it would have looked like a snake. A snake with a wicked set of upper and lower fangs and an underslung bottom jaw.

"You like for Master's dinner?" Yi said, showing Remo the firm white belly, then smoothing his hand along it.

The cutlass-fish, or hairtail, was a stone bitch to clean—imagine trying to fillet the meat from a shoestring—but it was one of Master Chiun's special favorites. The skinny fish was native to the waters around Sinanju, the Korean village where the Master had been born, nearly a century ago. Even in the late sixties, before the Korean government's rapid push to industrialization, the vicious, delicious predator had been plentiful. Due to the current availability and quality problems, the two assassins' mostly rice-and-fish diet rarely featured Yellow Sea hairtail.

Remo looked over the entire skin, checking for telltale clear blisters and weeping, bloody ulcers, evidence that the fish had been taken from polluted waters. And, to his delight, found none. "I like very much," he said to the fishmonger. "Please wrap him up."

With a matador flourish, Yi tore a sheet of white butcher paper from a big roll mounted on his cutting table. "You make Master happy meal tonight," he said as he passed the long, slender package over the counter.

As Remo stepped out of Mr. Yi's fish market, a gruff baritone voice barked, "Hold it right there."

Remo stared down the barrel of a blue-steel Beretta. It gleamed with fresh oil. Three more men stepped up on the storefront sidewalk, bracketing him with raised weapons. One held a snub-nosed nickel-plated revolver, another had a stubby-barreled combat-type pump shotgun, and the last brandished a Taser stun gun. All four were Baby Hueys, big and doughy, and dressed in what looked like official SWAT uniforms—black armored vests, black skintight leather gloves, black T-shirts and BDU pants. They had communications headsets clamped on their wide heads, and shiny gold badges hung on cords around their thick necks.

Not LAPD, Remo thought.

Stenciled in bright yellow across the front of their body armor were the words Bail Recovery Enforcement Agent.

Bounty hunters.

"Don't move," said the guy aiming the cocked 9 mm pistol at the middle of Remo's forehead. The bounty hunter's own skull was shaved to the skin, leaving a dark shadow of receding hairline. He sported a black goatee, and the tattoo on his hairy forearm bragged I Make Shit Happen. From a distance of six feet, he smelled like a cross between a burned-out coffeepot and an old cigar butt.

Remo smiled at him. Not an inscrutable smile-mask like Mr. Yi's; this baby came straight from the heart, radiating generous sympathy and warmth, and a patience that matched the serenity of the evening. Sometimes, once in a while, he found himself slipping into this persona and he wasn't quite clear why. But it made him feel as though he were floating above all problems, without taking anything from his lethal edge.

While the other three covered Remo, Goatee referred to a flimsy sheet of fax paper, holding it up to compare the blurred, virtually useless photo with the thick-wristed, 160-pound guy holding the long package. "William M. Ransom," he said.

"That's not me," Remo told him. "Whatever this is about, I think you've made a mistake."

The bounty hunter with the .357 snub-nose got a chuckle out of that.

"According to the bench warrant, Mr. Ransom," Goatee went on, "you're wanted in the state of Oregon for a little over twenty-three thousand dollars in outstanding traffic tickets. Seems you skipped bail. The contract you signed with the bondsman, a Mr. Tretheway of Portland, authorizes us to return you to that jurisdiction, by force if necessary."

"You've got the wrong guy. I'm not a bail jumper."

"You drive a 1994 white Camaro Z28 with the personalized Oregon license plate WEIRDMAN."

"No, I don't."

Goatee flicked at the fax with his Beretta's muzzle. "The police report's all right here in black-and-white.

Your whole rap sheet. Says you fancy yourself some kind of big-time Dungeons & Dragons role-player." Grinning, he aimed the pistol at the parcel under Remo's arm. "What've you got in there, Ransom? Is it your Singing Sword?"

"Maybe it's his Magic Wand," the bounty hunter with the Taser stun gun snickered. "Ooooooh, Mr. Wizard, are you going to turn us all into toads?"

"Unfortunately," Remo said, "somebody's beat me to it."

"For a skinny little shithook, you've got a real smart mouth," Pump-gun snarled. He wore his black ball cap backwards, and the adjustable white plastic tab cut deep welts into the meat of his forehead, after the style of the day. "Smart mouth's something we can fix...."

"Why don't you take a look at my ID?" Remo suggested. "That'll straighten everything out. It's in my hip pocket."

Goatee deftly removed his wallet, scanned the New Jersey driver's license, then passed it over to his colleagues.

"Well?" Remo said, holding out his hand to the last man for the return of his property.

Taser made no move to give the billfold back. "This license looks like a phony to me, and not a very good one," he said. "And the last names on these credit cards are all different. 'Remo Ito,' 'Remo Kalin,' 'Remo Barbieri.'" He checked the driver's license again. "Why don't you explain what that means, Mr. Remo?"

"Means we just scored a grand apiece," Pump-gun chimed in gleefully.

Remo felt the first stirrings of annoyance intrude on his calm. Of course the license and credit cards were fakes. They had to be. That was one of the problems with being declared dead prematurely: your real name got buried along with the empty coffin. Officially, Remo *Williams* was a former Newark cop who had been electrocuted more than two decades ago by the state of New Jersey for a murder he didn't commit. Electrocuted and then resurrected so he could serve as a roving hitman for CURE, an ultrasecret, virtually autonomous intelligence-gathering, crime-fighting organization. The fact that the ID he now carried was so laughably poor could be laid at the feet of his one and only boss for all those years. Recently, Dr. Harold Smith had refused to pay for any more top-quality documents, accusing his assassin-employee of going through assumed identities "like Milk Duds." Remo suspected that Smith had started doing the forgery himself, to save money. To make matters worse on the annoyance front, the long package was starting to leak; hairtail slime was slowly dripping down the inside of Remo's arm.

"I say we cuff him nice and tight," Goatee said, "stick him in the trunk and haul his sorry ass up to Portland to collect our dough."

The quartet of Baby Hueys began to close in.

Remo decided it was time to make his excuses—and his exit. "The road trip sounds great, a real hoot," he told them, "but I've got to get home to cook this puppy." He opened the end of the package and showed them the green-fanged snake head.

"Christ on a crutch!" Snub-gun exclaimed.

"It's probably part of one of his twisted black-magic rituals," Taser said.

"I think we ought to pound the little bastard flat and fold him twice before we stash him in the trunk," Goatee suggested. "I think it'd do him a world of good."

At this point, Mr. Yi appeared in the shop doorway, smiling as big as all outdoors.

"Stay back, this is official business," Snub-gun growled, holding up his phony gold badge for Yi to see.

Remo spoke a few words of fractured Korean, asking Yi to please not concern himself with this unimportant matter, that it was under control.

"I call 911?" Yi offered.

"Ask for two ambulances," Remo said. "These guys won't all fit into one."

"What was that mumbo jumbo you laid on the gook?" Taser snapped as the still-smiling Yi retreated into his shop.

"I told him you're mistaking me for somebody

else. Better take a closer look, before something bad happens..."

"The shrimpboat's trying to tell us he works out," Pump-gun scoffed.

"Looks to me like he does wrist curls, big time, and forgets about the rest," Goatee said. "Some reason for that?"

"It's all in the wrist," Remo confided.

"Did this peckerwood threaten us?" Snub-gun said, outraged as the idea finally sank in. "I think he just threatened us!"

"Let's take him down," Pump-gun urged.

Taser had a better suggestion. "Shit, let's do a Rodney on him."

While Taser kept Remo covered, the others put away their guns and pulled out black rubber truncheons.

Snub-gun waggled his foot-long sap under Remo's nose and said, "Role-play this...." The bounty hunter thought for sure he had a solid grip on his trusty truncheon, but then it was gone, vanished, his hand empty. Just as suddenly, the blunt weapon reappeared out of the ether, its lead-weighted tip violently colliding with the point of his chin. With a bone-splintering crunch, his jaw hinges gave way and flying teeth skittered across the sidewalk.

"Muhhhh!" he cried, clutching his face in both hands.

It all happened so quickly that it caught the other bounty-hunters flat-footed.

Taser recovered first. He aimed the stun gun at Remo's chest and fired from a can't-miss distance of six feet. With a *phut* of compressed air, the microdarts launched, trailing the fine copper wires that connected them to the hand-held power source.

Remo could see the little darts racing for his chest. At just the right instant, he blew a quick puff of breath. As the burst of air escaped his lips, it cracked like a small-caliber gunshot. The *chi*-powered gust veered the tiny missiles wide of their intended target.

Goatee shrieked as the twin darts caught him in the top of the right thigh, sending fifty-thousand volts coursing through his body. For a heartbeat, he went bug-eyed rigid, then his head drooped. As his chin dropped to his chest, his knees went rubbery soft. In slo-mo, he slumped down to his hands and knees, then to his face on the sidewalk. He lay there motionless, except for the kicking, solo dance of his right leg.

Pump-gun discarded his truncheon and made a grab for his shoulder-slung side arm.

A bad choice.

Without apparently moving from the spot on which he stood, the hairtail still safely tucked under his arm, Remo threw the bounty hunter fifteen feet through the air. Pump-gun landed with a hollow thunk, belly first on the car's hood, caving it in. Unconscious, he slid off the right front fender like a 280-pound over-easy fried egg.

Remo reached out for the guy with the stun gun. With a downward slash of a single razor-sharp fingernail, the assassin neatly slit through the front of the Kevlar body armor. Before the bounty hunter could get his hand on the butt of his pistol, Remo groped inside the foot-long gash for his pound of flesh. And catching hold of it, he wrung it out like a fistful of wet socks.

"Yeeee, Mama!" yelped Taser, dropping to both knees on the sidewalk with a shuddering thud.

"Who am I?" Remo asked him.

"You're a fucking maniac!"

"Who am I?"

Desperation filled the man's eyes.

"Think, think," Remo urged him.

"You're *not* William Ransom," the bounty hunter wheezed.

"Bingo." Remo slightly loosened his grip. "Now, *what* am I?"

The man with the Taser squinted up at him, teeth clenched, anticipating more pain.

Remo smiled. "I YAM WHAT I YAM."

"Huh?"

"A wrist joke. Forget it. Time for night-night." Cocking his middle finger against his thumb, Remo delivered a precisely measured snap to the side of the bounty hunter's head. The man's eyelids fluttered shut, and he went limp. Remo eased the unconscious man onto his back.

As Remo retrieved his wallet, Yi reappeared in the shop's entrance. He seemed pleased by the sight of all the downed bodies, but then again, he always seemed pleased.

"You come tomorrow," Yi said in English, "I have sand eel for Master. Very fresh. No parasites, or money back."

Remo left the parking lot, whistling. As he crossed Olympic Boulevard, the sounds of approaching ambulances made a seesawing counterpoint to his off-key hornpipe.

REMO AND CHIUN'S vacation rental was on a side street a few blocks from Mr. Yi's shop. Since its inception, the surrounding neighborhood had passed through three sets of ethnicities—white, black and Latino—before becoming largely Korean. Remo would have preferred Malibu or even Santa Monica; the location had been Chiun's choice. Although the Master of Sinanju often claimed to enjoy being around "his own people," the farther they got from the fishing village of Sinanju, the less use he had for them. A person from Seoul might as well have been born in Namibia. Or Afghanistan. For Remo, the whole "my neighbor, my brother" thing was made even more laughable by the fact that in the ten days since their arrival, Chiun had left the house only once.

Remo turned down the narrow concrete walkway that divided a double row of clapboard dollhouses. The little court of eight bungalows had been built in the 1930s. All the houses were white, and they'd been painted and repainted countless times without proper sanding between coats—nowhere on the siding was there a square foot without a spall, a burst blister or a painted-over dust ball. Stunted orange trees decorated the walkway. A sign of the times, every front door had a black steel security screen, and every window was barred.

As he put the key in the lock, Remo heard the blare of a TV commercial through the door. Though he couldn't make out the words, he knew the spot had to be selling either trucks or beer, the cornerstones of "Friday Night Football." He opened the door onto a cool, dark, postage stamp of a living room that seemed even smaller because of the projection TV that covered the entire rear wall. At Chiun's insistence on the day of their arrival, Remo had arranged delivery of the seventy-two-inch Mitsuzuki Mondiale from a local Rent-to-Own appliance and furniture store.

Three-foot-high beer bottles danced the Macarena in the gloom of the window-draped room. In front of the Mitsuzuki, a little man with a face like a yellow raisin sat on a La-Z-Boy recliner. In a long silk kimono, with his TV tray at his side and the *TV Bible* opened to the night's playbill, reposed the deadliest killer on earth.

"You haven't moved a muscle since I left," Remo complained as he shut the door.

A slender hand appeared out of the cuff of the silk robe. The Master of Sinanju raised a long-nailed finger to his lips and shushed his inconsiderate pupil. In the erratic light of the TV, he was flipping through the little magazine's full-color-insert section.

"You're not reading that godawful gossip crap again?" Remo said. "Can't you see all the stories are just unpaid ads for upcoming shows? The whole damned magazine is self-congratulating boosterism run amok."

Chiun pressed the *TV Bible* over his heart and said, "Only a fool scolds a cat for licking its own behind."

There was no arguing that one.

So Remo didn't bother trying.

He turned for the tiny kitchen. After depositing the hairtail on the counter, he set the lightly oiled wok on the gas burner to heat and started a pot of jasmine rice. As the Mondiale's enormous quartet of speakers blasted an all-too-familiar theme, he stuck his head back out of the doorway.

With an opening montage of fireworks, Lycra-clad, gyrating cheerleaders, superb computer graphics and raucous country-rock fanfare, "Friday Night Football" was under way. Huge helmets in the competing teams' colors—pumpkin orange for the L.A. Riots and crustacean red for the Maine Lobsters—collided and exploded into a sea of glittering fragments.

Which dissolved into a three-shot of the show's hosts in the stadium broadcast booth. As if anyone with a functioning brain didn't already know who Chunk, Sal and Freddy were, the network superimposed their first names under the live picture. Chunk was the former offensive lineman and now the color commentator, Sal was the canny play-by-play guy and Freddy the brainy statistic-and-trivia king. All three of the media personalities wore matching navy blue blazers, but there the similarity ended. Sal and Freddy could have used Chunk's sports coat as a two-man tent.

In Remo's opinion, Chiun's long-running fascination with the boob tube had taken a decided turn for the worse. The Reigning Master of Sinanju had become a pro-football junkie. Though his understanding of the fine points of the game left much to be desired, Chiun had caught the fever.

"We've got a good one for you tonight, folks," said Sal. "A real grudge match between two of the league's newest expansion teams...."

"If anything, that's an understatement," Chunk said. "If you don't believe me, just take a look at some tape we shot during warm-ups. Even the team mascots hate each other."

Images of a man-size velour dog-thing with a huge head, and a man-size red foam lobster with one big claw flooded the screen. A nose-to-claw shouting match ended with a flurry of blows exchanged and the two mascots rolling around on the artificial turf.

"Ol' Lootie the Coyote is really giving it to Claw-boy," Freddy said.

"The bad feeling goes from the bottom up, folks," Sal said into the camera as it switched back to the booth, "from the towel boys to the general managers. Like I said, we've got a humdinger tonight. Stay tuned."

The network switched to a commercial break: half-ton pickups danced the Macarena.

"Haven't you noticed that those three bozos always talk that grudge-match stuff before the kick-off?" Remo said. "And that no matter what they say, the game always sucks royal. Why on earth are you watching it? Even the shopping channel is less predictable."

"I'm doing it for your sake," Chiun admitted.

"Why doesn't that surprise me?"

"Because my selfless regard for your betterment is nothing new," Chiun answered. "I make many sacrifices so that you will be prepared to take up the mantle of Master when I pass on."

"And how, pray tell, is 'Friday Night Football' going to help me become a better assassin?"

"Surly One, games are the yin and yang, the living, beating heart of a people. By watching your professional sport, I'm able to study the inner workings of the American mind. I do this so I can understand you, my pupil, more completely. Only then can I raise you beyond the limits of your native-born mediocrity. Only then can I help you be all you can be.''

"Face facts, you're rotting your mind, Chiun.''

The Master dismissed Remo's concern with a toss of his hand. "Western culture cannot harm me. I observe with great detachment, from a high perch of wisdom. Besides, this entertainment of yours is very weak compared to the excitement of Korea's national games...."

"Teeter-totter and kite flying?''

Miffed at the tone of Remo's remark, Chiun pulled his hands into the baggy cuffs of his kimono and ducked his chin down into its round collar, a turtle retreating into its brocaded shell.

Back in the kitchen, Remo checked the rice, which was already filling the room with its fragrance. Before he took the hairtail from its package, he opened the kitchen window. He pried the fish's jaws apart and hooked the upper fangs over the edge of the windowsill. Then, holding the hairtail out straight with his left hand, he used the point of his razor-edged fingernail to make a slit in the skin all the way around the head, just behind the gill plate. In a single motion, he stripped the entire skin down to the tail, turning it inside out like a sock.

Remo flopped the skinned fish back on the counter and started the tedious separation of the greenish meat from the backbone with flicks of his guillotine nail. He sliced the resulting twin fillets into two-inch chunks, dipped them in beaten egg and dredged them in seasoned flour. As he drizzled a little more peanut oil in the wok, a cry came from the living room.

"Aieeee!"

Remo abandoned the stove. "What is it? What's wrong?"

"Orange team has poked the peach."

"Pooch," Remo corrected.

Chiun waved impatiently for silence. Moses returned from the Mount, the color commentator was speaking.

"Well, guys," Chunk said, "let's hope that first-play fumble doesn't set the tone for the rest of the game. Otherwise, we could be in for a long evening."

"So what else is new," Remo muttered.

"That muffed catch on the kickoff turns the ball over to the Lobsters on the Riots' ten-yard line," Sal announced.

The camera cut to the Lobster sideline, where the Maine cheerleaders, known as "the Tails," cavorted with highly choreographed enthusiasm as their offensive squad took the field.

While the squads changed, Freddy started adding stats and gossipy trivia tidbits to the list of players' names that appeared on the screen. When he got to the Riots nose tackle, he said, "Whoa! That's got to be some kind of a typo. The roster has Boomtower weighing in at 502 pounds!"

"Can we get an iso shot of him?" Sal asked.

The camera zoomed in on the defensive players as they waited for the Lobster offense to come out of their huddle. Amid the milling orange uniforms, Number 96 loomed large indeed.

"What's happened to the Great Pumpkin?" Freddy said.

"Tonight he looks more like the Incredible Hulk," Sal quipped.

"I gotta tell ya, folks, I've never seen a physical transformation like this," Chunk said. "You know we like to poke some fun at the overweight players from time to time. And we've stuck it to Mr. Boomtower on more than one occasion. But tonight against the Lobsters, he's really turned it all around. Folks, no exaggeration, Bradley Boomtower is truly enormous. Look at the thighs on him! They're as big around as my waist!"

"The only question is," Sal said, "what can he do with it?"

Remo decided to watch one play to find out.

Of course, it was typical FNF. At the snap of the ball, Boomtower took one step and slipped, falling on his face, and before he could get up, the play was over—the Lobster deep corner-end-zone pass had floated way out of bounds.

"Wow, that's a sorry start for the Great Pumpkin," Freddy said. "Flat on his mug on the carpet. I don't think he even made contact with an offensive player...."

"He's calling the head linesman over," Sal said.

"There's something wrong with the Astroturf," Chunk added.

All the officials gathered at the line of scrimmage, apparently examining the playing surface. Whatever they were looking at was concealed from the camera by their huddled backs.

"Let's replay that in slo-mo," Sal suggested, "and see if we can pick up what happened."

The slow-motion replay did in fact show why Number 96 had lost his footing. With his initial burst of speed, with a single push of his forward leg, Boomtower's cleats had ripped up a yard of green carpet. That's what had tangled his feet and tripped him.

"How'd he *do* that?" Freddy said.

Which was exactly what Remo was asking himself.

While the grounds crew made a quick, temporary repair to the artificial turf, Boomtower took off his shoes and threw them to the sidelines.

"He's playing barefoot," Sal said, with his trademark firm grasp of the obvious.

"There have been quite a few barefoot kickers, but never barefoot nose tackles," Freddy said. "We may have a major story in the making here tonight, folks."

"The oil is starting to smoke," Chiun declared without taking his eyes from the big screen. "You must clean the wok and start over."

"Yeah, yeah," Remo said, but he made no move

to return to the kitchen. The players were lined up and ready to go.

At the snap of the ball, Number 96 surged between the center and the tackle, and as he did so, he delivered a left-handed blow to the middle of the center's back, dropping him like a load of bricks. Effortlessly, Boomtower sidestepped the offensive tackle's attempted block. He was well into the backfield as the Lobster quarterback rolled out for another pass. With Boomtower charging in his face, the quarterback reared back for a second throw to the end zone. He got the ball off, a wobbly, wounded duck that dropped incomplete, and for all his trouble took a tremendous square-on hit from the Riots nose tackle. Like it had been rocket launched, the quarterback's helmet flew off and sailed downfield; he crashed to his back under a quarter ton of Boomtower.

Number 96 jumped up at once and started doing his pelvic-thrusting, head-juking sack dance.

"What a hit!" Chunk gasped. "Hoo-wee, that had to cost the Lobster eight-figure bonus baby some brain cells."

"It'll make this year's highlight film for sure," Freddy said.

Sal was less sanguine about the situation. "Uh, the center's still down and he's not moving," he said. "Neither is the QB. I think they're both hurt. Yep, here come the trainers."

The camera closed in on the fallen center. The

trainer crew rolled the big man over onto his back, and then they did something the football-viewing audience had never seen before: they started giving him chest compressions to try to restart his heart. Meanwhile, players from both teams were yelling excitedly, waving at the sidelines and pointing at the downed Lobster quarterback.

"What's going on over there?" Freddy said. "Get a tighter shot."

They did. In middle of the man's shoulder pads, the neck hole of his uniform yawned. It was empty.

"Oh, Jesus, where's his head?" Chunk cried. "Where's the quarterback's fucking head?"

"Look in his hat," Chiun suggested, snuggling deeper into the La-Z-Boy.

The camera zoomed in on the missing helmet, which rested top side up on the carpet at midfield. There was a face inside it, and remarkably the chin strap was still buckled. The angle of the shot produced a disturbing illusion: it looked like the QB had just poked his head up through the Astroturf for a quick peek around.

From his expression, he didn't like what he saw.

The feeling seemed universal.

Players from both teams turned away from the red helmet, some of them slack jawed with horror, others bent over at the waist, puking through their face guards. This while Bradley the Fighting Vehicle Boomtower continued to strut his stuff: slow-motion moonwalking, he struck classic bodybuilder poses to the beat of the sideline photographers' flashguns.

Understandably incensed, the Lobster bench rose up en masse and attacked the showboating nose tackle, burying him under a heap of bodies. Not to be outdone, Boomtower's whole team rushed onto the field to try to defend him. The roar of the hometown crowd drowned out Chunk, Sal and Freddy as the stadium police surrounded the wildly shifting, hundred-man dog pile.

Then, abruptly, the network cut away from the live-action melee to a row of triple-bacon cheescburgers dancing the Macarena.

"Fifteen yards," Chiun proudly announced.

Remo shook his head to clear it. Smoke from the burning wok hung heavy in the room. "What's fifteen yards?"

"The penalty for roughing the passer."

As Remo opened his mouth to speak, the telephone rang. It was the scrambled line.

3

Like the tire of some gigantic earthmover, the landmark sign loomed over the flat white cinder roof of the Big-O doughnut shop. Dramatically lit from beneath on both sides, the dimpled stucco ring could be seen for blocks up and down busy Sepulveda Boulevard. No doughnut known to man was ever so huge, so pink, so utterly indigestible.

Chiz Graham stood under the Big-O's red awning, watching through the service window as a plump, short Latina girl in a white paper hat and long braids finished pulling together his order from the rolling racks of freshly baked treats. The clerk was *so* short she had to reach up to push the pair of wide, flat boxes across the counter to him.

"Por favor, Señor Cheez..." she said, straining on tiptoe to stick her bare arm through the service window. Fingers gloved in clear plastic offered him a black permanent marker.

Chiz uncapped the broad-tipped markie, and with big, looping flourishes, autographed the inside of her brown forearm from wrist to elbow. He wrote, "Warmest wishes, Chiz Graham."

"Muchas gracias," she cooed, cradling her autographed arm to her bosom like a newborn babe.

"De nada," said the movie star, scooping up the boxes.

As he turned for the waiting limo, the girl clawed herself above the level of the counter so she could watch the action-film Adonis walk away. At his broad, densely muscled back, she aimed a shrill, undulating cry: the same hair-raising sound voiced by female *ballet folclórico* dancers—and chickadees in heat. She punctuated the "I am Woman" yodel with a heartfelt *"Estupendo!"*

Long accustomed to having girls go glassy-eyed at the sight of his massive, jutting buttocks, Graham paid her no mind. All he was thinking about was the fragrant burden—the forty-eight oven-fresh doughnuts—he carried. His jaws ached in anticipation of their succulent, deep-fried goodness. He felt a ferocious urge to sit down on the curb and eat every single one of them himself.

But he knew if he did, there would be pure hell to pay.

As he reached for the limo's rear door, it swung open. Crouched inside, in the midst of the litter of empty paper bags from the BurgerMeister up the block, in her black Gucci tank top, matching leather micromini and stiletto-heeled ankle boots, was Puma

Lee, the movie star's even bigger movie star of a wife. The ravishing, tawny-skinned, raven-haired grade-school dropout pronounced her screen name "Poo-mah," not "Pew-mah," and everyone in the show-biz know followed suit.

Without a word, the leggy beauty snatched one of the boxes from him. Before he could get the limo door shut, Puma was stuffing heavily sugar iced cinnamon-apple fritters into her face with both hands. Chiz sat in one of the jump seats, as far away from her as he could get. Hunched protectively over his own flat of treats, he started ramming assorted glazed doughnuts into his mouth. For Chiz and Puma, the act of eating had become an athletic event, in this case, the twenty-four-doughnut sprint. Neither wanted to be the last to finish, because neither wanted to share the stub end of the final cruller with the other. Rainbow sprinkles and shards of icing glaze flew left and right, as did the grunting, gulping sounds of their frantic swallowing.

The noise was such that the uniformed limo driver lowered the one-way privacy window to make sure his passengers were both all right. In his rearview mirror, he watched the highest-paid actors in motion-picture history make total pigs of themselves.

It was common knowledge in Tinseltown that between the two of them, Chiz and Puma pulled in a minimum of thirty million dollars per film. Puma invariably commanded a good deal more money than

Chiz—and the salary gap was a touchy subject. He had been typecast by the industry as an action-adventure star who showed his bare behind; Puma had a much wider dramatic range. She was perfectly believable taking off all her clothes not only in summer shoot-'em-ups, but also in historical romances, modern-relationship pictures, cancer tear-jerkers, disaster flicks and Shakespearean rehashes.

The driver wrinkled his nose as he caught a whiff of something dank and musky floating through the window from the back. He'd read the tabloid stories about how the celebrity couple always bathed in vintage sauvignon blanc. He decided that whatever liquid they soaked themselves in, they didn't use soap. Having hauled around Hollywood types for half his adult life, the driver thought he'd witnessed every conceivable eccentricity of the filthy rich. But even a binge-ing Orson Welles couldn't hold a candle to these two. Like wild animals, Chiz and Puma sought out and gobbled the lowest forms of junk food. And the question the chauffeur kept asking himself was how could people who ate so bad look so good?

By the time the limo driver exited the parking lot and merged with oncoming traffic on Sepulveda, four dozen assorted doughnuts were history. He started to accelerate in order to change lanes for the freeway ramp.

"No, pull in there," Chiz told him, waving to the right.

"Excuse me, sir," the driver said, "but we're going to be late for the benefit if we stop again—"

"He told you to pull in!" Puma snarled.

End of discussion. "Yes, ma'am," the driver said flatly.

Their new destination was Tito's Tacos, another fast-food landmark of West Los Angeles. It lurked in the shadow of an elevated section of Interstate 405. With the double-parked limo blocking half the small lot, Chiz trotted up to the outside service window.

"*¿Que quieres, señor?*" asked a guy with pomaded salt-and-pepper hair, long sideburns and a pencil-thin mustache. For forty years he had been folding tortillas at the same location, and in an identical white polyester guayabera shirt. Awaiting Chiz's response, he held the stub of a pencil poised on a paper pad. Over his shoulder, one of the cooks—a shorter, wider version of the counterman—lowered stainless-steel baskets of tacos into boiling vats of dark amber oil. A peculiarity of Tito's cuisine, the *picadillo* meat was already packed inside the folded tortilla shells when they were plopped into the deep fryer. This meant that as the meat was heated, it soaked up oil like a sponge.

"Give me a dozen beef tacos with double guacamole," Chiz said. Then he thought better of it. "No, wait a minute. Hold the tacos. I'll take a couple of quarts of that, instead."

The taco bender seemed irritated as he used what little was left of his pencil's eraser on the order pad.

Looking up, he said, "*¿Que quieres—frijoles, men-udo?*"

"*No. Déme la grasa.*"

Chiz's unusual request confounded the seasoned counterman.

"Yeah, you heard me right," Chiz assured him. "I want the deep-fry oil. Pour it in a couple of those jumbo drink cups. Make them to go."

Puma scowled at her husband when he returned, practically empty-handed. "Where's the tacos? You were supposed to get tacos!" She wasn't just disappointed; she was furious. And venting her fury, she seized handfuls of the back seat's gray Corinthian leather, which parted under the points of her long red fingernails like so much pebble-grained tissue paper.

Chiz would never have admitted to actually being afraid of his better half. Such a thing ran counter to his image, public and self. After all, it was he who had carved out a celluloid career by battling armies of terrorists, mutant zombies, hair-shirt barbarians, and it was he who had whipped their evil butts, all by his lonesome. But of late, whenever Chiz considered thwarting Puma's expressed wishes, he thought about it long and hard.

He handed her one of the big cups. "Try this instead."

Puma tried to sip through the straw and got nowhere—it was already soundly plugged with congealed grease. She took off the plastic lid, cracked the white film of beef fat with a long nail and daintily sipped at the brownish *picadillo*-spiced oil underneath.

The sip quickly became a gulp.

"I figured, why not cut to the chase?" Chiz told her as he raised his own cup to his lips.

They were licking away their fry-oil mustaches as the limo climbed the 405 on-ramp, heading for Hollywood. Two exits from Sunset Boulevard, they passed a freeway billboard advertising Chiz's new action flick. The movie's title, *Big Bore*, was supposed to refer to weapon caliber, as in elephant gun. That no one had caught the unfortunate double entendre until after the picture was in distribution was a prime example of Murphy's Law.

The billboard's airbrush painting showed a three-times-life-size Chiz stripped to the waist with a massive chromed Magnum revolver braced on his inner thigh. The yard-long, vent-rib barrel was raised in a highly suggestive fashion. Across the top of the billboard, huge letters proclaimed Tougher...Bigger... Harder. Beneath the banner, a row of infinitely smaller type credited the review quote to Nigel Plimsole, of the *Agoura Weekly Advertiser*.

As the billboard zoomed by, Chiz couldn't help but recall the strain of getting into shape for *Big Bore*. Prior to the filming, he'd spent six hateful months with personal trainers and holistic-diet consultants. It wasn't just vanity that drove him to buff out for his movie roles. His fans expected it of him. His fans and his producers. When your bare ass was up there on the screen, twenty feet tall, you'd better be able to bounce quarters off it, baby.

The problem was, Chiz Graham was slipping into his mid-thirties. Forget about bulking up—it took more and more effort just to keep in shape what muscle he had. Between films, he had taken to hiding his burgeoning layer of flab under loose shirts and baggy slacks.

No more.

A shit-eating grin spread over the movie star's internationally recognized, square-chinned mug. His flab-hiding days were done. Tonight all he was wearing above the waist was a custom-tailored red leather vest with extralarge armholes designed to showcase his deeply tanned and monumental biceps and lats. Thanks to a miracle of modern science, without having lifted so much as a finger, Chiz was totally megabuffed. His body fat was under ten percent. Muscle mass up by thirty percent. Strength more than doubled. And it all came from a two-by-two-inch adhesive patch. Which, as far as he was concerned, was worth twice its million-dollar-a-year price tag.

Chiz wasn't wearing the drug-dispensing bandage stuck on his bum, where it would certainly have shown through the skintight seat of his red cycling shorts. He'd applied it below the shorts's waistband in front, where it blended nicely into the gridwork of his abs. Puma wore her patch as high as possible on the inside of her right thigh.

The dark-haired screen queen sat there, alternately flexing her arms, transfixed by the pop of her own sleek, powerful muscles. After the quart of warm taco grease, Chiz could almost see his own biceps growing in size, too. He felt the pleasure-pain burn in the core of the muscle, like he'd just done 150 reps of dumbbell curls.

A few minutes later, the limo pulled up in front of the Venom Club. On the marquee, a pink-and-green-neon rattler coiled and struck, coiled and struck every few seconds. At Tinseltown's newest in spot, it was said, the crème de la crème could let their hair down among their own kind. The assembled paparazzi and crowds of fans on the sidewalk were kept behind a velvet-rope cordon by a phalanx of bouncers.

The nightclub's ponytailed head of security opened the limo door for them. In his trademark black leather trench coat, leather pants and cowboy boots, Pismo Pete quickly ushered Chiz and Puma through the entrance, beneath a huge banner that said Oxfam Benefit Gala.

Inside on an elevated stage, under a huge rotating glitter ball, tall, thin and beautiful people boogied to retro seventies rock. The main body of clubgoers surrounded the long buffet table in the center of the room. Chiz and Puma said their hellos, waving, air-kissing cheeks, moving quickly through the mob to the front of the food line.

Without bothering to pick up a plate or utensils, Puma plucked a big sticky gob of blue cheese from the top of a spinach-salad mountain. She only had it in her mouth a second before she spewed it back over the heaped greenery. "What was that crap?" she gasped, wiping her lips with the back of her hand.

A guy in a white uniform and chef's hat scurried over at once. "It's Virtual Gorgonzola," he told her. "A cheese-flavored tofu product. Not to worry. It's completely fat free, like everything else we're serving here tonight. So, just enjoy…"

But Puma's attention—and her anger—had already wandered.

Chiz looked over his shoulder and saw whom his wife was staring at with such focused malice.

Vindaloo.

The tall, blond, former world-class model turned movie actress was Puma's only real competition for global box-office supremacy. The baby-smooth Swede had piled her plate high with a rich-looking chocolate dessert. When Vindaloo smiled at Puma, there was no-fat mousse cake all over her perfect white teeth.

Right off, Chiz knew there was going to be trouble.

4

"The illustrious Emperor beckons," Chiun announced as the scrambled link to CURE's headquarters continued to chirp. The Reigning Master of Sinanju made no move to get up to answer the phone himself, even though he was closer to it. With his words, Chiun was just pointing out the existence of the irritating noise, on the off chance that his one and only pupil had somehow failed to notice.

From decades of experience, Remo knew there was no purpose served by standing fast. His butt cast in concrete, Chiun wasn't going to budge from the La-Z-Boy, even if the phone rang all week. Remo crossed the smoky room and turned on the speaker phone. "What's up, Smitty?"

Without preamble, a very distraught Dr. Harold W. Smith said, "Turn your television to 'Friday Night Football.'"

"Exalted One," Chiun warbled, "it is already our privilege to be witnessing that glorious contest."

"Then you saw what just happened to the Maine quarterback?"

"If you ask me," Remo said, "it was a little over-the-top, even for sweeps month."

"We have the makings of a major problem on our hands," Smith continued. "Please switch to Channel 8."

Chiun picked up the Star Trek Next Generation Phaser remote-control unit from the arm of the recliner. The Master of Sinanju didn't question the purpose of the order or grouse about missing the rest of the game as he would have done if Remo had made the request. After all, his Emperor had spoken. According to the ancient code of Chiun's predecessors, the generations of highly sought master assassins from the Korean peninsula, fealty—and the choice of light entertainment—invariably went to the guy with the most gold. Like a good and faithful servant, Chiun pushed the channel-change button.

The Mitsuzuki's giant screen blipped, and a man and woman appeared. They were seated behind a stylishly modern desk that conspicuously lacked a modesty panel. More annoying than their perfectly sculpted hairdos, than his impeccably tailored gray Armani silk suit or her red Adolfo, more annoying even than his reliance on dimples to drive home a point or her habit of crossing and recrossing her long legs under the table, were their matching, synthetically earnest expressions.

"Peephole USA" was one of those tabloid-news magazines that specialized in "T and T." Titillate and

Terrify. And its producers were only truly content when they accomplished both objects in the one-minute feature story. With respective dimples and upper thighs bared, Jed and Molly were doing their standard chitchat wrap-up of a tale called "When Easter Bunnies Attack—the Texas Day Care Nightmare."

Chiun immediately read the handwriting on the wall. "You wish these two people dead for unspeakable crimes against the Emperor? Say no more. Consider it done."

"Off with the talking heads," Remo concurred.

"Shh. Just listen for a minute," Smith instructed them.

With a whirlpool flourish of computer graphics, "Peephole USA" plunged into its next feature, which was entitled "What's Got into Great-Great-Grandpa?"

"By now," began Molly's giggly voice-over, "all of America's heard about the past-ninety Southern senator and his beauty-queen girl toy. Well, this time tomorrow, Senator Ludlow Baculum and Bambi Sue Stimple will be on their honeymoon. It's her first, and his thirteenth. Last night's 1-900 viewers' poll tells us you think old Lud's robbing the cradle, but is little Bambi robbing the grave?"

As the screen filled with a panning shot of poolside at a Malibu Beach mansion, the "Peephole USA" reporter offered a few tidbits of pertinent background: that this was the May-December marriage to end all,

Bambi being sixty-nine years her intended's junior, and that Baculum was the chairman of the powerful Term Limits and Election Finance Reform Ongoing Investigation and Research Committee.

To the strains of "Baby Love" by Diana Ross and The Supremes, the camera closed in on the pool's shallow end, where the former Miss Nicotine, glowing with youth and health, splashed around in her black thong bikini. At the deep end, Senator Baculum swam in slow, deliberate circles with his eyes and nose just above water. His bald, liver-spotted head bobbed like the top of a well-pickled egg. A fine fringe of silver hair brushed the tops of his large, protruding ears—ears with unusually pendulous lobes. The camera tightly framed the senator as he dog-paddled to the ladder and made his dripping exit from the pool.

"My, oh, my!" gushed Molly breathlessly. "What's got into great-great-grandpa?"

The crepe of the senator's chin formed a kind of international date line. Below it, Ludlow Baculum was neither stooped nor sagging nor withered. He was, in fact, a different man.

He was Tarzan.

To Remo, it looked like one of those computer-video morph tricks he'd seen a hundred times on MTV. The ancient Sunbelt legislator appeared to have monumentally broad shoulders, huge, densely chiseled muscles and zero body fat. In his zebra-striped

Speedo, he padded across the pool deck with the animal grace of a teenager. As Baculum toweled himself dry, the camera lingered a fraction of second on the zebra stripes, just so Molly could gush, "My, oh, my..." one more time.

"What exactly is the problem here, Smitty?" Remo asked.

Chiun snorted at his pupil's impossible thickheadedness. "Obviously," he announced, "our Emperor wishes to make this Bambi creature his private concubine. Is the old man with a young man's body an impediment to Emperor Smith's pleasure?"

"Just watch!" Dr. Smith barked through the speaker with uncharacteristic impatience.

Then "Peephole USA" ran the "before" tape. It was a segment of a video taken eight months before, at the wedding of Baculum and his twelfth wife, a twenty-three-year-old part-time waitress at a highway restaurant outside of Mobile, Alabama. The ceremony took place in the honeymoon suite of the Holiday Inn next door to the girl's place of casual employment. On the tape, Ludlow looked every one of his ninety-plus years. Hunchbacked, sallow skinned, his shirt collar a mile too big, the senator used a walker to make an excruciatingly slow approach up to his wedding cake. As he did so, he leered, rheumy-eyed, at his gum-snapping bride's round bottom. Behind the wedding cake, along the wall, a row of oxygen tanks and a full-size defibrillator unit were visible.

"Until two weeks ago, *that* was Senator Ludlow Baculum," Smith declared.

"Peephole USA" cut back to Jed and Molly, who half turned in their chairs in order to react to the freeze-frame comparative shots behind them.

"Has Ludlow Baculum found a fountain of youth?" Jed asked his national audience. "That's what everyone on Capitol Hill wants to know, but so far the good senator is keeping his own counsel on the subject. Molly, you have to admire the guy for wanting to die with a smile on his face."

"From what I just saw, he isn't going to be the only one smiling tomorrow morning," Molly said as she did her scissor-leg shtick, extraslow.

Jed fanned himself with his blank sheets of copy while dimpling for the camera.

"I still don't see a problem," Remo said.

"Ah-hah!" Chiun exclaimed. "At last all becomes clear. You wish to trade this old man's young body for your own, and he is resisting the chance to be of service. Tell us where you want him delivered, Exalted One. Be assured there will be no further delay."

A noise came through the speakerphone.

Remo would have sworn it was the sound of grinding teeth, only it was much, much too loud.

5

Puma Lee had blood in her eye as she stalked her nemesis through the shifting press of the club crowd. Lanky in a hot lime spandex minidress, Vindaloo walked with an infuriating little-girl hop in her gait that set her shoulder-length white-gold hair a-swish and her various rounded baby-fat parts a-jiggle.

There was no longer any jiggle to Puma.

Bands of steel and cables of Kevlar interlaced under her almost transparently thin skin. Her breasts had lost a full cup size; once luxuriantly soft and resilient, they had turned to granite. Beneath her rock-hard bosom burned a desire more terrible than any she had ever felt.

And what she felt, felt so right.

People said things to her as she passed by, showering her with greetings, salutations and praise, fawning shamelessly because of who she was. She couldn't hear their words over the pounding of her own pulse in her ears. Their bright, eager faces meant nothing to her, either. Her fellow party-goers might as well have been stalks of tall, dry grass—spindly things to be pushed aside and walked over.

Ahead of her, the Swedish actress passed the entrance to the men's room, which was marked with a sign that said Hiss. Vindaloo pushed through the other swinging door, the one marked Not Hiss.

Only when Puma Lee entered after her quarry, stepping into the blindingly white tiled bathroom, did her sense of hearing return to normal; as the door swung shut, it came back with a rush of pressure against the sides of her head. The bathroom she surveyed was deserted; the Swede was nowhere in sight. To Puma's left, the brushed-steel stall doors were all closed. It was so quiet that she could hear the sawing, sixty-cycle hum of the fluorescent lights above the mirrored sinks.

Then, from the end of the row of doors, it began.

Sudden. Thunderous.

The ralphing bark of the sea lion echoed in the narrow, tiled room.

A sound Puma recognized at once. Recognized and expected. Like most successful high-fashion models, Vindaloo was a puker. Had the Swede not been so thoroughly addicted to the hurl, her sylphlike form would have quickly assumed the waistless sausage shape dictated by her Scandinavian-fishwife genetics.

Again, the sea lion called.

Oxfam's buffet spread might have been no-fat, but that didn't mean it was no-calories. Which left a figure-conscious individual with two options: lose it or wear it home. From the upchuck arpeggios raging in the bathroom's last stall, Vindaloo was hell-bent on getting rid of every last smear of that chocolate mousse cake.

Puma Lee sympathized with the need to vomit after taking one's absolute fill. And not simply to void unnecessary calories, as Vindaloo was doing.

One also vomited to make room for more.

As she closed in on her unsuspecting enemy, for the first time in her charmed life, Puma Lee knew exactly what she wanted.

She wanted it all.

Money. Possessions. Adoration. Acclaim. Power.

Not just the mixed grill, the polite taste of each entrée that untold thousands of wanna-be actors would have gladly sold their souls for. Puma Lee already had the fattest lamb chop, the biggest prawn, the juiciest filet, and it was not enough.

Puma wanted it *all*.

She even wanted the wanting.

The raven-haired actress had decided on her course of action the instant she'd laid eyes on her blond counterpart. There was no final straw, as such. No smirky expression from the Swede at the buffet table had tipped the balance. No ultimate, unforgivable stab in the back. No unfairly bestowed Academy Award. No plum lead role recently stolen.

Like other corporate giants, like auto makers or

chemical companies, the two female megastars competed head-to-head for sales in the world market. As with other international conglomerates, when there were big profits and substantial losses on the line, industrial espionage ran rampant. Puma's underpaid screenwriters and sacked script doctors routinely fled to Vindaloo's studio, and vice versa, their heads bursting with ideas already under development, if not in production. Scripts appeared as if by magic on executives' desks in both camps, leaked by the competition's CPAs, security guards and night janitors. With the opposite camp's material in hand, a team of skilled hacks could quickly pound out a new star vehicle, and one just different enough to avoid successful legal action.

Which went a long way to explaining why every year the movie mills released two "flight attendant in jeopardy from terrorists" films, or two "just passed the bar woman lawyer in jeopardy from clients" films, or two "Las Vegas dancer in jeopardy from the mob" films. Whichever actress had started the process of cloning the other's work, up until tonight it had become the common practice of both, in order to hedge their box-office bets.

After tonight, all bets were off. What Puma had endured in the past, the irritating threats to her territory, she would endure no longer.

Puma stepped to within a foot of the door of the last stall. She reached for the door handle and gave it the lightest of tugs. The lock latch rattled in its striker plate.

"Occupied!" Vindaloo groaned from the other side.

Through the sizable gap between the door and its frame, Puma could see the Nordic princess on her knees before the porcelain god. She tugged at the handle a little harder.

Removing her finger from down her throat, Vindaloo cried, "For Christ's sake, didn't you hear what I said? Go away!"

That was not in the cards. Puma made a flat blade of her right hand and, as if the door had been made of two layers of aluminum foil instead of two layers of eighth-inch sheet steel, she thrust her fingers through to the other side.

At the shriek of splitting metal, the Swede twisted around and saw the woman's hand poking through the rip in the door, the long, perfectly manicured fingers turning the inside lock button.

"What do you want?" Vindaloo bawled as the door slowly swung open. When it came to a full stop and she saw who the intruder was, she had her answer. And it was murder.

Even though the door was no longer a barrier to Puma's desires, in her rage she stripped it off its hinges, and in the same motion sent it crashing sideways into the line of mirrors behind her.

Like a spooked rabbit, Vindaloo scuttled under the

dividing wall between toilet stalls. Puma lunged for her, but not in time. The Nordic model's slim ankle slipped out of reach.

Undaunted by the steel partitions, Puma pursued her prey, cleaving through the intervening walls with downward slashes of her arms. She made the astounding feat look easy, as easy as the way a circus poodle breaks through a paper-covered hoop. But there was no mistaking the difference. In the tiled room, the impacts of her arms flailing upon the steel boomed like a squadron of jets breaking the sound barrier. And instead of bits of brightly colored tissue paper fluttering about, shards of red-hot metal sang through the air.

Somewhere, under the din of Puma's single-minded attack, Vindaloo squealed desperately for help.

CHIZ STOOD at the end of the buffet table, staring at the women's-room door as he waited for the shit to hit the fan. He hadn't tried to calm his bride or to divert her from her purpose because he'd known it wouldn't have done any good. Her strength was such that he could no longer dominate her physically. As an icon of alpha-maleness, he understood Puma's need to control her own turf, to have free range within boundaries of her own making. He also understood—and shared—her lust to destroy something living, to rip it apart for the best of all possible reasons: because she could do it.

The mob milling around the party food practically begged to be torn to shreds. But as luck would have it, Chiz could find no one to focus his homicidal urges upon. No Vindaloo counterpart. Like a school of bait fish, the benefit crowd was a shifting, dizzying mass of virtually identical targets. And on top of that, unlike his wife, Chiz still felt caution in the presence of so many. He wanted to do bad things, but was held in check by the fear of being caught and punished. The action-adventure star considered his new desires a consequence of the bigger, better body he inhabited. As his power and muscle mass increased, so had his contempt for those who were weaker.

A noise cut through the vintage rock and roll, the rumble of talk and laughter, and froze every person in the room. It sounded like someone had rammed a truck into the bathroom wall. A very big truck. The club's floor rippled underfoot as the noise boomed again and again.

When the disk jockey cut off the music, everyone could hear the shrill screams.

Then Chiz smelled it. Over the spicy aromas of the buffet table and the various costly unguents and perfumes of his fellow guests, he caught the odor of freshly spilled blood. And lots of it.

Before anyone else could connect the dots, and with a speed no one in the club could match, he raced for the women's bathroom. The door opened as he reached it, and Puma Lee stepped out, spattered from head to foot in blood.

People standing close by saw her like that, and with the sounds that might have been explosions fresh in their minds, began to yell, "Bomb! Bomb!" Panic spread like wildfire through the crowd.

Chiz took advantage of the general pandemonium and replayed a scene that had appeared in virtually every movie he'd ever made. He scooped the damsel in distress in his bared, bulging arms and rushed her to safety—in this case, the fire exit.

WITH HIS CREW OF BOUNCERS busy calming and evacuating the crowd, it fell to Pismo Pete to be first to enter the women's bathroom. He didn't want to do it, but he had no choice. Even though there was a possibility of another explosion, the job couldn't wait for the Hollywood cops and the paramedics. If a bomb or bombs had been set off by terrorists or some lunatic fan, somebody had to go in at once and check for survivors. After all, a big-time celeb could be down and hurt, even dying inside.

As he pushed open the door, the ex-outlaw biker and sometime stunt double thought he was prepared for what he might find, but he was wrong. He'd never seen so much blood. It was spattered everywhere on the white floor and walls, making them look pink. And every toilet-stall partition had been jaggedly breached down the middle, as if slashed by a chain saw.

What kind of a bomb was precise enough to do a thing like that?

Equally puzzling was the absence of any lingering odor of explosives, no pall of smoke in the room, no sign of heat scorching anywhere. Glass from the shattered mirrors crunched under the stacked heels of his cowboy boots, but amazingly the lavatory's high, narrow windows remained intact.

Behind him, the bathroom door swung open a crack, and one of his bouncers said, "Need any help, Pete?"

"Stay the fuck out," he growled over his shoulder. "This is a one-man job until I say different."

Something dripped from the ceiling onto the cuff of his ankle-length leather trench coat.

"Shit!" he said, wiping off the splat of blood with the heel of his hand. Then he looked up. Beads of red clung to the ceramic-tile ceiling like a nightmare dew. One of the ruby droplets broke free and hit him square on the chin.

"Jesus," Pismo Pete gasped, quickly rubbing it away.

"Don't think about it, just fucking do it," he muttered to himself as he hurried down the line of stalls, hoping to find a survivor, expecting to find a body or bodies.

He found no one, no grisly litter of body parts,

either, but he did notice that each of the toilet-tank tops was slightly askew and he couldn't miss the bloody handprints all over them. Water ran in all the toilets, like they'd just been flushed. Or their tank balls were stuck.

Cautiously, the security chief entered the last stall and, doing his best to avoid the gory smears, he swung aside the tank's heavy porcelain lid.

Long blond hair swirled in the pink water, momentarily obscuring the pale face that lay beneath, trapped under the arm of the tank float.

Evidence that sunk the bomb theory, once and for all.

6

"What would you like, Dr. Smith?" asked the woman behind the serving counter at the Folcroft Sanitarium cafeteria. The clock on the wall behind her read 10:49 p.m., eleven minutes until the food concession shut down for the night.

"I'd like to be home," Smith told her as he surveyed neatly arranged dishes of orange Jell-O, fruit salad and vanilla pudding sitting on a bed of flaked ice. It was another one of *those* nights. No home cooking for him. No delightful "Matlock" rerun to settle his meal. And later, as he drifted off to sleep, there would be no wide, warm, wifely backside in a flannel nightgown pressed against his own. Once again, in the name of duty, Dr. Harold W. Smith had been forced to sacrifice his simple comforts.

"I don't see any prune whip," he complained.

"If it isn't already set out, Dr. Smith, I'm afraid it's all gone until tomorrow."

Smith scanned the cafeteria case until he located his second choice. "Then I'll just have the shredded beets."

"That's all you're going to eat?" the counter-woman said, aghast. "Good grief, you're not a caterpillar. You can't live on beets. You need something more substantial under your belt. Look over here, we've still got some of tonight's special beef stew...."

Smith followed her plastic-gloved finger to the wide stainless-steel serving pan. Embedded in pasty, dark brown sauce were yellow bits that might have been potatoes, orange bits that might have been carrots, green bits that might have been peas and gray, gristly chunks that were most probably meat. The woman picked up the serving spoon and stirred in the shiny golden grease that had floated to the surface.

"How 'bout a nice big plate of piping-hot stew?" she asked him. "If you're going to work late again, it'll help you keep up your strength."

The doctor shuddered at the idea. Past middle age, he was a spare-looking man who had given the best part of a lifetime to the enjoyment of Spartan pleasures. His ideal main course was his wife's famous meat loaf, which consisted of five parts uncooked oatmeal to one part ground chuck, all bound together with her own family-secret moistener of corn starch dissolved in warm tap water. Maude precooked this confection in the microwave on high for twenty minutes to fully render the fat and juices. After a thorough draining, which included some manual compression, she baked the loaf in her conventional oven at four hundred degrees until it gave off a noise like a snare drum when she thumped it with the back of a spoon.

"I'll just have the beets, thanks," he said.

"You're going to turn into a beet one of these days," the counterwoman warned him as she filled a small ceramic bowl with a heap of dark purple shreds. "Or a puddle of prune whip."

"I do appreciate your concern," Dr. Smith said as he accepted the dish from her. "But I'm afraid I have a very sensitive stomach. I have to be extremely careful what I put in it."

Sitting down in the deserted eating area, he took three paper napkins from the dispenser, flattened them one on top of the other, then tucked the triple layer into his collar. With the front of his gray suit thus defended from accident, Smith ate quickly and confidently, tipping the bowl so he could spoon up every last drop of the ruby juice.

After bussing his single dish, Dr. Harold Smith trudged back down Folcroft's well-waxed hallway. He'd been doing the same job, in the same location, for more than three decades. His work had nothing to do with the business of the sanitarium, which existed largely, if not completely, to conceal the nature of his work. From his second-floor office overlooking Long Island Sound, Smith tracked current events both at home and abroad, ever alert for any threat to the republic. His secretary and the mainframe computers deep in the bowels of the brick building were his only company. And that suited him just fine.

Computer science had been his chief passion for better than thirty-five years. At the height of the Cold War, as a midlevel CIA programmer, he had combined the then fledgling field with his innate skill as a forecaster of future events. His predictions were not only based on mind-boggling rows of numbers, reflecting shifts in industrial production, annual rainfall and immigration rates of certain insect pests; they also factored in reports from CIA field operatives on the ambitions and mental states of key political figures. Sometimes it turned out that the critical element in an equation wasn't a dictator's relationship with the Kremlin, but how he got along with his live-in mother-in-law.

The accuracy of young Smith's analyses eventually came to the attention of a visionary new President, who had immediately sensed his patriotism, dedication and moral rectitude. Before his murder in Dallas, that President had done some oracling of his own. He had become convinced that, Cold War appearances to the contrary, internal threats not external ones were the real danger to the nation's survival. The limits of his constitutional powers prevented him from protecting democracy from its true enemies: the criminals eroding it from within. He created CURE as a temporary measure, a stop-gap to steer the country past the bad patch he was certain it faced. CURE was designed around the singular talents of Harold W. Smith. It was a one-man black-ops show with no direct support staff, no money trail leading back to Congress. Smith's task was to deploy his unique abilities to identify and defuse potential disasters. He had the authority to do whatever it took to ensure the survival of the nation, and his secret brief included the power to target selected individuals for assassination. Smith's only overseer was the Commander in Chief himself.

Since that bright late-November day so long ago, he had worked with a succession of Presidents, resolving a succession of do-or-die problems. Some of the Chief Executives had been pleased when they learned of CURE's existence; others had not. Whether they approved or disapproved, it changed nothing. The covert intelligence network Harold W. Smith had built had already acquired a life of its own. As is so often the case, what had been originally intended as temporary, had out of necessity become permanent.

As Smith shut his office door behind him, he decided he felt a little better for having eaten something. It had been a very frustrating day for the director of CURE. Like Chicken Little, he was having trouble convincing anyone of the danger he saw ahead.

The current President, when informed of the situation via CURE's direct line to the White House, had said, ''So, let me understand you correctly, Dr. Smith. By taking this hormone drug you're talking about, I can eat all the french fries I want, and in the process actually get thinner and more physically fit? And you want my okay to put the kibosh on it?''

To the Commander in Chief, the drug known as WHE—Wolverine Hormone Extract—had sounded like a hell of a deal.

To Smith, it sounded like a sign of the times.

Painless self-improvement had been a growth industry in the U.S. for more than twenty years. Much of its dogma was based on the assumption that you are what you're thinking. According to its glib promoters, it was possible to restructure any or all parts of your life just by playing a tape loop of thoughts over and over in your head. *I am happy. I am sexy. I am rich.* Conveniently enough, these positive image-shaping thoughts didn't have to be original, and could be rented from those doing the promoting. In a society devoted to improvement by self-hypnosis, personal growth no longer required actual striving and real hardship. Therefore, change had no down payment, no sacrifices. It was easy and fun, and there were no irreversible dire consequences.

The prospect of instant, painless self-reinvention gave Smith cold shivers. To his way of thinking— and he was a man who had worn the same brand and color of suit, tie, shirt, socks and underwear to work for the past thirty-five years—a life without a center point was no life at all.

Historically, the failure rates of these kinds of bogus personal-growth schemes ran close to ninety-six percent, so their impact on society was largely indirect. They were time-wasters, energy sappers. Snake oil. But Dr. Smith saw in their very proliferation a disturbing long-term trend. The American people had somehow convinced themselves that an easy way out had to exist, and they were hell-bent on finding it.

Bottom line—the nation was primed for something like WHE. Unlike heroin, cocaine and methedrine, the drug was not illegal. It was too new for that. WHE produced neither euphoria nor hyperactivity; instead, it altered the basic chemistry of the human body, turning fat to muscle virtually overnight.

Painless self-improvement.

The hard-body Holy Grail.

WHE not only made muscles bigger. It made the users more aggressive. More territorial. And, as had been demonstrated on "Friday Night Football," prone to outbursts of unimaginable violence.

Over the past few hours, Smith had run dozens of computer simulations, and the results always came out the same. As long as the drug was refined from its natural source, the endangered wolverine, the distribution and societal effects would be limited. Because of the expense, only the very rich would have access to it. The resulting epidemic of mayhem would be unpleasant, but containable. Once WHE had been successfully synthesized, however, it would be cheaper to produce than aspirin, and in short order, available on every street corner, if not in every corner health-food store. His most optimistic projections showed that within eighteen days of the synthetic variety's first appearance, every major city in the United States would be under martial law. After another eighteen days, society as we know it would have dissolved. Those not taking WHE by day thirty-six would be hunted down and killed by those who were.

Hearing the news, the President had heaved an audible sigh and said, "That bad, huh?"

Indeed it was.

Smith had first learned about the disruptive potential of the experimental drug over a year ago, while conducting a routine survey of academic-research activity. The director of CURE had tried to sink the Purblind University project through the usual channels—and thought he had succeeded by arranging for the suspension of all research funding. Most of Smith's behind-the-scenes manipulation of critical events was in this subtle, nonviolent vein—very promising careers just went belly-up, for no apparent reason. Hired assassins he saved as a last resort; among other things, they were expensive. In this case, Smith had waited too long to call in Remo and Chiun, CURE's enforcement arm. The biochemist in question had vanished with all his research, and set up shop somewhere offshore. So far, Smith hadn't been able to locate him yet.

A bell-like tone made the director swivel around in

his chair. It came from a color television set bolted high on the wall. The Emerson was part of CURE's global Intel uplink, and was monitored by sophisticated computer programs that would alert Smith to anything truly newsworthy.

What he was looking at now was a news flash from Los Angeles about a movie star's murder at a chichi Hollywood club. The bulletin cut to dramatic video that showed the actor Chiz Graham carrying his bloodied actress wife, Puma, to a waiting limo. They both had bodies like comic-book superheroes. It was the effect of WHE; of that, Smith had no doubt. As the limo zoomed away down Sunset, the voice-over narration said, "Although she was first believed to be a victim in the brutal attack that has left megastar Vindaloo dead, police now confirm that Puma Lee is a suspect in the bizarre killing."

This is how it begins, Smith thought.

7

Bambi Sue Baculum, her blue eyes as big as saucers, gazed at what lay across the palm of her new husband's hand and said, "I knew you were in good shape for your age, darling, but I never expected *anything* like this."

"Sweetheart, you ain't seen nothing yet," the senator assured her.

Without further fanfare, and for the fourth time in a little over an hour, ninety-something Ludlow Baculum mounted his apple-cheeked bride. They had already made love from one end of the Malibu beach house to another. Their violent coupling had tipped over lamps and end tables. Now they christened the ocean-view living room's sunken conversation pit, rumpling and disarranging the couch cushions in their bliss.

Not even in his early teens had Lud felt so magnificently potent. Like the rest of his body, his wedding tackle was totally buffed. It wasn't simply a matter of having the necessary rigidity. The desire was there, too. Overwhelming desire. It burned like a high gas flame under the saucepan of bubbling oatmeal that was his geriatric brain. He suffered no distracting thoughts. His mind did not wander. It was completely focused on the pleasure he was getting and giving. Senator Baculum had never felt so alive.

As had been the case with the previous encounters, it was over very quickly. And as before, satisfaction had left the senator undiminished—no Señor Limp Doodle here. Lud was famished, though. The adhesive patch on his jutting rump itched as he walked naked across to the kitchen counter. With his bare hands, he attacked the remains of a cold prime rib roast, stripping away the rind of dense white fat and gobbling it down. Melted by the heat of his overstuffed mouth, grease ran down his chin and over his massive white-haired pectorals.

From the edge of the conversation pit, Bambi Sue cleared her throat meaningfully. When he looked over at her, she said, "More please, darling..."

"You really like it, don't you?" the senator said.

"I'll never get enough of you," she cooed. "You are a miracle worker. You're Superman." As he climbed back down into the conversation pit beside her, she let out a gasp. "God, I don't believe it!" she said. "Honey, I'm sure it's gotten even bigger."

On an irresistible impulse, Ludlow grabbed his new bride by the neck and started shaking her about.

That felt good, too.

HALF AN HOUR LATER, Ludlow Baculum stepped alone and nude out on the beach house's rear deck. In the pale light of the moon high overhead, the splashes of blood drying on the upstanding member of the U.S. Senate looked black. Bambi Sue had finally got enough sex. And so had he.

Lud stuck a fingertip in his mouth and, using the edge of his nail, tried to dislodge a piece of his late wife's neck that was stuck between two of his three remaining natural teeth. Failing to loosen the bit of trapped skin, he turned back for the house, walking through the broken slider door, past the shambles of overturned furniture and the bloody mess he'd left in the conversation pit.

He'd finally located some dental floss when a convoy of flashing red-and-blue lights started down the drive.

He paid them no mind.

That's what lawyers were for.

8

Carlos Sternovsky stopped for a much needed rest. After eight months in the Far East, he still wasn't used to the combination of high heat and humidity. He whipped out a cotton handkerchief, tipped back the broad-brimmed straw coolie hat he wore and mopped his dripping brow and cheeks. Ahead of him, trudging up the aisle between rows of elevated, shaded steel cages, a freshly drawn jug of wolverine blood in either hand, was a pair of half-naked Taiwanese laborers. They moved cautiously with their cargo; they knew to drop it might cost them their lives. Sternovsky's only burden was a notebook computer, a cybernetic log he used to keep track of which lab animals he had most recently phlebotomized. While he caught his breath, he watched the rag-diapered workers climb the shallow incline to where his electric golf cart sat parked.

All around him, covering the landscape in neat lines, were seventy rows of seventy cages each. The nearly five thousand live wolverines they contained had been imported illegally, and at tremendous expense, from Siberia by Family Fing Pharmaceuticals of Formosa. The cost of housing and maintaining the animals was equally staggering.

But the investment had already begun to bear fruit.

Thanks to an ample budget, a large, well-trained laboratory staff and state-of-the-art equipment, Sternovsky had been able to chemically isolate the active neuropeptide agent from wolverine blood. Which made it unnecessary to sacrifice an animal to get the required raw material from its hypothalamus. At this stage of product development, the wolverines had become hormonal dairy cows, and were bled on a rotational basis. Long gone were the salad days of Donny and Marie; like prize Jerseys, the lab animals had code numbers tattooed into their ears.

Sternovsky stuffed his hankie back in his shorts and shuffled up the slope. As he approached the golf cart, the Taiwanese laborers set the rattan-wrapped jugs in the back, alongside a dozen others on a bed of flaked ice. When they turned toward him, he could see the plastic clothespins they wore clamped on their noses; the tips of which were tourniqueted a startling white against the brown of their faces.

Twenty-two acres of nothing but wolverines in sweltering tropical heat created a stench that was an instant emetic for most people. On top of that, a worker couldn't walk down the lines of cages without drawing a volley of musk spray—and the wolverines usually hit what they were aiming at. As Sternovsky got behind the steering wheel of the electric cart, the two laborers used a weak stream of water from a row-side hose bib to rinse the oily, yellow-green gunk off their arms and legs. The drawing of blood had become Sternovsky's job by default. No one else with the technical skill would go anywhere near the "Stink Ranch," as it was called. No one else was immune to the smell.

He putted the cart around the two men and up the hill, past the corrugated silo that held the wolverines' dry-pellet food. Everywhere he looked, he could see half-naked workers lugging buckets, shoveling, pushing wheelbarrows. Feeding, watering and excrement removal went on nonstop, from dawn to dark.

At the top of the low hill, the scientist drove around the trailer where he lived and did most of his work. He took the single-lane road down the other side of the slope. The company road was string straight. It ran along the top of a dike that separated two tracts of marshy scrubland. In the distance a mile ahead, the setting sun lit up the flanks of the main Family Fing Pharmaceutical complex, turning its alabaster walls, immense holding tanks and mazes of pipelines a rosy gold.

The Family Fing fortune had been built on sales of a product line called Imposter Herbalistics, which offered imitation black-bear gall bladder, white-rhino horn and Bengal-tiger pizzle in easily digestible, powdered form. The Fings specialized in making in quantity what nature or man had made scarce. They did this by first isolating the active agent in the folk medicine, then they used specially developed strains of bacteria as microscopic manufacturing plants. These bacteria were genetically tailored to give off the desired chemical compound as part of their ordinary waste. The synthetic end product was guaranteed to be chemically identical to the real thing and so, Family Fing's advertisements claimed, was just as safe and effective.

Imposter Herbalistics were sucked up on a daily basis by millions of Asians who could now afford to treat themselves with the best, and by holistically minded Westerners who were eager to sample the native cures of the Pacific Rim, but unwilling to have the death of a rare critter on their consciences. Of course no one asked where Family Fing got the raw material on which its bacterial magic depended. In point of fact, the company's ongoing experiments with endangered animals had pushed more than one species to the brink of extinction.

As Sternovsky and Family Fing well knew, the main difference between the Imposter Herbalistics line and WHE was that the new drug actually worked.

The research biochemist backed the golf cart up to a loading dock, where workers in crisp white jumpsuits and matching fiberglass hard hats were lined up, waiting to carry the blood to the preprocessing area.

As the scientist got out of the cart, the foreman of

the transfer crew stepped over to him and said, "Papa Fing, he want see you up top. He say you no wait. You go now."

Sternovsky nodded. But before he could enter the plant proper, he had to suit up. Inside a steel Quonset hut beside the front entrance, he kicked off his rope sandals and climbed into a sterilized jumpsuit with built-in booties and gloves. Since he sometimes made five trips between ranch and plant in a day, covering up the wolverine dirt was quicker than an antiseptic shower, and it accomplished the same thing. He traded his coolie hat for a white paper shower cap and headed for the complex's elevator.

The building's air conditioning was pure bliss, even through the plasticized-paper jumpsuit. He got out on the tenth floor. Though no pharmaceuticals were made in this part of the structure, the halls were kept spotlessly clean. The entrance to the office suite of Fillmore Fing, founder and CEO of Family Fing, was in the middle of the corridor and marked by an intricately carved ebony-and-ivory arch.

As he entered the reception area, Sternovsky could hear Fillmore Fing's voice booming from the boardroom. The biochemist understood very little of spoken Chinese, but he recognized these words because he had heard them so many times.

"What have I done to deserve this betrayal?" the elder Fing repeated as his private secretary ushered Sternovsky through the double doors. Dressed in a gray pin-striped suit from Savile Row, the plump drug tycoon stood nose to nose with his number-two son, Fosdick, who was the head research chemist for the family business. Except for the sad state of Papa's hairline, and the clear snot bubble blowing in and out of Fosdick's right nostril, their faces could have been mirror images.

Upon Sternovsky's arrival, Fillmore Fing ceased his tirade. He walked over to his desk and selected a massive Cuban cigar from a mahogany humidor. He immediately lit up, puffing hard.

Fosdick hurried to follow his father's lead. His hand trembled as he fumbled around in the humidor.

"Hey, Fos, over here..."

Fillmore's oldest son, Farnham, sprawled on a white leather couch. He wore a gaudy Hawaiian print shirt under a baggy black silk sports jacket, baggy tan silk pants and a pair of handmade Italian loafers. Farnham Fing was the company's director of international sales. At present, he was enjoying being the son not on the hot seat.

Fosdick threw his brother a cigar, and when his father's back was turned, wiped his runny nose on the inside of his lab-coat cuff.

For a minute or two, the three Fings didn't utter a word. They concentrated on putting as much smoke into the air as they could. It was necessary because even a sterile jumpsuit couldn't contain the aromas of wolverine ranch that Sternovsky had brought with him.

Only when blue smoke hung thick in the board-room did Fillmore lower his cigar and address the American. "We've had a major setback in the stage-three trials," he said in perfect British-public-school-accented English. "Thanks to the sloppy science practiced by my offspring..."

"But things were going so well at midday," Sternovsky said in shock. "What on earth happened?"

"Tell him," Fillmore instructed his younger son.

"There have been some unforeseen developments over the last few hours," Fosdick admitted.

"Show him, you idiot!" Fillmore prompted.

The head chemist, his head lowered in shame, switched on the boardroom's VCR.

At the bottom of the television screen, the time, date and title identified the segment as the surveil-lance-monitor tape of Test Subject Four. It wasn't for scientific-documentation purposes alone that Family Fing scrupulously recorded the progress of its drug trials; Farnham planned to use the evidence of rapid morphing as part of his global ad campaign. The tape showed a huge man pacing back and forth in his room in the plant's medical wing. His name was Toshi Takahara. A former professional sumo wrestler, he had been taking a synthetic form of WHE for three days. In that time, his voluminous flab had retreated like a melting glacier, revealing Himalayas of newly formed muscle.

"He seems highly agitated," Sternovsky said.

Farnham laughed at the observation. "You'd be agitated, too, if you started growing a tail."

"What? That's impossible!"

"That's what we thought at first," Fosdick said glumly. "Shortly after 2 p.m., Test Subject Four complained of severe discomfort and pressure at the base of his spine. We examined him and discovered a sizable nodule that had not been present at morning rounds. Because of its growth rate, we were pretty sure it had to be a cancerous side effect of the hormone. We did an immediate biopsy, of course."

"And?"

"It's not a tumor. It's healthy bone."

The video zoomed in on the Japanese man's broad backside, bared for an examination. His behind now sported what looked like the docked tail of a Doberman.

"I don't understand," Sternovsky said. "This can't be happening."

"There's more," the elder Fing told him. He waved impatiently, and Fosdick fast-forwarded the tape. When he stopped it, the sumo wrestler was on camera again. Holding the hem of his hospital gown out of the way with his teeth, Takahara carefully urinated in each corner of his room.

"He does that every fifteen minutes. More often if the staff tries to clean it up."

"Good God!" Sternovsky said as the realization hit him. "He's marking his territory."

"We seem to be losing Number Four," Fosdick said.

"We're on the verge of losing much more than that," Fillmore snarled. "All I have built in my life is about to come crashing down around me. Based on overoptimistic projections, I committed two hundred million dollars to the construction of a new pharmaceutical plant in Union City, New Jersey. Because of the sheer incompetence of my own flesh and blood, the new product will not be ready for distribution in the States by the December 31st deadline."

That deadline was key to Farnham's marketing strategy and Fillmore's financial house of cards. It was calculated to put the hormone on the shelves of health-food stores already retailing Family Fing products in time for the New Year's resolutions of seventy million overweight, out-of-shape, fat-loving Americans. The Fings' U.S. legal counsel intended to temporarily sidestep the need for FDA approval by calling the drug a "nutritional supplement."

Long enough for Family Fing to net a few billion dollars in clear, sweet profit.

"You," Fillmore said, pointing an accusing finger at son Fosdick, "have put a knife in your father's heart."

Even in the throes of a tantrum, the elder Fing always gave the impression that there was not a hair out place *anywhere* on his body. Sternovsky had noticed this curious trait the first time he laid eyes on the man, back in Pennsylvania. Fing had gotten wind of his work during a VIP tour of the university. Fillmore was a supporting member of the International Society for Pharmaceutical Advancement, which underwrote Purblind research to the tune of seventy-five million dollars a year. Though Fing contributed generously to the cause, it hadn't bought him what he wanted—the respect of his peers. The other pharmaceutical giants looked down on Fillmore Fing because he had made all his money on "ethnic homeopathics."

"What about the others in the test panel?" Sternovsky asked. "Are they having the same kind of negative reactions?"

"We're getting some behavioral problems," Fosdick answered. "Extreme irritability. Violent and destructive outbursts. The same things we've seen with the natural hormone, but the effect is much more exaggerated."

Sternovsky winced. Those side effects hadn't stopped Fillmore from prematurely market-testing the earliest form of the drug. By selling the refined natural product at an astronomical price to a few select international celebrities, he had managed to recoup some of his initial investment.

"There's got to be something wrong with the formulation of the synthetic," the American said.

"It's chemically identical to the natural hormone," Fosdick countered.

"It can't be," the biochemist told him. "You've miscalculated somewhere."

"Think!" Fillmore commanded his number-two son. "Think what the mistake might be!"

Fosdick swallowed hard before he spoke. "It's possible that there's an impurity we've failed to remove from the bacterial product, and that impurity is interfering with the desired reaction. If that's the case, we've been unable to locate it using our most sophisticated equipment. Another possibility is that a naturally occurring but vital impurity is missing from the manufactured compound. The synthetic hormone may be simply too pure for human consumption. This might explain why it seems to be taking effect so much more rapidly than the natural product."

Sternovsky had another idea. "It's also possible that we're getting a cascade effect that has nothing to do with the presence or absence of an impurity. The changes in blood chemistry related to sudden fat depletion could be bringing on a chain reaction of somatic and psychological effects."

"What you're both saying is, you haven't got a clue," Fillmore said.

"Yes, Father," Fosdick admitted.

"I have a suggestion," Sternovsky said. "We

should immediately divide our test subjects into control groups. We can wean two off the drug completely. Reduce the dosage of two more. And maintain current levels in the last two."

"No," Fillmore said emphatically.

"No?"

"The real question here is commercial viability. Commercial viability and meeting our production deadline. What we need to know is, do the test subjects regard the worst of these side effects as so negative that they'd stop buying the drug in its present form? To answer that, we must maintain the current dose in all our subjects."

"But these are human beings, not lab rats!" Sternovsky protested.

"Wrong," Fillmore declared. "These are human beings who have agreed to act as lab rats."

"Do you really think anyone in their right mind would consider the growing of a tail to be an 'acceptable' side-effect?"

Fillmore shrugged. "If it were marketed correctly, it could easily become a fashion statement...."

Sternovsky opened his mouth to speak, but he was so flabbergasted that no words came out.

From the luxurious comfort of the boardroom's leather couch, Farnham Fing laced his fingers behind his neck and in a cheery voice said, "Welcome to Family Fing."

9

After driving around in circles in Simi Valley for twenty minutes, Remo took matters into his own hands. Every time his map reader gave him a direction, he headed the opposite way.

"Turn right," Chiun said.

Remo went left.

"I said right." Chiun indicated the direction with a long-nailed finger.

"Sorry," Remo said.

Actually, the only thing Remo regretted was that he'd let the Master of Sinanju decide their route after they got off the freeway. Chiun's plan, it seemed, was that they stealthily spiral in on their destination from a distance of several miles, presumably so it could not escape them. The alternative—that Remo should read the map and Chiun should drive the rental car—was unthinkable. Chiun didn't drive. Which was a lucky break for the residents of Simi Valley and their insurance companies.

"Go left," Chiun instructed.

Remo went right.

"We are going the wrong way."

"Oh, sorry..."

In three minutes, they pulled into the parking lot outside the L.A. Riots' sprawling training camp and general headquarters. The scheduled press conference was just starting as they pushed through the crowd of reporters and camera crews.

At the porticoed entrance to the main building, standing in front of a cluster of a dozen or more microphones, were three men: one huge, one large and one tiny.

"For those of you who don't know me," the little one said as he stepped up to the bouquet of mikes, "I'm Jimmy Koch-Roche, Mr. Boomtower's legal representative. I'm going to deliver a short prepared statement on behalf of Mr. Boomtower and the L.A. Riots organization, then I'll answer your questions, briefly."

"Is he standing in a hole?" Chiun asked Remo.

"No," replied the grizzled-looking reporter right behind them, "he *is* a hole."

The famous gunslinger attorney, even in five-inch lifts, only came up to his client's waist.

"What we've all experienced," Koch-Roche began, "the shock and horror of last night's tragic events on the football field, will live in our memories forever. But in the cold light of day, we, as a civilized society, have to ask ourselves two important questions. First, were these events unexpected, and second, who's really to blame?

"I don't have to tell you that football at the professional level is a violent and dangerous game, and one that quickly takes its toll on athletes. The average league career works out to a little less than twenty-two months. Most of the players have been in the sport since grade school—they know what they are getting themselves into. They play despite the danger, because they love it. And because they love it so much, they play even after they've been injured. That's the real tragedy here. The deaths of the Lobster quarterback and center were preventable. One hundred percent preventable."

"Don't ya just love the guy?" the grizzled reporter muttered.

On cue, head coach Dangler passed the attorney a large manila envelope.

"Thank you, Harry," Koch-Roche said as he opened it. He whipped out a sheaf of X rays and waved them at the camera lenses. "What I have here is incontrovertible proof that my client is innocent of any crime. These X-ray films were taken two weeks ago at the Lobster training center in Bangor. They indicate spinal weaknesses in both of the deceased players, weaknesses that should have kept them out of last night's game, if not out of professional football forever. Mr. Boomtower acted, as did the entire Riots organization, on the assumption that their opposition was to a man fit to step on the playing field. Unfortunately, that assumption was incorrect. We contend that the responsibility for what happened last night lies elsewhere. I'll take your questions now.''

''What kind of weaknesses are you talking about?'' one of the reporters asked. ''Can you be any more specific?''

Koch-Roche referred to a slip of paper clipped to the top X ray. ''In the case of the Lobster center,'' he said, ''a congenital abnormality of the thoracic vertebrae at T-4. In the case of the quarterback, an untreated hairline fracture of the cervical vertebrae at C-1 and C-2. Sadly, these men were disasters waiting to happen.''

''Do you expect an indictment for manslaughter soon?'' another reporter called out.

Koch-Roche shook his head and then rhymed, ''There's no crime, he'll do no time. Next question.'' He pointed at a guy wearing a network red blazer.

''What about the league?'' the man asked. ''Isn't it reviewing permanent sanctions, and a possible lifetime expulsion for your client?''

''I am confident that Number 96 will be back in orange and black for next week's game.''

A rumble of shock passed through the crowd.

''What do you say to the rumors about illegal drug use by your client?'' was the next question.

''That's slanderous rubbish. He's random-tested

like every player and has never shown a positive result for outlawed drugs.''

The reporter shot back with a quick follow-up.
''Then how do you explain the sudden change in his
appearance and his enormous weight gain?''

''I don't have to explain it. Next question.''

At this point, Bradley Boomtower bent over at the
waist and whispered something into Koch-Roche's
ear.

Watching this, it occurred to Remo that the football
player's finger span, thumb to pinkie, was almost as
wide as his attorney's shoulders.

''Okay, okay,'' Koch-Roche said, waving Boomtower off. Then he amended his previous remark.
''My client attributes his added muscle mass to a new
diet and herb regimen legally imported from Asia. All
perfectly natural, I can assure you.''

The grizzled guy had a question of his own. He
shouted it through a cupped hand. ''After seeing what
Mr. Boomtower did to those two Lobster players last
night, do you really expect people to swallow this
crock about preexisting injuries?''

''Each person is free to make up his or her own
mind, of course,'' the attorney answered. ''But based
on the evidence, I am confident that my client will be
fully exonerated.''

Something beeped annoyingly. Koch-Roche
reached under the jacket of his three-piece suit and
drew out his cellular phone. He turned away from the

microphones before he spoke into it. The conversation was short. When he turned back to the audience, he announced, "That's all we have time for today. Thank you for your patience, ladies and gentlemen."

Deaf to the protests of the reporters, the trio ducked through the smoked-glass front doors of the Riots' HQ.

"So, who're you guys with?" the grizzled newsman asked Remo. He was looking around their necks for the press IDs they didn't have. His photo ID indicated he was Les Johnson, from "National Sports Hotline."

"I'm Remo Wormwood, *Folcroft News-Dispatch*."

"Never heard of it."

"A biggish small-town daily. It's East Coast. Long Island."

"And you?" Johnson looked at Chiun, who said nothing.

"This is Dan Tien," Remo told him. "He's the sports editor from *North Korea Today*."

"Gee, I didn't know they followed pro football in North Korea."

"They get it on satellite TV now," Remo said. "Along with curling and bass fishing."

"Teeter-totter is very popular over there, too, isn't it?" Johnson said to Chiun. "I saw your national team in the Olympic trials. Very impressive legwork."

"It's all in the breath," Chiun confided. "Everything comes from the breath."

"I wouldn't presume to argue with you there, Dan."

"Say, Johnson," Remo said, "if a daring and enterprising reporter was of a mind to, how would he go about sneaking into the Riots' training center?"

The veteran newshound made a sour face. "Bad idea, Wormwood. The worst idea I've heard in a long time. Look around. Why do you think this pack of jackals is standing around, playing pocket pool, instead of rushing into that building and pursuing the biggest story of the year? Do you think we are a kinder, gentler media?"

"Yeah, I kinda wondered about that. There don't seem to be any guards on the entrance, either."

"Oh, there are guards, all right. They're on the inside, watching, waiting for the chance to bust some heads. The Riots' security staff is made up of proball wanna-bes and washouts. They're big and they're mean, but not nearly as big and mean as the players. Even if you managed to get close enough to ask them a question, the players won't say 'boo' to you without authorization from the team front office. What they will do if they catch you inside is break all your arms and legs and pitch you in a Dumpster. The gulls will pick out your eyes, Wormwood."

"We're talking purely hypothetical here," Remo insisted.

"You're sure?"

"Sure, I'm sure."

"Well, in that case, I'd go around to the delivery entrance and hide there until I could duck into the storage area. Say, wait a minute! Where are you two going? Didn't you hear what I said? Hey!"

The newsman watched Remo and Chiun disappear into the crowd.

10

The tall man in the orange-and-black T-shirt tapped on the wall beside the warehouse's interior door. Something metallic clacked, the door opened and the security guard vanished through it.

Before the door closed, Chiun was up and moving.

His one and only pupil sensed the opportunity, too. But sadly, after so many years of diligent instruction, a fraction of an instant later. The Reigning Master of Sinanju glided across the concrete loading dock like he was on roller skates. Behind him, he could hear the huffing of Remo's breath and the thundering clump of his huge feet.

Chiun heaved a sigh. Just when he thought his student had finally achieved a level of masterly perfection came the disappointment. The inevitable disappointment.

It wasn't the teaching that wore a man down, he thought.

It was the reteaching.

Three decades of experience with this pupil had confirmed his belief that whites could not retain knowledge for more than a few days. Of course, they could remember their Social Security numbers, their last names and the necessary procedure for opening a tube of toothpaste. The important things, the subtle things, were beyond their ability. Like breathing. And running. Perhaps it was time to once again drag out the long sheets of rice paper for poor Remo. First, he would have to relearn to walk barefoot over the flimsy stuff without tearing it. Then to run over it. And finally, to run in the ridiculous, stiff-soled Italian shoes he chose to wear.

Being the world's only teacher of Sinanju was a job requiring infinite patience, complete dedication and daredevil aplomb. In other words, Chiun thought, it was right up his alley. The problem was, and had always been, the pay.

There was never so much as a nugget of extra gold for all the overtime his student's limitless shortcomings forced upon him. No, it never counted when negotiations came up for a new contract and the payment in gold. They always divided the amount Chiun wrangled from Smith. Not an equal division, of course—what need did Remo have for gold when he enjoyed the honor of working with the Reigning Master of Sinanju? Also, Chiun had a greater responsibility—his birthplace, the entire village of Sinanju.

Years and years ago, at the start of Remo's training, the Master had tried to talk his employer into discarding the idea of his taking on a pupil. Chiun had argued that a pupil was redundant, that for the right price the Master himself could do all the assassinations. But Emperor Smith had foreseen a problem with Chiun's moving unnoticed through a society of whites—something an assassin had to do in order to succeed. Today the Emperor's wisdom had proved itself once again. It was because of Remo's overwhelming, all-reflective whiteness that Chiun had blended in so well with the reporters out front.

It was said that an acceptance of one's fate was the first step on the road to serenity. Though Remo had completed the rites that prepared him to be a master, he had lapses. Clearly, the fate of Chiun was to be joined at the hip to a perpetual student. Such a thing was not unheard-of in Korean culture. In the celebrated Pansori novels of his homeland, every noble hero was balanced by a comic footman, a Chong-wook.

That was Remo.

His Chong-wook.

With all due haste, the Master closed the distance between himself and the door that led from the warehouse to the training center proper. To the right of the door, set at chest height in the wall, was a ten-key touch pad that controlled the lock. It was very much like the keypad of his treasured Star Trek Next Generation Phaser TV remote control. Above the rows of numbers was an LED readout. Chiun held his palm close to, but didn't touch the keys. He moved his hand back and forth slightly, as if heating it over a candle flame.

"What are you doing?" Remo asked as he finally arrived behind the Master. "You couldn't have seen the code that guy used."

Chiun didn't waste time on a reply. The razor tip of his crooked fingernail clicked on the plastic pad. He tapped on three of the keys.

The warm ones.

"This could take all day," Remo complained as the words "No admit" blinked on the LED screen.

Chiun tapped in the same three numbers, but in a different sequence.

"No admit. No admit. No admit."

"We don't *have* all day, Little Father."

On the fourth try, the lock shot back.

"Dumb luck," Remo snorted.

Chiun shook his head. "Luck had nothing to do with it."

"Then how did you open it?"

"It would take me ten years to explain it to you, and a week later you would have forgotten it all. Instead of wasting time on lessons too complex for the simple whiteness of your brain, let us proceed to do as the Emperor has commanded."

Inside the training center, the halls were wide and low ceilinged. There were no windows to the outside, only doors leading to interior rooms. Some of the doors were made of glass. On the trot, Remo and

Chiun passed a small surgery and an extensively equipped X-ray room. Beyond that was a hydrotherapy center. Remo looked through the porthole in the door. Two of the half-dozen stainless-steel tubs were occupied, but the player they sought was not there.

As they moved by an open office door, the man inside glanced up from the pile of papers on his desk. He wore the white uniform of a physical therapist. He looked startled to see them. They were already forty feet down the hall when they heard the sound of a chair scraping back. The therapist stuck his head out the door for a second, then ducked back in his office.

When Chiun saw the three big men in orange-and-black T-shirts charging down the hall toward them, he knew the man in white had called for help. The security guards filled the corridor as they lumbered, shoulder to shoulder. When they stopped a few feet away, the one in the middle raised a small black object to the side of his face and spoke into it.

"Yeah, we got 'em. Nah, we can handle it."

The security guard in charge was, even by the standards of his hirsute race, notably hairy. His pale face, except for a patch of forehead and the area under the eyes, was covered by a curly black beard, trimmed close. The hair on his head was long on the sides and in back, after the fashion of the new-country-music stars of the glorious Nashville Network. The hair on his forearms looked like his beard, but was untrimmed.

"What do you and Kung Fu there think you're doing?" the large hair-covered man demanded of Remo.

The question immediately put Chiun's back up. "What does he mean by 'Gung Fu'?" the horrified Master asked his pupil. "Does he mistake me for a Chinese? Is he blind? How could he mistake *this* for the wide-nosed face of a barbarian?"

"I mistake you for a dumb shit," the security guard informed him. "About to be a dead shit."

"Kung fu's a Chinese martial art," Remo explained. "My friend here's Korean. To him, it's a big deal. Something to do with a thousand years of invading armies, domination, rape and pillage. Go figure…"

"Put a lid on the double-talk," the head guard said. "You two are trespassing on private property of the L.A. Riots. A crime punishable by the kicking of your butts."

"Look," Remo said, "we just want a word with one of the players. Two minutes and we're out."

"Buddy, you're already out."

At a silent signal, the other two security men closed in on Remo, a pincer move calculated to sandwich and overpower him. They didn't bother protecting themselves in a serious way, as they outweighed their target by a hundred pounds each. Because of the size differential, they were willing to absorb a punch or two in order to get their big hands on him.

Giving Remo first crack was their mistake.

And they only got one.

At the same moment, both guards lunged. It looked like a football play they had practiced thousands of times. Only they ran it at what seemed to be one-quarter speed. When the guards' fingers closed, they snatched only thin air. For an instant, the two men stood frozen, unable to grasp why they hadn't grasped the intruder's neck. With their arms extended straight out from the shoulder, the lengths of their torsos, from armpit to waist, were open to attack.

Ribs snapped like bread sticks, dry and crisp.

Both guards dropped to their knees. As they clutched their sides, foreheads pressed to the floor, they wheezed and gasped for breath.

"Too slow," Chiun commented. He wasn't referring to the fallen guards, whose fighting skills were laughably childlike. The comment was directed at his pupil, Chong-wook, the ironic footman. Then the Master unleashed what might have been his ultimate insult. "If they had been Gung Fu," he told Remo, "they would have caught you."

"Hey, now, that isn't fair...."

The big hairy guy leaped, glomming onto Remo's back. Using all his weight, the security guard tried to drive the dangerous trespasser into the orange-and-black Congoleum.

"Whoop!" Remo said, twisting at the waist. Not a power twist. A timing twist.

The hairy guard flew over his shoulder and

slammed headfirst into the wall with a mighty thunk. As the man's body slipped to the floor, it revealed a face-shaped indentation in the Sheetrock.

Chiun didn't give the remarkable depth of the concavity so much as a glance. "We've wasted enough time here," he said, stepping over the unconscious body.

"The weight room must be just up ahead," Remo said to the Master's slender back. "Hear the iron plates clanking? And the rap music?"

Chiun stopped short.

"What's wrong?" Remo asked him.

"An evil smell." Chiun fanned a hand in front of his slender nose. "It is the stink of a fatty-red-meat-eating urine-dribbler."

"Don't look at *me* like that."

"You don't eat red meat, so it couldn't possibly be you."

"Thanks so much for the vote of confidence," Remo said. "Given our present location, though, that nasty aroma could be coming from anyone or anywhere."

"This is no ordinary smell," Chiun countered. "It's like what rises from a low clump of bush after a gentle spring rain."

"You mean cat pee?"

Chiun glided ahead and turned the corner into the weight room, which was big enough to accommodate the entire Riots team. The walls were lined with floor-to-ceiling mirrors, and the floor was taken up with great steel contraptions and racks of dumbbells and barbells. As Remo followed Chiun through the doorway, the starting offensive line of the L.A. Riots looked up at them from the bench-press area. Sweaty, towering men, whose combined weight was somewhere around three quarters of a ton.

Remo smiled at the men in orange and black. Out of the corner of his mouth he said to Chiun, "Johnson had said they were bigger and meaner than the security staff. He forgot to add younger."

A guttural growl came from beyond the offensive players. At the squat rack, a monster man held an Olympic bar balanced on his impossibly wide shoulders. The heavy steel bar was bowed in the middle by the tremendous weight at both ends. Bradley Boomtower let eight hundred pounds of iron crash to the deck.

"He is the one who smells," Chiun announced, pointing an imperious finger at the offender.

"Just the guy we want to see," Remo said.

As the second-most-dangerous man in the world took a step forward, the two guards, two tackles and the center spread out to block his path. A grove of redwood trees in numbered, XXXL sweatshirts.

"We've got business with your big guy, there," Remo said.

"And what exactly is your business?" the center said, testing the heft of a seventy-pound dumbbell.

"A glorious and time-honored trade," Chiun answered at once. "We are assassins."

Remo gave the Master a look of dismay.

Behind the offensive line, Boomtower howled with rage and began to advance.

"Stay back, F.V.," the right guard said, holding up his hands. "You're in enough hot water already. You get in any more trouble and you'll be out of the lineup next week."

"We need you against Portland, man," the right tackle said. "That Parakeet air attack will pick us apart without your pass rush."

The offensive linemen edged closer to Remo.

"Our time in the gym is very special to us," the center said, still armed with the dumbbell. "We don't like being gawked at by geeks and gooks in our most private moments. You guys sound like you might be crazy, fucking escapees from Atascadero, but that doesn't cut you any slack with us. My friends here are going to hold your arms and legs down while I beat your heads to mush with this. From the chin up, you're gonna be nothing but a red stain on the carpet." He waggled the dumbbell.

"Hey, Chiun, I might need a little help here," Remo said. "Chiun?"

The Reigning Master of Sinanju slipped his hands inside the loose sleeves of his robe. A gesture that needed no further explanation.

There were only five of them.

The pupil was on his own.

"That's it, old-timer," the left guard said, "you just wait there, nice and still, and we'll see to you in a minute."

Remo meanwhile had picked up a football from a bin on the floor. Thick wrist flexing, he gripped it with his fingertips on the laces. His knuckles whitened, and his fingers dug deeply into the ball.

It exploded in his hand like a party balloon, only much, much louder.

The noise made the offensive line pause in their advance.

"Is that little trick supposed to scare us?" the left tackle said.

Remo selected another ball from the bin. "I'm asking you real nice to clear a path," he told them.

"What're you gonna do, hurt our ears again?" the center said, laughing.

Remo dropped back to pass, pumped once. The Riots didn't take the fake, so he let fly.

The offensive line thought it was another fake.

Only Chiun saw the ball leave Remo's hand. It traveled twenty feet before the pointed end made contact with the middle of the center's heavy-boned chin. Again the ball compressed until its seams exploded. The impact snapped back the huge man's head, driving him into a watercooler, which tipped over as he dropped to the carpet. His fellow players ducked and used their hands to deflect the flying pigskin shrapnel.

Remo picked up another ball and slapped it into his open palm.

The right guard bent over the center. "Louie's out cold," he said. "That skinny little punk KO'd him with a pass. Jesus, he's spitting teeth."

"Assassinate this," the right tackle snarled, scooping up the object the center had dropped.

Remo ducked, allowing the seventy-pound dumbbell to fly over his head.

The other players followed suit and started chucking dumbbells at him. Remo didn't even try to get out of the way. As the heavy objects rained down on him, end over end, he swept them aside, deflecting them right or left with the backs of his wrists. Dumbbells clanged on the floor and bounced, rolling every which way as the Riots emptied the racks of weights.

"Get the fucker!" the left tackle cried, rushing over to the stacks of iron plates. "Flatten his ass!" He picked up a thirty-five-pound plate like it was a pizza pie and sent it spinning, discus style, across the room at Remo.

But to Remo, the plate moved through the air so slowly that even a small child could have avoided it.

The spectacle bored Chiun. There was no subtlety to it. He withdrew his hands from inside his sleeves and covered his shell-like ears to protect them from the crash of weights hitting the floor. As the four big men used up all the metal plates, they grew visibly weaker. Patches of sweat appeared on their chests and under their arms. Their breathing became labored. They leaned on the steel contraptions for support.

Chiun carefully watched the man Emperor Smith had sent them to interrogate. Number 96. Animal Man. Chiun had never seen a creature quite like him. A creature with such density of muscle. The corded flesh on the backs of his arms looked like the mooring lines of a freighter. And the covering skin was almost blindingly shiny, stretched tight, almost to the splitting point. Nothing the least bit subtle there, either; as such, he was hardly a worthy opponent for a Master of Sinanju.

Chiun could sense Number 96's desire to enter the fray. The man was chomping at the bit. What held him back? Not fear, certainly. Like the others, he was too ignorant to be afraid. Perhaps another desire, a more powerful one, kept him in check?

Even from across the room, Animal Man's smell was overwhelming. That Remo couldn't detect it didn't surprise Chiun. A man who had once indulged in the cheesy burger, the Camel, the Budweiser, couldn't be expected to have an undamaged sensory system. The aroma Number 96 gave off wasn't the smell of a human, not even a dirty human. This puzzled Chiun.

In point of fact, the Master hadn't paid much attention to the background details of the mission as laid out by Emperor Smith. Something about a drug. Such things were usually unimportant, mere trifles when compared with the truly significant— how he could leverage upward the gold payment for the next negotiation.

When Bradley Boomtower suddenly turned on his heel and headed for the nearest exit, Chiun was after him like a shot.

"Hey, get that guy!" the right guard wheezed.

Before the offensive line could respond, the Master had slipped past them.

11

Bradley Boomtower let the eight-hundred-pound load roll off his shoulders and crash to the weight-room floor. His intention was to snatch hold of the two intruders who had violated his territory with their ghastly fish smell and then tear their soft bodies into thin, bloody strips. His outrage at their presence inside his domain was too terrible to be held in check by the threat of league banishment or by the upraised hands of his fellow players. Boomtower could no longer think in terms of the future. As far as he was concerned, next week's game might as well have been next century's. There was no longer a barrier between what he felt like doing and what he did. The barrier that kept human society from ripping itself apart. In a way, what he possessed, or what possessed him, was absolute freedom; in another way, it was absolute slavery.

To get his hands on those who muddied his urine-marked perimeter, Boomtower would have thrown aside his teammates. He would even have killed them if they had tried to stop him.

The enormous nose tackle took a step forward, then hesitated as another, even more powerful need filled him. All around the squat rack were heaped empty boxes of Manteca. It had been eight minutes since his last "energy" snack. And already the hunger pangs were starting up again. These were no sudden cravings for a particular food. He wasn't responding to mouth-watering mental images of pork chops or rib roast. The feelings of aching emptiness were so intense that they were impossible to ignore. The inside of his belly clanked and shuddered like a length of steel chain caught up in the blades of a madly revving lawn mower.

A small bit of the pre-WHE Bradley Boomtower remained, self-aware, imprisoned in the giant body. And that man, who had earned a business degree from a Big Ten college, who had over eight million dollars in cash stashed in a Cayman Islands bank, was frightened by the intensity of the urge. And by the fact that he was eating more and more, and was never satisfied. Only for a second did this fragment of his original personality surface, then it was sucked under, down into the whirlpool of wolverine neuropeptide.

Boomtower spun away from the spectacle of flying dumbbells and pushed out the weight room's exit. Ahead of him was the Riots' deserted practice field. As he loped across the five-lane track that circled the playing area, he sensed someone or something behind him.

He turned and saw the old fish-eater. He wanted to turn and kill the intruder, but the ache in his belly would not permit it. At the back of the near end zone, he broke into a trot. A trot for Boomtower in his present physical condition was like an all-out sprint for anyone else. For a ninety-year-old Oriental, it should have been impossible.

Should have been.

The fish-eater not only matched his sudden burst of speed, but even gained on him.

Confidently, Boomtower increased the pace to a sprint. High-kicking, he could feel the huge muscles of his quadriceps shudder at each impact with the natural sod. His size-18 feet felt light and quick under him. And they were. Since he started using the patch, he was easily the fastest man on the team. Faster even than Regional Parks, the NCAA hundred-meter record holder.

The biggest and the fastest.

His superbody sliced through the air, which screamed around his ears. He passed the twenty-yard line, the fifty, and with the opposite goalpost looming large, took the opportunity to look back over his shoulder. He expected to see the old man falling back somewhere around seventy yards behind, or perhaps even collapsed on the field. Instead, to his shock, he discovered the old guy running right at his back.

Well, maybe *running* wasn't the right word.

It didn't appear that the Oriental geezer's legs were

moving at all. And his arms weren't pumping, either. He had his hands tucked inside the baggy sleeves of his robe. Yet, there he was, serenely drafting in the wake the nose tackle left behind.

Boomtower blinked once, and like the *pop!* of a dream coming to a sudden end, the old man was gone. When Number 96 turned his head back toward the goalpost, he witnessed a vision that made his jaw drop. He saw the fish-eater descending, from a height of at least thirty feet, his robe flapping in the breeze. The old man's somersault ended as his slippered feet came down on the goal post's cross bar. He stood there, not waving his hands around for balance, but rock steady like he was standing on flat ground.

Boomtower didn't plan on stopping, but the fish-eater dropped from his perch, light as a feather, right in front of him, blocking his path. The absolute strangeness of all this made the nose tackle skid to a halt.

"Get out of my way!" Boomtower said. The sweep of his enormous right arm sent a rush of wind that stirred the tiny old man's straggly beard. The Oriental did not so much as blink.

Beyond the end zone Boomtower now faced, beyond the track, was the training center's parking lot. From where he stood, he could see his white 500-class Mercedes two-door with its one-way windows, its gold-plated bumpers, side-trim molding and wheel covers. Two days before, he had had both the front seats ripped out. No bucket seat on earth could contain his five hundred pounds. He had had a specially designed leather-upholstered bench seat installed. Also, the frame and shocks on the driver's side had been reinforced to keep the vehicle from listing too much to the left. Boomtower wanted to get to his car and drive to the nearest source of dietary fat without further delay. Over the power lines, he could just make out the gaudy signs lining the main boulevard, signs that advertised All Things Fried.

Craftily, he inched forward on the little fish-eater. And when he was well within reach, with a mighty grunt he unleashed a backhanded swing at the old man's head, a blow intended to send him flying, if not kill him outright.

Between the start of the movement and its conclusion, something very unexpected happened: his fist made contact with nothing. Which sent him tilting off balance on the edge of his left foot. Before he could catch himself came a touch that felt like a hint of breeze. A touch so soft he might have imagined it. Just there on his right hip. Instead of knocking the old man into the cheap seats, it was Boomtower himself who went suddenly hurtling through the air. He landed with a sickening crunch, twenty yards away, near the sideline.

As he scrambled to his feet, he once again faced the slip of an Oriental.

"In you, I sense a great void, a terrible hollowness," Chiun told him, shaking his head.

"Hungry," Boomtower growled, starting to lunge forward, in the direction of his Mercedes. "Got to eat."

"No."

When the little man raised his slender hand, with its extremely long fingernails, the football player paused.

"This hollowness I sense is different," Chiun explained. "Not a vacuum of the belly that can be filled with material sustenance. This is a vacuum of the spirit. You are strong, but you are also weak. And your weakness is so great that your strength is more than negated."

"Hah!" Boomtower said, thumping his massive pectoral with a balled fist.

"Under all that flesh of yours, you are still a piddler."

"Why, I could pop your little yellow head like a pimple!"

"No, you couldn't."

Boomtower lunged for the scrawny neck in the Mandarin collar. Silk brushed his outstretched fingertips; of that he was sure. And then with a jarring starburst of impact, he found his face buried to the ears in the coarse sod. Spitting dirt and strands of Bermuda grass, he looked up.

"As I said," Chiun went on, "the animal power

that you possess is chaotic, undisciplined. Ungrounded. It appears indomitable, but that is an illusion of physical form. Your strength lacks the focus of careful meditation and long study. It fails to tap the inexhaustible *chi* force of the universe. And because of that, it is as empty as a child's balloon. Perhaps it is good enough for your American football, but even the simplest strategies of teeter-totter would be beyond your grasp. The lesson here is that shortcuts do not always lead you where you want to go.''

"Where I want to go is over there," Boomtower said, nodding in the direction of the parking lot. "Stand aside."

"I have questions for you, from my Emperor."

"Screw your Emperor. And screw you, you crazy motherfucker."

"Those options are not available. My Emperor wishes to know the source of your newfound animal strength."

Boomtower could wait no longer. His internal pangs were too powerful. They even overwhelmed his instinctive fear of this strange little man. Reverse pivoting, he tried to get the Oriental moving the wrong way. For his trouble, there was an explosion of pain in his shin, and a simultaneous and sickening crack of bone. Bradley Boomtower dropped to the turf, clutching his right leg below the knee with both hands.

"You broke it!" he moaned. "Jesus, you broke my leg!"

The fish-eater's strike had been so swift, he hadn't appeared to have even moved. He stood there completely relaxed, his high forehead unlined, a slight smile on his ancient, withered face.

"Perhaps we can talk now?" Chiun said.

The nose tackle dived for him, broken leg and all.

Though the distance between them was less than a yard, Boomtower missed his target by a wide margin. And when he hit the ground, he had a shattered right forearm.

"I'm not enjoying this," Chiun assured the shrieking Goliath as he stepped closer. "I am an assassin by trade, not some ham-fisted torturer. Killing is what I do best. So you see, I would much prefer to kill you. And I will do so if you do not answer."

"Go to hell."

The nose tackle took a left-handed swipe at Chiun's ankles that didn't even come close. Then he struggled up on his one good leg. In his eyes was the naked fury of the jungle, of the wounded beast. Boomtower looked as if he would have gladly torn off his broken arm and used it to beat Chiun over the head.

"I do not understand your stubbornness," the Master of Sinanju said, clucking his tongue. "Have I not proven to you that your overwhelming strength is of no value in the face of my weakness?"

Growling from low in the pit of his stomach, Boomtower lunged with all his strength. And this time his fingers closed on silk brocade.

12

"You guys had enough?" Remo challenged, tossing the football a foot or two in the air and catching it.

The Riots offensive line lay draped over the weight-room benches, sweat soaked and panting. Only the left guard had strength enough to wave his hand in surrender. The four linemen had transferred every pound of movable weight from one side of the room to the other in their attempt to squash the dude in the black T-shirt and chinos. And now that wiry guy stepped, unfazed, over the resulting piles of iron plates, the heaps of dumbbells.

"That was fun," Remo said. He tossed the football back into the bin as he headed for the exit door. "We'll have to do it again real soon. I got to tell you something, though. It's no wonder you're always at the bottom of your conference. You guys are really out of shape...."

Outside, Remo quickly located Chiun, who stood at the far end of the practice field. He also saw a large form slumped motionless at the Master's feet. It was their quarry, Bradley Boomtower. Remo broke into a run. As he crossed the fifty-yard line, he saw Boomtower make a sudden grab for Chiun's ankle.

Remo's immediate thought was Oh, shit!

To an untrained eye, the scene in front of the goalpost appeared to suddenly blur, as if obscured by heat waves rising from the earth. To an untrained eye, it appeared that two figures maintained their relative positions. As a student of Sinanju, Remo saw things much differently. He saw the huge man lifted by the small one, whirled around his head like an orange-and-black pillow, then bounced on the turf. Lifted, whirled, bounced. Five times. *Boing. Boing.* And when the bouncing stopped, the two were in exactly the same spot as when they had started.

Remo knew without taking a pulse that the football player was dead. Chiun stood in the center of a churned-up ring of sod. It looked like the turf had endured a twelve-play goal-line stand.

"Did you have to kill him?" Remo said.

"Stupid question. I wouldn't have killed him if I didn't have to."

"We needed information from him."

"His mind was confused. He couldn't answer even the simplest of questions. The chaos inside him was too strong."

"You couldn't have just knocked him out?"

"I did him a favor."

"Yeah, maybe. But where does that leave us?"

"Examine his backside."

"What?"

"Pull down his pants and you will find the source of his animal nature."

"Yeah, right..."

"It is a small plastic patch on his right buttock."

When Remo looked more closely, he could see the outline of the square through the tightly stretched Lycra fabric. "What is it?"

"It is where the bad smell begins."

"No doubt. But it has something to do with the drug, too?"

"Of course."

As Remo struggled to draw down the football player's skintight pants, he muttered, "God, I hope *this* little scene doesn't make 'Peephole USA.'"

He exposed Boomtower's behind and a two-by-two-inch patch of adhesive. Remo recognized it as a time-release drug-delivery system, like that used for nicotine.

When Chiun reached down to peel off the patch with the tip of a long fingernail, Remo brushed his hand away. "No, don't touch it!" he exclaimed. "If you get some of the active ingredient on your fingertip, it'll go straight into your bloodstream."

"Why do you shudder so violently?" Chiun asked him. "Is it because of your concern for my safety?"

"What else?" Remo said. And he forced from his mind the image of a five-hundred-pound, five-foot-nothing Chiun running amok in Los Angeles.

13

When the homicide unit of the Hollywood police rang the doorbell of Puma and Chiz Graham's palatial mansion, it was answered not by a uniformed maid or butler, but by a very small man in a three-piece pin-striped suit.

"Good morning, Detectives," Jimmy Koch-Roche said.

The lead investigator, a burly man with a shock of snow white hair, produced two folded documents from inside his plaid sports jacket. "We have a warrant to search these premises, Jimmy," he said. "And a warrant for the arrest of one Puma Lee, also known as Harriet Louisa Smootz, on a charge of first-degree murder in the death last night of the actress Vindaloo."

Koch-Roche examined the papers, then handed them back to the officer. "All properly done, Detective Hylander," he said. "My client is prepared to surrender herself into your custody at this time. I caution you that she will make no statement to you outside my presence. And as to your search of the premises, I would like to remind you that this house contains numerous priceless works of art and irreplaceable antiques. Please instruct your forensics people to be very careful.''

The tiny lawyer led the officers into the mansion's dizzying foyer, which soared three stories high to a domed greenhouse ceiling, and was quite warm and humid. The white marble floor and walls were lined with tiers of exotic plants. Among the green-and-yellow-and-pink-striped leaves, rare orchids hung from chunks of bark in the perpetual drizzle of an automatic watering system. Koi fish spattered with color swam in the dark blue garden pool.

''Your high-profile clients seem to be having a run of bad luck,'' Detective Hylander said as they filed into the mansion proper. ''Sort of a mini-crime wave, in fact. This is the third time in less than twenty-four hours that we've had one of your people in on murder charges.''

''Nothing I can't handle,'' Koch-Roche assured him.

Puma Lee and her husband rose from the Art Deco love seat as their lawyer and the police entourage entered the overfurnished but vast living room. It looked more like an art gallery or antique showroom than a place where people actually lived. Puma was dressed in stark contrast to her public image. Instead of revealing as much of her astounding figure as possible, she concealed it under a very conservative, past-knee-length beige silk suit. Chiz wore one of the extra-baggy shirt-and-pants outfits that had previously hidden his between-picture flab. The attempt to conceal their extreme muscular development, urged by their legal counsel, was only partially successful. If one looked closely, one could see the outlines of Puma's massive quads under the silk skirt, and Chiz's baggy Hawaiian shirt couldn't conceal the breadth of the shoulders and depth of the chest it hung from.

Detective Hylander read the movie star her Miranda rights, then asked her if she'd care to make a statement. It was all polite and routine.

Jimmy Koch-Roche replied for her. "No, she wouldn't care to make a statement," he said. "On advice of counsel."

"Then I guess it's time for a trip down to the station," Hylander said.

Puma glanced down at her attorney, who nodded in agreement. From the love seat, she picked up a large leather purse, which matched the color of the suit. The purse was so overpacked its sides bulged out.

"Better leave that here, ma'am," Hylander said, reaching for the shoulder strap.

For an instant, the eyes of the cop and the movie star met. And locked. Hylander froze like a rabbit caught in high beams. The tendons in Puma's neck twitched as her gaze held him fast.

Jimmy Koch-Roche interceded at once. "It's okay,

Puma," he assured her, lightly touching the back of her hand. "You won't need the purse. If you take it, it will only prolong the booking procedure. Everything that's in there will have to be logged with the police clerk. And we want to get you out on bond as quickly as possible."

Knowing that its weight in junk food would have dropped him to his knees, the attorney let Chiz take the purse from her.

"Jimmy and I will follow you over there," Chiz told his wife as the police led her away. "Don't worry. We'll bring whatever you need."

After they'd gone, Chiz slumped back down on the love seat and said, "What a fucking mess!" Then he glowered at the tiny lawyer. "And it's all your fault."

"Wait a minute," Koch-Roche protested. "Didn't I warn you that the drug was experimental? I told you up front that there might be side effects. I sure as hell didn't put a gun to your heads and make you take it."

"So says the pusher man."

"Look," Koch-Roche snapped back, "strip the patch off your ass right now. Give me the rest of the supply you have. And I'll refund your money. I'll write the check right now."

Chiz considered this, then he dry-swallowed. "I'd go back to the way I was?"

"Fat and forty."

"Thirty-six!"

"Whatever. It's your choice. I gave the same option to your wife a few hours ago and, as you know, she turned me down flat. What do you say, Chiz? Wanna give up the new hard body?"

Chiz pulled at his world-renowned chin and grimaced. After a moment, he said, "Can you get her off the murder charge?"

"Piece of cake. And I can do it for under ten million."

"But her handprints are all over the crime scene!"

Koch-Roche tut-tutted his client. "This is the law, Chiz. Facts mean nothing. It's all in the interpretation. The *right* interpretation. I'll bring in a dozen expert forensic witnesses who will testify that Puma left those prints while struggling with the real assailant, who was in the process of ripping Vindaloo apart. I'll show that the prosecution's blood evidence came as the result of a valiant but failed attempt by Puma Lee to save her colleague's life. By the time I'm done talking, the mayor will award her a certificate of heroism. Maybe the city will even put up a statue."

"So there's really nothing to worry about?"

"What do you mean?"

"No reason to stop taking the drug."

"Like I said, that's completely up to you. A personal decision. If you don't want it, I'll buy it back. Believe me, there are plenty of others standing in line to get their hands on it."

"No, I'm talking about what's happened to Puma.

The Venom Club and Vindaloo. I mean, what if I go berserk like that? What if I happen to kill somebody?''

Koch-Roche shrugged his narrow shoulders. "As far as legal consequences go, as long as you've got the bread to pay for a proper defense, conducted by yours truly, there won't be any.''

14

Before he drove out of the mansion's eight-car garage, Chiz Graham removed the convertible top of his custom-made, cream-colored Excalibur sports car. Jimmy Koch-Roche had suggested that he take his own wheels to the police station and drive Puma home personally. He'd also suggested that Chiz put the top down so the army of waiting photographers could record the happy event in its entirety. In the hope of coloring the water for potential future jurors, Koch-Roche wanted a public display of confidence from Chiz. Strong, committed husband supports wife's innocence. The usual drill.

Chiz made good time on the freeway. As he took the exit nearest to the station house and pulled onto the city streets, he realized that he was going to arrive a few minutes ahead of schedule. Because he was starting to get a bit hungry himself, and he figured that Puma would be famished after her ordeal, he decided to make a brief stop at a minimart to pick up some tasty snacks for the return trip.

He drove past the double row of gas pumps and

parked out front of the SpeeDee Mart. When he walked through the automatic doors in his skinny, blue-tinted, wraparound sunglasses, no one recognized him. The store clerk, a rail-thin Pakistani, was preoccupied. From his station behind the cash register, he was nervously checking the antitheft mirrors along the back wall, trying to keep track of a half-dozen teenage shoppers. The do-rag sporting low-riders, ball caps backward, were gathered over by the dairy case, apparently comparing prices on whipping-cream aerosols. The clerk was trying to see if they were slipping the cans into their enormously baggy clothing.

A few yards farther down the wall, a trio of overweight Hollywood housewives in tentlike caftans was sucking down sixty-four-ounce, sugar-free, all-you-can-drink sodas while making moon eyes at the ice-cream case. Their facial expressions as they continued to sip their diet sodas all said the same thing: *Well, maybe just one DoveBar, because I've been so good*

The SpeeDee Mart's only other customer, a sales-rep type in a short-sleeved dress shirt, pocket protector and wide tie, was over by the coffee corner, tapping steaming brown fluid from a stainless-steel urn marked Irish Mint Mocha into a very large thermos cup.

Chiz took a wheeled cart and started down the narrow aisles. He was drawn at once to the hot-food section by its wonderful aroma. Under warming lights was a tray of chicken tidbits, deep-fried to golden perfection. The grease in the bottom of the pan remained liquid from the heat. Chiz dumped the entire tray of Gobs O' Chicken into a pair of foam containers, pouring the grease over the top like it was Sauce Bernaise.

He left one container open on the cart's little raised shelf and began to eat as he shopped. As he quickly discovered, the snack food contained a special surprise. Every time he crunched down on a gob of chicken, a squirt of warm grease was released from within. There was hardly any meat inside the nuggets—a minuscule speck of flesh surrounded by seasoned batter and fat.

Delightful.

He filled his mouth, packing his cheeks with them.

SpeeDee Mart's other warm treats were less appealing to him because of their disappointing fat content. Hot dogs on rotisserie spits. Hamburgers overcooked by hours under the warming lights. There was no coating to hold in the succulent grease. And to make matters worse, the display units had screened floors that allowed the dripping fat to fall out of sight, and out of reach, into collectors somewhere below the counter.

As Chiz started in on the second quart of chicken gobs, he was no longer thinking about Puma wasting away in a jail cell. With a luxuriant glow in his expanding muscles, he was thinking about dessert.

About rows and rows of half gallons of full-fat ice cream waiting for him in the dairy case.

"Mister sir," said a reedy voice at his elbow. "No. No. You no can do that...."

Chiz looked around at the SpeeDee Mart clerk, who was in a most agitated state. The man was literally hopping from one entry-level jogging shoe to the other. The plastic name tag pinned to his red-and-white-striped shirt pocket said Hi! I'm Bapu.

"I weigh chiggen *before* you eat," protested Bapu.

The movie star tipped his skinny sunglasses down his nose. "Do you know who I am?" he demanded, reaching for another gob.

Evidently not.

The clerk blinked at him, then, seeing another golden crusty nugget vanish between the big man's shiny lips, he moaned. "Oh, mercy me. You will stop, please. You will stop now, mister."

"Where do you keep the butter?" Chiz asked him as he licked the inside of the foam container.

Bapu answered automatically, "Aisle three, dairy case." Then, snapping out of robot-clerk mode, he clutched his curly mop of hair in both hands and said, "Oh, my, oh, my, you've eaten them all! What am I to do?"

Chiz rolled his cart toward the back of the store. There was considerable congestion around the wall of glass cases at the rear. The teenagers were huddled around the whipped cream and cottage cheese and had the refrigerator door standing open. The three fat women were jammed elbow to elbow as they comparison-shopped the quart prices of Ben & Jerry's and Häagen-Dazs. The sales rep was examining the rows of shrink-wrapped, maxi breakfast burritos while sipping at his steaming mug of Irish Mint Mocha.

Over the infectiously cheery Muzak—"Hey, Little Cobra" as performed by the Vienna Philharmonic— came the sound of angry reptiles.

A chorus of hissing.

And the unmistakable smell of aerosolized animal fat.

If the teenagers had had the price of a huff between them, everything might have turned out differently. Chiz might have filled his cart, paid his bill and left for the police station without incident. But as it was, imminent disaster rode the minimart's air-conditioned air.

Chiz locked on to the source of the sweet and creamy aroma.

"What are you doing?" Bapu cried as, peering around Chiz's bulk, he saw the teens huddled around the discharging canisters. Whipped cream was all over their faces, the glass door, the floor. "Oh, please, please, let me by!" he told Chiz.

The clerk made the mistake of not only touching the movie star, but of trying to get between him and the mounds of delightful white fluff. To all outward appearances, Bapu was trying to beat him to it.

Without taking his eyes off the huff party, Chiz reached out casually and snatched hold of Bapu's neck. His hand completely encircled it. And when Chiz squeezed, it made the clerk's eyes bug out.

Seeing what was happening, the sales rep dropped his coffee mug and tried to back away. He bumped into the teenagers and the fat ladies, who completely blocked any path of quick retreat.

With a seemingly effortless flip of the wrist, Chiz both snapped Bapu's neck and flipped him in an arc over aisles three and four. Out of sight, he landed with a soft thud on the floor.

The sales rep opened and closed his mouth, but no sound came out. He looked to the other customers for help, but they were all too focused on what they were doing to pay attention.

On the other side of the teens, one of the fat ladies hefted a quart of Häagen-Dazs and, peering through granny glasses on a beaded cord, said, "Well, the label says the flavor is the same, but how do we know the taste is the same?"

Another woman held a quart of Ben & Jerry's, and was likewise reading the ingredients. She shook her head. "I can't tell them apart from this," she complained.

The third woman took a quick look over her shoulder. Not seeing the clerk, she turned back to her friends. "There's only one way to find out," she said, grabbing for the lids.

The fresh scent of fat set Chiz to drooling. Profusely. Great ropy strands of saliva swayed from his chin. His breathing became short and ragged. Whatever the smell was coming from, he wanted it.

All.

The movie star reared back his cart, then rammed the front of it into the sales rep's shins, making him fall forward into the basket. Before the guy could cry out, Chiz had him by the throat. He likewise snapped the man's neck and sent him flying, out of sight, over the rows of shelves.

His muscles popping from the two quarts of gobs he'd just consumed, Chiz rammed the front of his cart hard into the mass of teens.

"Hey, butt-fuck!" said one in a knit cap and superbaggy plaid shirt. "Watch it! You're messing with our high." He had liquid white stuff all down his shirtfront.

Chiz backhanded him against the refrigerator case, driving his head and shoulders through the glass door. The teen bounced off the steel racks inside and flopped forward over the side of the cart. Chiz dumped his limp form off onto the floor.

The other five kids gawked at him, red eyed, foam nosed, propellant brained. As they did so, they lowered their Reddi Wip cans.

The fragrance was maddening.

Fat without substance.

It was worthless to Chiz, and that infuriated him.

The movie star couldn't have stopped himself even if he'd wanted to. He jerked the steel cart over his head and brought it crashing down on the petrified youths. They had nowhere to run. Bellowing his rage, Chiz used the cart like a hammer to pound the huffers into the black-and-white acrylic tile. Brains and blood flew in all directions as the cart crashed into them repeatedly.

The three ladies, their granny glasses and caftans spattered with gore, just stood there, clutching the opened ice-cream containers to their bosoms. Each of them had an ice-cream finger and mustache.

Now, there was fat as fat was meant to be.

An entire wall of it.

Like a knacker man in a slaughterhouse, Chiz brought his balled fist down on the closest woman's head. She dropped in the aisle, instantly dead. The other two suddenly found their feet and scooted around the corner, heading for the SpeeDee Mart's front exit.

Chiz paid them no mind. He filled his arms with half gallons of ice cream and moved out of the spray of carnage to enjoy his little feast.

When the police found him fifteen minutes later, he was sitting on the floor in the middle of aisle two, surrounded by a litter of empty Häagen-Dazs containers, eating almond-mocha fudge with his left hand and Ding Dongs with his right.

15

In order to prepare himself for yet another press conference, Jimmy Koch-Roche had retreated to the relative solitude of the Malibu sheriff's substation men's room. Facing the washbasin counter's long mirror, but unable to see his reflection because the top of his head was two feet below its lower edge, he puffed out his chest and recited sotto voce, "The only crime of Senator Lud is that he was too much of a manly stud."

Words echoed in a jumble in the tiled room.

The attorney sighed and shook his head. It wouldn't do. Too many syllables. If you wanted the media to pick up on a quote, it had to be both short and memorable. Once again, he referred to his well-thumbed rhyming dictionary.

After a moment of reflection, he tried again, this time opting for a slightly different vein. Picking up the tripod-tipped cane, a theatrical prop intended for his client, Koch-Roche gestured forcefully in the air. "Ninety years is too far gone, to hump your sweetie to the great beyond."

Ugh, Koch-Roche thought as his own doggerel resounded around him. That one wouldn't work, either. Not only was it too long, but it focused attention in a highly dangerous area. An area the attorney wanted at all costs to skirt. It would be much better, he decided, to play down the rough sex and work on the love angle. More words rhymed with *love* than *sex*, anyway.

He returned to his dictionary. He was still puzzling over the problem minutes later when a deputy sheriff stuck his head in the men's-room door. "Your client is being released from custody now, Jimmy," the officer said. "The animals are waiting for you out front."

Koch-Roche put away his rhyming dictionary. The senator would get no snappy verse at this juncture. As the attorney had learned the hard way, a bit of poorly constructed rhyme could do more damage to a case than a defendant's fingerprint on a murder weapon. Better to present no rhyme at all, even though the media crowd outside would be expecting it. And if Koch-Roche remained stumped for a way to put a poetical spin on the senator's legal position in the days ahead, he knew he could always call in a ghostwriter or two. The coffee-shop counters of Los Angeles were packed with out-of-work hacks.

Koch-Roche pulled out a small hand mirror and in its reflection smoothed down the sides of his hair. Then he checked his teeth for bits of spinach from his lunchtime salad.

"Jesus, Jimmy, don't you ever get tired of the goddamned circus?" the deputy asked him.

"Why would I?"

"Because it's always the same show."

"In case you hadn't noticed, Deputy," Koch-Roche explained as he put away his mirror, "I'm not the one shoveling up the shit out there. I'm the fucking elephant."

With that, the attorney left the bathroom and joined the newly freed Senator Baculum in the sheriff's substation hallway. Even Koch-Roche, who had witnessed the other recent miracles wrought by Family Fing Pharmaceuticals, was still amazed at the change the drug had made in the decrepit old man. Before taking WHE, Lud had been so stooped over that he and his lawyer had been almost the same height. Now he towered above his counsel. Koch-Roche found himself staring at the senator's jawline. Because there were no major muscle groups in the face to expand and fill out the voluminous, loose skin, as had happened all over the rest of his body, his head from the wattle line up still appeared very much ninety-plus years old.

Bizarre.

As Koch-Roche had requested, the senator was wearing a pair of blue silk pajamas and matching robe. The loose-fitting garments helped to conceal the enormity of his chest, arms and legs. Also adding to the sick-room atmosphere was the portable oxygen tank on wheels. A white-uniformed male nurse pushed the tank, which was connected by a clear plastic line to Lud's nostrils, and another male nurse carried an emergency medical case with a big red cross on the side.

"Remember, Lud," Koch-Roche said, "hunch over and wheeze for the cameras. And don't answer any questions. I'll do all the talking."

"I'm getting hungry again," the old man said.

It was a warning, not a request.

"I have everything waiting for you in the ambulance," the attorney assured him. "We'll be out of here in two shakes, but for the sake of your defense we need some positive coverage to counter the press the prosecution has been getting about the crime scene. This is very important to our case." Koch-Roche handed his client the tripod cane.

The senator glowered down at the little man in the three-piece suit, but he accepted the walking stick. Then he let his back droop and his shoulders sag. The spring in his step faded, and as he moved, he shuffled along in his slippered feet.

"The mouth, Lud. Don't forget the mouth...."

Senator Baculum let his mouth hang open.

Two deputies opened the substation's front doors, and the male nurses helped Koch-Roche's client through them. The senator immediately faltered for the cameras and was helped by his attendants into the waiting wheelchair. This was greeted by volleys of exploding flashbulbs and shouted questions from reporters. Raising his little arms for calm and order, Jimmy Koch-Roche stepped forward and faced the press.

16

"This is déjà vu all over again," Remo groused as, from the back of the throng of press types, he watched the shrimpboat lawyer step up to the very low, growing bush of taped-together microphones. Behind Koch-Roche, with a burly nurse at each elbow, Senator Ludlow Baculum sat slumped in a wheelchair, his hands on his knees.

A very strange looking ninety-plus-year-old, Remo thought. Not the least bit shrunken and frail, even though he was severely bent over in the chair. In particular, Remo was struck by the way Baculum filled out his silk jammies and robe. Even though he was seated, the legs stretching out the pj's were most impressive. Legs were always the first to go with advancing age, yet the senator's apparently hadn't gone anywhere—except huge.

"He's the same age as you," Remo said to Chiun. "Check the size of the calves on him."

"He has the stink," the Master announced, crinkling up his nose.

Then the miniature barrister spoke into the clustered mikes, his amplified voice booming over and hushing the restless crowd.

"I'm Jimmy Koch-Roche and I'm Senator Baculum's attorney," he began. "I'll be answering any and all questions for him today." The lawyer half turned to his client. "As you can see, the senator is in no condition to respond himself."

"Why did he kill poor Bambi?" shouted a reporter. His words hung in the air for a second, then the rest of the press took up the cry.

Koch-Roche waved his little arms. "Wait just a damned minute now! I'm going to set some ground rules. I won't answer stupid questions like that one. Every one of you knows that just because the sheriff arrested my client doesn't mean he did anything criminal."

Another reporter hollered, "Rumor out here is, Lud was found by the sheriff naked and covered head to foot in her blood."

"You should know by now I don't comment on unsubstantiated allegations like that."

Which only invited a shouted follow-up from the other side of the crowd. "Was rough sex involved in Bambi's death?"

The attorney pointed at his stoop-shouldered client once more. "For Pete's sake, all of you, stop mouth-breathing and take a look at the poor man. He's nearly a hundred years old. What kind of sex, rough or otherwise, do you think he's capable of?"

"Does that mean you're going to use the 'hero defense' again?"

Before the attorney could reply, another reporter restated the question. "Are you claiming that Lud tried to save Bambi from an intruder on their honeymoon?"

Koch-Roche shook his head. "I can't comment on what my strategy will be. Our time to talk is running out. The senator is clearly exhausted by his ordeal. I'll take one more question."

It was a doozy.

"If Lud is cleared of all charges," cried a woman wearing a network blazer, "does he plan to marry again?"

"As you can see, Senator Baculum is deeply grieved by his sudden and tragic loss. I can assure you he is not thinking about the future at this time. Thank you and have a good day."

A phalanx of uniformed sheriff's deputies parted the mob so Koch-Roche, his wheelchair-bound client and his attendants could reach the waiting ambulance.

Because Remo and Chiun stood well back, at the rear of the crowd, they were able to move quickly around its outer fringe and get very close to the ambulance's back doors. Not close enough to strike, but close enough to get a good look at the operation. It took both attendants and two deputies to lift the senator and his wheelchair inside. As they set his chair down, Remo got a glimpse of the ambulance's interior. Bags of burgers, literally dozens and dozens of them, were lined up on the floor. The reek of hot, semirancid animal fat coming from them made Remo's throat constrict and his stomach muscles clench.

As the ambulance attendants reached for the rear doors, the senator twisted around in his wheelchair. He already had one of the bags torn open and with both hands was mashing a greasy, four-inch-thick sandwich into his mouth. His eyes were slitted with pleasure. Drool and escaping grease glistened all down his chin and neck. Then the doors slammed closed.

With sirens blaring, the ambulance sped away. It had a three-cruiser escort.

"Come on, Little Father," Remo said, "we've got to follow him."

Because of the ambulance's spinning lights and wailing sirens, it wasn't in theory a hard thing to do. The problem was, every other member of the crowd had the same idea. All the reporters and their crews dashed for their cars and satellite-dished minivans. And in a matter of seconds, Pacific Coast Highway was like the Daytona 500 in pursuit of the speeding ambulance. The best Remo could do with the underpowered rental car was maintain position dead in the middle of the pack.

The ambulance turned onto the Santa Monica Freeway, and in short order led the honking, swerving entourage to the emergency entrance of Marshall Connors Memorial Hospital.

Immediately, some of the media vehicles turned off for the hospital's parking area. Other drivers pulled up onto the sidewalk and highballed it across the lawn for the emergency entrance. Amazingly, those daring souls skidded their vehicles to a stop without colliding with each other or with any of the madly scattering pedestrians. The car and van doors flew open, disgorging reporters and video cameramen, who raced to get a picture of the senator as he was carried from the ambulance.

"I'd better find a place to park," Remo said.

"No, wait," Chiun commanded. "All is not as it appcars."

"Don't tell me. You're getting a news flash from the satellite dish in your head?"

Chiun clucked his tongue. "If your senses were not so impaired, you too would know that the man we seek is at this moment leaving by the building's side exit."

"And how would you know that?"

The Master reached a slender hand out the open passenger window and wafted the air to his flared nostrils. "Go that way," he ordered, pointing with a long finger. "And hurry!"

Remo leaned on his horn and turned right, forcing his way between the jam of backed-up media cars. He drove over the landscaped concrete island, onto the hospital front lawn and then around the side of the hospital. When he came to the wide redbrick entry walkway he turned again, this time for the street.

"What car did he get in?" Remo demanded. "What the hell am I supposed to be looking for?"

Chiun stuck his head out the window and, his scraggly beard flapping in the breeze, shut his eyes and took a deep, slow breath. "That way!"

Remo bounced over the curb and back onto the road, fishtailing around oncoming traffic.

"Are we getting closer?" he asked.

Chiun sampled the air. Then he opened his eyes and pointed again. "That one!" he exclaimed. "The stinker is in that one!"

The vehicle the Master had identified was a stretch limo, navy blue, with a silver TV antenna on the roof.

"Gee, I wonder who the limo belongs to?" Remo said as he closed the gap between the cars.

The limousine's personalized California license plate read MY-T-MAUS.

Even though Remo sang a bar or two of the theme song for him—"Here I am to save the day!"—Chiun didn't get it. The cartoon show had been off the air for decades before the Master had picked up his nasty TV habit.

The limo turned onto an on-ramp for Interstate 5 North. After traveling six or seven miles, it exited the freeway and headed into the hills of Brentwood. Once they got onto the city streets, Remo dropped back a bit to avoid being seen.

"You realize we have a much more serious problem on our hands with this one," he said to the Master.

Chiun gave him a deadpan look.

"Ludlow Baculum is a U.S. senator," Remo explained. "His security team will most likely be either federal agents or enforcers from whoever is importing the drug."

"So?"

"So they will not wait to use deadly force against us."

"If they are in the employ of this inhuman monster, then they, too, must die."

"No, Chiun," Remo said. "Listen to me. If the security is federal, it works for the government, not the senator. We work for the government, too. Indirectly. We can't kill those guys for doing their job. And we can't kill the senator, either."

"But Emperor Smith—"

"He wants a live subject to interview. We can't have a repeat of what happened on the football field."

"It was I who captured the stink patch...."

"Yes, but that's all we got." Remo waited for the message to sink in, then he said, "And there's another thing. It's a crime punishable by death to kill a member of the U.S. Senate. If we do that and get caught, even Smith won't be able to save us."

"Do you suggest that *I* might be the one to lose control?"

Remo grimaced; no way could he miss the outraged tone of the Master's voice. "Lighten up, Chiun," he told his companion. "All I'm saying is, this time let's try and not slaughter the man we're after."

Chiun appeared to sulk, his hands and neck disappearing inside the cuffs and collar of his brocaded robe.

"Sheesh," Remo said.

Ahead, the limo slowed to a crawl as it approached a pair of tall white steel gates on the left. Gates that immediately opened, allowing the limo to enter a tree-lined asphalt drive. Remo kept on driving. The estate was ringed by a twelve-foot-high perimeter wall, which in turn was topped with tastefully rendered iron spikes. Remo continued on up the hill. As he rolled past the gate, he got a look at the men guarding the entrance. In suits, ties, shades, headsets and carrying mini-Uzis, they were Feds for sure.

Remo parked a couple of blocks farther on, in front of a gardener's pickup truck, the bed of which was loaded down with bags of grass and yard tools. The gardener in question had ear protectors on and was in the middle of mowing the front lawn of a three-story Spanish-style home.

"Let me handle the guys at the gate," he told Chiun as they got out of the car.

The Master, still miffed, said nothing.

As they passed the pickup, Remo grabbed a rake and a limb trimmer on an aluminum extender pole from the back. "Here," he told Chiun. "Carry this."

The Master accepted the rake in silence.

The two of them crossed the street and walked down the hill toward the white gates. As Remo and Chiun approached, through cascades of purple-and-pink bougainvillea, they could see the blue limo parked under the mansion's porticoed auto entrance. The huge home was without frills: modern, multilevel, with lots of glass exterior walls. They were about ten feet from the gate when the two security men on the other side moved into position.

The Fed who wore his pale brown hair in a supershort crew cut spoke crisply into his headset, "We've got a pair of bogeys at nine o'clock. Stations Red and Blue on intruder alert."

With the limb trimmer resting over his shoulder, Remo stopped in front of the gate.

"Move on," said the Fed.

"We're supposed to do some pruning inside," Remo told him.

"No, you're not. Move on, lawn boy."

The security men shared a smirk.

Remo set the tip of the long metal pole on the sidewalk and stepped a little closer to the gate's bars. "My partner here," he said, gesturing at the little old Oriental with the rake, "is the world's foremost expert on the monkey puzzle tree. He's made time in his busy schedule, as a personal favor to Mr. Koch-Roche, in order to inspect a suspected fungal outbreak on a museum-quality specimen on the grounds. I don't think Mr. Koch-Roche will be amused if you turn him away.''

The crew-cut Fed gave Remo an irritated look, then spoke again into his mike. "Station Yellow here," he said, sizing up the men on the other side of the gate. "We've got a couple of guys claiming to be gardeners at the gate. See if they're expected. One's an old Jap—''

Remo hadn't quite reached the optimum position for the strike he had planned—the tip of the pole was a little too far to the left—but he knew he had no choice but to go for it. Chiun had already whipped the handle of his rake around, and was thrusting it between the steel bars like a lance.

With a loud crack, the wooden handle splintered against the crew-cut Fed's body armor, but not before Chiun had delivered a paralyzing shock to his diaphragm. The Fed crumpled and dropped to his side, curling up in a fetal position on the drive.

Crew-cut's partner had his hand on his mini-Uzi when Remo made his own thrust. The long aluminum pole bowed in the middle as its butt made solid contact with the man's chin. The bend in the pole absorbed some of the blow's power, which was still sufficient to stun the Fed and make him drop his weapon.

Remo quickly scaled the gate and used the lever to open it for Chiun, who with great dignity walked through the opening and stepped over the fallen form of the crew-cut Fed.

The Master paused to kneel beside the wheezing man.

"Korean," Chiun said slowly and distinctly, as if addressing a child. "I am Korean."

17

Senator Ludlow Baculum carefully peeled the adhesive patch from his right buttock. He observed the entire operation in the master bathroom's floor-to-ceiling mirror wall, while standing on the gold marble steps leading up to a vast, Mayan-temple-motif bathtub. Having removed the spent patch, the senator carelessly discarded it over his shoulder, mesmerized as he was by the sight of his own behind.

Ludlow's butt was monumental. Not even as a young man had it jutted so firmly, so solidly. As he walked up and down the bathtub steps, he could see the various muscle groups rippling under skin stretched thin as an overinflated balloon.

Oh, he was a manly man indeed.

Even if Koch-Roche had been charging ten million a year for the patch, Lud would have paid it gladly. The wonder drug had resurrected him from the dead. Though his mind was still razor sharp, he had been trapped in a decaying, ancient hulk of a body.

His was the tragedy of the aging horndog.

His sexual desires were still intense as ever, but he

no longer had the physical wherewithal to satisfy him self or anyone else. Before he'd started taking the drug, when he had put his palsied, liver-spotted hand upon a young woman's naked body, the sensation was dim, as if he were groping through many layers of fabric. Even his sense of touch had been dulled by time.

That his continuing interest in women had become a joke, a widely circulated joke, had stung the senator most bitterly. But it hadn't stopped him from chasing women young enough to be his great-great-granddaughters. Because he was hampered by his walker and oxygen tank, Baculum's Washington, D.C., staff—comprised entirely of women under thirty—could usually avoid being cornered by him in the office. Elevators were a different story. As he slipped into his mid-eighties, Ludlow Baculum had spent many happy and profitable hours lurking in the back of a crowded car, his fingertips poised for a quick pinch or a shuddering grope.

All that was past.

Now he had a new body to match his desire.

After an absence of a little more than a quarter century, Lud the Stud was back.

The senator peeled the backing off a new patch and stuck it on his other buttock. Then he did some Mr. Universe poses in front of the mirror, squinting ferociously so he could focus on his popping biceps and hulking traps without donning his specs. It didn't matter to him that he still had a ninety-plus-year-old face, no hair and three teeth. Thanks to more than thirty years of carefully cultivated PAC contributions, of corporate under-the-table payoffs, he was filthy rich. Pretty young women could often overlook a bit of toothless blotch face when it controlled a few hundred million in purely liquid assets. Especially the type of pretty women he was attracted to: screamers in the sack with shoe-size IQs. His taste in lady friends hadn't changed since Woodrow Wilson took office.

What Lud anticipated, now that he had a world-class bod, was fewer serial marriages and many more casual love partners. Many more. Not only would he be faster on the grab, but given his more attractive physique, his prey would be less likely to try to escape. In the long run, the senator figured to break even on the price of the drug because the cost of his prenuptial agreements was bound to take a precipitous drop.

Lud barefooted across the marble over to the sink counter, where he had left the remains of his most recent snack. He poked around in the bottom of the translucent paper sack and came up with a tiny shard of overcooked french fry and a few grains of salt. Which he quickly consumed. Then he held the bag up to the light. It was drenched in grease. He could feel it all slimy under his fingers. Delicious but inaccessible grease.

Well, not quite.

The senator wadded the bag into his mouth and chewed and sucked the oily goodness from the paper. When he was done, to make sure he hadn't missed any, he swallowed the bolus down.

As he licked his lips, he heard soft singing from the next room.

And he smelled Woman.

In the past ten hours, his sense of smell had become most amazingly acute. Even the faintest hint of the opposite sex was for him a beacon, a Klaxon, a war cry. From her aroma, the senator judged the woman's age at twenty-two, well into the range of his target zone. And he guessed that she was Latina.

He ducked his bald, spotted head around the bathroom doorjamb.

Right on both counts.

Jimmy Koch-Roche's live-in maid was bent over the queen-size bed, fluffing up the pillows.

"¡Hola, Lupe!" Lud said, stepping into the bedroom.

The girl looked up from her work. The friendly smile on her face vanished as she saw that the man who had hailed her was both naked and fully aroused.

Lupe was no delicate flower. Though short in stature, she weighed a good 160 pounds. Her working clothes weren't the frilly, short-skirted French-maid outfits sold in sex-fantasy shops, but the cotton, sensible, no-nonsense, loose-fitting pants and shirt jacket of a nurse or beautician. She had no waist to speak of, and therefore no apparent hips. She wore her hair twisted up into a bun at the back of her head.

None of which mattered in the least to Senator Baculum, whose dander was most definitely up.

"*¡Venga aquí, Lupe!*" he said, opening his huge powerful arms to her.

Lupe let out a yelp and ran over the bed in her pink Reeboks, trying to reach the hallway door and, she hoped, safety.

Lud was too quick for her. He blocked the exit with his massive body.

"Come to me, my little *frijole negra,*" the senator cooed.

Lupe had no intention of doing anything of the kind. She dashed back over the bed and through the bathroom door. She slammed the door shut, shot the bolt and started yelling for help at the top of her lungs.

The senator booted the heavy door off its hinges with a single kick, then walked over the fallen door. The maid was nowhere in sight. At first, he thought she might have escaped out a window. But behind the frosted glass of the huge shower stall, he saw her shadow. She cowered there, too scared to utter a sound.

When Lud jerked open the door and stepped in, Lupe slumped down the wall to the floor, covering her head with her arms. She was sobbing, her black hair falling around her shoulders.

"Don't cry now, Lupe," Lud said in a soothing voice. "I'm not one of your wham-bam-thank-you-ma'am Latin lovers. I'm from the old school of romance. I believe in foreplay, foreplay, foreplay...."

With that, he dragged her bodily from the stall by her hair, sank his three teeth into her shoulder blade and started shaking her around the room like a terrier with an old knotted sock.

"FREEZE!" said a voice behind Remo and Chiun as they mounted the low, broad steps to the mansion's side entrance. The command was followed immediately by "Get your hands up!"

Remo turned to face a very excited young man with a very stubby machine pistol. The mini-Uzi's red laser-sight dot jitterdanced across the breast of his black T-shirt.

"Please don't point that thing at me," Remo said, lifting his hands. "It makes me nervous."

"Shut up!" The young Fed shifted his aim to Chiun. "You, too. Get 'em up!"

The red dot played over the Master's scrawny throat and brushed his smiling lips.

"What're you grinn—?"

Before the federal agent could finish the word, let alone his sentence, it was over.

He had been rendered unconscious by what appeared to be a wave of a hand, a gesture that never actually made contact with the side of his head. The vacuum, the back draft created by Chiun's movement, had caused the young man's skull to lurch violently sideways and his brain to slam into the walls of that bony chamber.

After disarming the agent, Remo and Chiun entered the mansion. At once, they heard a woman's screams.

"Sounds like old Lud's at it again," Remo said.

And then came the sound of heavy running feet.

The running feet belonged to the rest of the mansion's security staff. Remo and Chiun were confronted by four more machine-pistol-toting Feds and a trio of Koch-Roche's personal bodyguards. The latter pointed blue-steel .40-caliber SIG-Sauer pistols at them.

"Stop right there!" shouted the Fed in charge. "Stop where you stand or we'll fire."

Remo raised his hands above his head. "We aren't going anywhere," he said. "Aren't you going to check out those screams? Or don't you understand Spanish for 'Please don't kill me'?"

"You are our only problem at the moment," the Fed said. A pair of big, mirror-surfaced aviator sunglasses was perched on top of his head. "Cuff 'em, Roberts."

"Somebody's getting murdered in the next room, and you're worried about a couple of gate-crashers?" Remo said in disbelief.

"Somebody's going to get killed in this room if you don't zip it in a hurry, pal."

Roberts gestured for Remo and Chiun to face the flagstone wall that framed the enormous fireplace. "Lean forward, hands on the wall and spread your legs," Roberts directed.

Remo and Chiun obeyed the man's order and allowed themselves to be quickly frisked.

"Okay," Roberts continued, "put your right hands behind your backs."

Even though the other six men had their weapons trained on the two suspects, even though they were watching as intently as was humanly possible, the little Oriental seemed to vanish. One second he had his hand behind his back, in an off balance and totally vulnerable position, and the next second he was simply and totally gone.

As Roberts spun around to face his colleagues, he looked up. "Shit!" he exclaimed. He was the only one who could see the old man, and there was nothing he could do about it. Chiun was hurtling through the air, the hem of his robe brushing the top of the twenty-foot-high ceiling. He soared past the lineup of security specialists, whose attention was still focused on where he had been, not where he was.

Then something hit Roberts in the side of the neck, and for him, everything went black.

At the same instant some fifteen feet away, the Master of Sinanju landed lightly on the balls of his feet and, once firmly grounded, roamed freely among the defenseless backs of his adversaries.

Everything soft and fluid.

Blows that started off hard as iron and ended at their targets as near caresses.

Without the all important follow-through, such strikes were not lethal—unless, of course, one of the men happened to have a steel plate in his head, in which case even the muted impact would have set it spinning like the blade of a runaway table saw.

As Remo carefully eased Agent Roberts to the floor, across the room armed men were falling like bowling pins. Between them, Remo could make out flashes of blue brocaded silk and the afterimage of a smile.

"All asleep," Chiun announced, slipping his hands back into his cuffs.

A piercing cry echoed through the mansion.

"Not all," Remo said.

Chiun nodded. "When the little head rules the big one, trouble cannot be far away."

"And Trouble Is Us...."

Remo led the way through the big house, following the sounds of struggle through the ground floor to its source.

Like a snowstorm spilling into the hall, kapok fluff floated out of the doorway to the master bedroom.

Remo entered first, low and quick. For a moment, he couldn't even see the woman, dwarfed as she was by the hugely muscled naked man who bent over her on the savagely ripped, partially de-stuffed mattress.

Then Remo caught sight of the soles of her Reeboks on either side of Ludlow Baculum's massive buttocks. The woman was furiously kicking her attacker and to some effect—there was pink smeared on the white treads of her traction soles.

"Senator?" he said.

Ludlow Baculum's ancient head snapped around on his corded, powerful neck. He smiled, and there was blood on his three teeth and tongue. He had the little woman's wrists pinned to the bed. Her clothes hung in tattered strips all around her.

"Go away!" Baculum snarled. "I haven't finished."

"Oh, yes, you have."

"I can't be bothered with this," the senator snarled. He called to the other room. "Roberts! Atkins! Get your butts in here!"

"You'll get no help from your hired hands," Remo said. "They've all been subdued."

Ludlow Baculum pointed a warning finger in the maid's face and said, "Don't you move. Not a muscle." Then he let her go and turned on the bed to handle the intruders by himself.

Remo noted the overlapping tread marks that ran across the senator's hips and thighs. "Man, oh man," he said with a laugh, "that little lady danced a stone flamenco on your doodle."

Baculum was not amused.

Sensing her opportunity, the half-nude maid shot off the bed and out the door.

"I'm going to kill you for that," the senator told Remo as hopped to the floor. "I can bend steel bars with my bare hands. I can kick through solid walls."

"That must be nice for you," Remo commented mildly.

"I'm going to rip your head off your shoulders and stuff it where the sun doesn't shine."

"Love to tussle with you, Lud, I really would, but I think you should play with somebody your own age."

When Remo looked around, the Master was nowhere in sight.

"I'd rather play with *you*," Baculum said.

Then the plundered mattress hit Remo square in the face. Before he could move to escape, the senator threw his body against the other side of the mattress, sandwiching Remo against the wall. From head to heels, he was not only held fast, but slowly being smothered.

"Now I've got you," Lud said as he dug in his toes, using his shoulder to wedge his victim tighter to the wall. With his free hand, the senator started ripping open the underside of the mattress, over the unmoving lump that was Remo. Through the hole he'd made in the ticking, he plucked away big clumps of kapok stuffing.

Soon to be big clumps of Remo.

"Pucker up, Buttercup...." the senator cooed.

18

Having taken to heart Remo's caution about the loss of a valuable source of information, and how dimly Emperor Smith would view a repeat of the football incident, Chiun was determined to capture their quarry alive. He recalled the ancient Korean proverb, "You can catch more bloodworm with fish paste than you can with bitter gall."

In search of fish paste, the Reigning Master of Sinanju padded into the mansion's kitchen, which resembled that of a modestly sized upscale restaurant. Everything was made of stainless steel. Sinks. Countertops. Range tops. The refrigerator doors set in a row along the wall.

Chiun opened all the refrigerator doors and stepped back to survey their contents. "If I were Animal Man," he asked himself aloud, "what would soothe my savage breast?"

He stroked his scraggly beard as he considered the problem.

There was meat aplenty on hand, cooked and raw. Cold standing rib roast, virtually intact. A partially dissected turkey. The nether quarters of a suckling pig. Mounds of aged steaks and chops.

He lifted the cover from a ceramic tureen.

Duck!

He took a tender leg from its congealed bed of sauce and nibbled daintily. Most excellent, he judged. Even cold, and perhaps four days old, it was far superior to Remo's meager cuisine. Try as he might, the man simply could not make a decent sauce. How many Saturday afternoons had Chiun made his pupil observe the magicians of the cooking channel? How many pages of notes had Remo taken down? All for nothing, it seemed. Remo's sauce was either thin as water or thick as glutinous rice. It either swam away from the dish it was supposed to adorn, or choked it, like so much concrete.

As Chiun gnawed the moist, dark meat from the bone, sucking it absolutely clean, he decided that flesh, even the fattiest kind of flesh, would not do the trick for Animal Man.

He turned his attention to the refrigerator that held a selection of high-calorie desserts. A wide array of flaky pastries, mousses and elaborate whipped cream cakes stood on the shelves before him. Yet something told him that even a five-layer Black Forest cake was not enough.

The job required something even more artery clogging.

Something so purely, so totally fat laden that the beast-senator could not possibly turn it down.

Chiun found what he was looking for in the kitchen pantry, which was jammed with various sacked, canned and jarred comestibles. The ten-gallon glass jar he sought stood on the pantry floor, its off-white contents the quintessence of fat. Bending his knees, he picked up the heavy jar and carried it back toward the master bedroom.

The Master could hear the sounds of violent struggle as he lumbered down the hall with his burden, and as he approached the open door to the bedroom, once again he saw bits of mattress fluff drifting out like snow. He stopped at the doorway, unscrewed the big metal lid and discarded it.

When Chiun entered the bedroom, his pupil was nowhere to be seen. The old man with a young man's body was holding the mattress against the wall with one hand and ripping at it with the other. Under the mattress was a man-sized lump.

A Remo-sized lump.

Then the senator thrust his hand into the hole he had made, and as if he were pulling a rabbit out of its hole, jerked Remo's head through the opening by the hair.

Chiun's pupil's face was very red all over, like it had been abraded with steel wool. The whites of the eyes were red, too.

"Do something!" Remo shouted.

"Of course," Chiun answered breezily. He reached into the big jar, grabbed a handful of the slippery white stuff and flung it at the back of the senator's bald head, where it landed with a wet splat over his neck and shoulders.

The effect was instantaneous.

Ludlow Baculum let go of Remo's hair and jerked his head around, his nostrils flaring wide. Still leaning against the mattress with his shoulder, the senator scooped some of the stuff off the side of his neck and pushed it into his mouth. A moan of pleasure escaped his withered lips. His rheumy eyes rolled up in their sockets.

From his raggedy porthole in the mattress, Remo croaked, "What the hell is it?"

"Fish paste to a bloodworm," Chiun answered.

"Well, for Pete's sake, give him some more!"

The Master made another mayonnaise snowball and hit Baculum square in the chops with it.

"Nuhhhgghhh," the senator gurgled as he used the edges of both his hands to scrape the full-fat dressing into his open mouth.

"Here," Chiun said, lowering his point of aim. He tossed a string of softball-sized gobs of mayo onto the bedroom carpet, leading Animal Man away from the mattress, and the still trapped Remo.

The distinguished Southern senator hurled himself facedown on the rug and, like a dog in pursuit of its own vomit, frantically licked and sucked up the slick white goo from the tightly woven carpet fibers. When he was through with one wet gob, he scrambled on all fours to the next, totally preoccupied with the task.

Remo pushed the mattress aside and stepped away from the wall. "That bastard almost had me," he said, pausing to pick a stray bit of mattress fluff off the tip of his tongue.

"You did an excellent job of keeping him here while I found the solution to the problem," Chiun said.

"Yeah, right. I sure didn't let him escape...."

"Now that we have the live specimen Emperor Smith desired," Chiun said, "all that is left is to render him senseless so we can bind him securely for transport."

"That honor is mine," Remo said.

Senator Baculum growled menacingly as Remo approached him, but he did not stop sucking the daylights out of the carpet. He remained on his hands and knees facedown, combing the short strands of carpet through his three surviving teeth.

Chiun watched his pupil carefully.

The angle of approach.

The coiling to strike.

The choice of fist.

The location and power of the blow.

He was pleased to see that Remo avoided the head completely. A ninety-plus-year-old brain could be a fragile thing, full of leaky vessels and bulging aneurysms, and it was the brain they needed for its information. Remo's strike was open-handed, and there was absolutely no follow-through. The target Remo selected was a small place on the back above the right kidney, a place where many important nerves came together.

Whap!

Senator Baculum let out a startled gasp and slumped face first into a puddle of his own slobber.

19

In his white sterile suit, Carlos Sternovsky rushed down the hall of the Family Fing Pharmaceuticals medical wing. At his side was Fosdick Fing. The lanky American took a single loping stride for every four of his Taiwanese counterpart. From the corridor ahead came a series of behemoth roars and a terrible crash of glassware and steel.

It sounded vaguely familiar to Sternovsky.

Like feeding time at the lion house.

"The deterioration started to accelerate about an hour ago," Fosdick informed him as they hurried along. "It is occurring in every member of the synthetic-drug test panel. We're getting physiological and behavioral abnormalities that are way beyond anything we've logged to date."

As they neared the first of the test subjects' private suites, the door jerked open and three uniformed female nurses scrambled out, shrieking and brushing frantically at their clothes. One of the nurses had a fresh bruise above her right eye and a bloody lip. They all had wet marks spattered over their uniform dresses, from shoulder to hem. Seeing the open door, an alert orderly jumped forward and slammed it shut.

"She attacked me," the bloodied, black-eyed nurse cried to Fosdick. "Then after the others pulled her off me, she sprayed us! God, somehow that great ugly cow managed to spray us all!"

"We were just trying to take a hair sample for analysis!" another of the victimized nurses said. She held up a pinch of short brown strands between her fingertips. There appeared to be lighter brown fuzz mixed in with the hair.

"Calm down," Fosdick said. "Please, all of you, calm down. Give those hairs to me." He took the sample from the nurse and placed it in a small plastic bag. "Now, go change your uniforms at once. And when you've done that, I want you to go outside and I don't want you to come back until you've regained your composure."

Sternovsky's attention was elsewhere. He was looking at the surveillance monitor of the room the nurses had just exited. Inside, Test Subject Two was naked. Her body fat hovered just above zero, and her current level of muscle mass was roughly equivalent to that of a male, six-foot-four-inch high-school senior. She sat on the edge of her hospital bed and in great agitation combed at her hair with her fingers.

Not the hair on her head.

The hair growing out of the tops of her shoulders. When the forty-eight-year-old romance writer had been admitted to the Fing medical wing four days before, she had weighed close to 350 pounds, less than forty percent of which had been muscle. The woman's weight problem had as much to do with her life-style and career choice as with her genetics. According to the medical history she had provided, all she did was sit at the computer and write.

And eat.

She had worked out a little reward scheme for herself. For every page of manuscript she completed, she gave herself a treat. A cookie. A bonbon. A bite of cake. A spoonful of ice cream. Using this positive-reinforcement scheme, she had produced forty-three novels in ten years.

After she'd completed her thirty-second novel, things began to go seriously wrong. When she submitted a current photograph for use on the back of the book jacket, her publisher rejected it, claiming that it made her look too much like an orangutan— her once passably cute face was lost in concentric rings of stippled white flab. This unfortunate development made book tours out of the question.

When the publisher began to suggest that a slender stand-in take care of the road work, the authoress panicked. She was caught in a terrible trap. Without the steady flow of treats, she couldn't write a word; without giving up the treats, she couldn't get the acclaim and adoration she had strived for her entire life. In her desperation to have it all, she had agreed to become a Family Fing lab rat.

WHE had seemed the perfect solution to her. Especially when its features were explained by a buttersmooth sales type like Farnham Fing. And it was a solution, up to a point.

"This isn't human hair," Fosdick said, holding the plastic specimen bag to the light.

Sternovsky tore his gaze from the monitor screen and the truly amazing definition of the woman's back muscles. "What?" he said.

"It's animal hair."

"Can't be," Sternovsky countered, leaning closer to the bag.

One look told him that despite what he knew—or thought he knew—about genetics, it most certainly was. Human beings didn't have a frizzy insulating undercoat. Wolverines, on the other hand, did.

"I don't understand," he said, a pained and helpless expression slipping over his face. "For this to have happened, WHE would have had to reprogram the test subject's DNA. Which is something we know it can't do...."

"It gets worse," Fosdick told him.

And he was right.

The sounds in the medical wing went from lion house to elephant house to ape house. And back again. The bellows of one test subject seemed to stimulate the others to cry out. Uniformed attendants ran from one side of the hall to the other, trying in vain to quiet the patients. The sounds of the staff's voices had just the opposite of the intended effect. The hallway reeled with booming crashes as the Fing lab animals hurled themselves against locked doors and windowless walls.

"Is your father aware of what is happening?" Sternovsky asked.

"He's monitoring everything that's going on from the boardroom," Fosdick replied.

"Hasn't he seen enough? Dammit, man, why haven't you sedated these people?"

"Father wants them conscious because that gives us more information. That's what this is about. Information."

A male orderly dashed up to the youngest Fing and said, "Number Five's started going into convulsions. You'd better hurry."

When Sternovksy and Fing reached the test subject's suite, they found the door already open and a handful of uniformed attendants standing just inside the doorway. The assembled staff seemed very reluctant to approach the massively muscled figure writhing around on the floor.

Understandably so.

Of the six test subjects, Number Five was the only one Sternovsky recognized. His name was Norton Arthur Grape. He was a meteorologist on a nationally televised morning news-and-talk show that Sternovsky had caught a few times while he was at Purblind. As with the romance novelist, Grape's size had begun to get in the way of his work.

Literally.

Over the past few months, the weatherman had grown to such monstrously wide proportions that his figure blocked three-fourths of the satellite weather map. Even his jovial attitude and beaming capped smile couldn't make up for this daily eclipse of America.

Like Test Subject Two, Grape was a pathological eater.

Food was not just the central focus of his life; it was the only focus. Between his rendering of the day's high and low temperatures, incoming hurricanes and cold fronts, his on-camera banter was always about what he'd eaten the night before, what he planned to eat that night, what he'd like to eat at that very moment.

That was then; this was now.

No longer a great marshmallow in a fifteen-hundred-dollar custom-tailored suit, the new Norton Arthur Grape, naked and megabuffed, kicked and shuddered on the linoleum, his purpling lips hidden under a foaming cascade of spittle.

"He's started to sprout fur, as well," Fosdick said. "See there along either side of the spine."

Sternovsky was no longer shocked by the callousness of the Fings, but he refused to stand idly by while someone suffered. "Fosdick, how can you just stand there? Do something for the poor man! For Christ's sake, he's a human being!"

Fosdick nodded to the male attendants. "Go ahead and put Number Five back in his bed. Let's get a heart monitor and EEG readout on him as quickly as possible."

The attendants approached the huge man very cautiously and carefully rolled him onto his back. As Norton Arthur Grape faced the ceiling, Sternovsky could see that his eyes were wide open, the pupils jerking up, then down, up, then down, in a rhythmic pattern.

"It looks like he may have stroked out on us," Fosdick said. "Father won't like that."

As the orderlies grouped themselves, two to a side, around the test subject and prepared to lift him onto his bed, Norton Arthur Grape's pupils snapped to center position.

Snapped and locked.

His hands moved in a blur as he suddenly, unexpectedly sat upright on the floor. Before the attendants could jump out of reach, he had snatched hold of two of them by the neck. As he squeezed their necks, their faces turned instantly purple-black.

"Back!" Fosdick cried as he retreated at top speed through the suite's open door.

Before Sternovsky could follow, he was knocked to one side by the scrambling orderlies. Because of the mad rush to escape, the biochemist was the last person to exit Grape's room before the door was slammed shut and bolted. As the American staggered back into the middle of the hallway, everyone could see that his white sterile suit was no longer white, but a gaudy speckle of tiny red drops.

From the other side of the door, an animal roar of triumph shook the very walls.

"He pulled their heads off," Sternovsky moaned as he sagged to his knees. "I saw him do it."

No one said a word.

Fosdick Fing looked down at the American without expression, his arms folded defensively across his chest.

Before Fosdick could back away out of reach, Sternovsky snatched hold of the lapel of his lab coat, pulled the research chemist's face down close to his own and shouted, "My God, he twisted those men's heads off like they were chickens!"

20

Jimmy Koch-Roche sat behind the steering wheel of his parked V-12 Jaguar four-door sedan. He was able to drive the vehicle thanks to a custom booster seat that allowed him to see over the dashboard and out the front windshield. He wasn't looking that way at the moment, though. He was turned toward the rear, watching his recently freed client stuff her beautiful face with pork rinds.

On the leather back seat of the Jag, Puma Lee—sex queen, fashion setter and homicidal maniac—ripped into yet another two-pound bag of lowbrow snack food. Once the package was open, she didn't bother picking out the chips of deep-fried animal fat with her fingers; that method was way too slow. Instead, she tipped the bag to her parted lips and shook it, letting the rinds fall into her mouth until it would hold no more. Without lowering the package from her lips, she chewed, swallowed and quickly shook again.

Needless to say, this gustatory technique was accompanied by considerable spillage.

The pork rinds tended to fragment and fly when

crunched. From her jawline down, Puma's world-renowned, shoulder-length raven tresses were flecked with bits of yellow, crispy pig fat.

Already the rear of the Jaguar sedan looked like the inside of a Dumpster approaching pickup day. Every place a stray shard of pork rind landed, it left a grease mark. Shreds of plastic bag, well lubed on the inside, were drawn by static electricity to the headliner, the front seats, the dash. The overspray of Puma's feeding frenzy, a combination of animal fat, fry oil and her saliva, coated the inside of all the windows like they'd been sprayed with PAM.

It was a detail man's worst nightmare.

Using the very broadest of yardsticks, Jimmy Koch-Roche could be seen as a detail man, too. A very well compensated detail man. He picked up after his careless clients, buffed their scratches, vacuumed their dirt, air-freshened their sullied reputations. And like his automotive counterpart, none of the nasty stuff he dealt with ever stuck to him.

There was never any chewing gum on Jimmy's size-5 shoe.

Which was the main difference between a lawyer/detail man and your average garbage collector.

That and the pay, of course.

The image, public and self, that Koch-Roche projected was that of a scrappy little bantam rooster. He was keen eyed, short fused and always ready for a fight. He dearly loved his job. Not just because of the money, though that was certainly a major part of it. He liked having other people come to him for help. Rich, beautiful, *tall* people with terrible trouble, almost always self-inflicted. The weaknesses of his clients, despite their physical gifts, made him feel superior. And in a court of law, he was. Before the bar, Koch-Roche was the Terminator, the brute to be reckoned with. That they—tall, strong, lovely—had to come to him, sometimes begging, and that they had to part with large portions of their net worth in order to secure his services, was too, too delicious.

Every night before he crawled into his little bed, Jimmy Koch-Roche thanked the Lord he was a lawyer.

Puma Lee paused for air, lowering the half-full bag of rinds. As she did, the lawyer could see that her face, from nose to chin, was encrusted with tiny bits of fried fat. The actress lifted her right leg, marveling at the swell of her own thigh muscles, at the definition between rectus femoris and vastus medialis. Her tanned, oiled skin shone like silk. On her face was an expression of perfect delight.

Vanity and narcissism, Koch-Roche thought. What would he ever do without them?

"How are you feeling now?" he asked the movie star.

"Famished," Puma said. "Where's Chiz? He was supposed to bring more food." She returned to the pork-rind feed bag.

"He still doesn't answer his car phone," Jimmy told her. "I hope he didn't have an accident on the way...."

A rap on the outside of the driver's window interrupted him. He turned to face a uniformed officer, who made a "lower the window" motion with his hand. The attorney hit the power button.

"Today is definitely your lucky day, Jimmy," the cop said as the glass glided down. "Ms. Lee's husband was picked up a few minutes ago at a convenience store in Hollywood."

"On what charge?"

"Charges, actually. I'm afraid you'll have your hands full with this one. It's nine counts of first-degree murder. And they got the whole thing on the store's closed-circuit video. Major ugly. Graham gave up without a struggle, though. He should be arriving here any minute."

The officer looked past the attorney, around the Jag's headrest, into the back seat. "Sorry to bring you such bad news, ma'am," he said to the screen goddess.

Puma crumpled up the empty bag of pork rinds and threw it on the floor. Then, with a depth of emotion she rarely showed in her professional career, she said, "Isn't there anything else to eat?"

21

"Isn't there anything else to eat?" Ludlow Baculum complained.

The old/young lawmaker was like a stuck record.

Or a tape loop.

And it was beginning to piss off Remo, big-time.

Bound securely hand and foot, the senator sat on the floor of the Koreatown bungalow in front of the Mitsuzuki Mondiale. Since he had regained consciousness, Baculum had been both lucid and passive, if completely uncooperative.

"No more food until we get some answers from you," Remo informed him. "We want to know who supplied you with the hormone drug."

"What difference does that make?" Baculum replied. "WHE isn't illegal to sell or possess. On the other hand, kidnapping is very much illegal. And the kidnapping of a U.S. senator happens to be a capital crime."

"So we've heard," Remo said without interest. "I'll bet you're glad you voted for that bill."

"Who the hell are you two?" the senator demanded. "Who do you work for?"

"That isn't the issue here," Remo answered. "We need information. The drug you've been using is dangerous."

"That's preposterous. Look at me. I'm a new man. Better now than I ever was. How has it hurt me?"

"Ask your late wife."

The senator glared at Remo.

"There will be serious national-security problems if the use of WHE continues to spread," Remo said.

"So you're trying to make me think you're working for our government?" Baculum scoffed. "I wasn't born yesterday, you know. Since when does the DEA hire hit men?"

Remo decided not to get into that area of discussion with the senator. CURE's involvement had to remain secret at all costs.

"If this potion is not illegal," Chiun said from the comfort of the fully reclined La-Z-Boy, "then why are you so concerned about protecting the people who are giving it to you?"

"Because it is a rare and very expensive commodity that I want to keep on taking for a long, long time," the senator told him. "If I make trouble for my supplier, if I make him angry, he might cut me off."

"Face it, Lud," Remo said. "You're already cut off."

"What's that supposed to mean?"

Remo picked a Ziploc bag from the TV tray and showed it to the senator. Inside was a used adhesive patch. "This was your last fix. I took it off your ninety-year-old behind myself about an hour ago, while you were still in la-la land."

For an instant, the light went out of the rheumy eyes.

"*No mas,* baby," Remo said. "We're just going to sit here and watch you revert to your former self. Got the walker and the oxygen tanks waiting for you in the back bedroom."

"Growing old," Chiun said solemnly, "is a bitter herb that should not have to be tasted twice."

When Ludlow Baculum looked down at his beautiful, still buffed bod, his lower lip started quivering, and in no time, hot tears were streaming over his cheeks. "You can't be that cruel," he insisted. "You just can't. It's inhuman. Please give the patch back to me. Please. I'll pay you anything you want. I'll give you anything you want. I can get you an ambassadorship. A cabinet post. A date with the First Lady."

"Let's cut the old crapola, Lud," Remo said. "You can't buy us because we aren't for sale. And no matter what you think, this isn't a kidnapping for ransom. Who sold you the patches?"

"No. I won't say."

Remo tried another angle of attack. "Why don't we get real for just a minute?" he said. "You are not being audio- or videotaped. You are not being observed through one-way mirrors. It's just you and us, Senator. And we all know that the drug not only gives you a bigger, better body, but it makes you do things that you wouldn't ordinarily do. It made you kill your bride on her wedding night. It's made others kill, as well. Somewhere inside that screwed-up old head of yours, you have to know what's happened. Exactly what's happened. You have to know how bad it is.''

Ludlow Baculum did not respond.

"He knows," Chiun said. "He knows and he doesn't care. He is Animal Man."

"Not for long now," Remo said, checking the clock on the living-room wall. "The effects of that muscle juice should have already started wearing off. It's happening so slowly you probably won't even notice at first. But after a while, things should start shrinking up and falling off.''

Remo turned to Chiun and said, "Maybe we should let him think about that for a bit? I gotta make a call, anyway.''

A look of desperation passed over the senator's face. Desperation and horror.

Remo picked up the speakerphone from the lamp table and waved for Chiun to follow him into the bungalow's tiny kitchen.

22

At the sound of the bell-like electronic tone, Dr. Harold Smith looked up from his computer monitor to the color TV bolted to the wall, hospital-room style. A swirl of graphics on the television screen was accompanied by the raucous, annoyingly repetitive theme music of "Peephole USA." The theme only had one joyous bar, which was played over and over again at every conceivable opportunity. As Smith tuned in, the show was already in progress; it was just returning from a commercial break.

The male host turned to the female hostess and, with his cheeks fully dimpled, said, "Molly, you're not going to believe your eyes when you see this next story. I know you're into personal fitness and you watch your diet like a hawk..."

Molly beamed at him. Under the set's desk, her long, slender legs slithered lovingly over each other.

After a slight hesitation, the dimpled man continued—the pause was calculated to increase the dramatic effect. "But wait till you get a look at the rich and famous people who've recently jumped on the workout bandwagon.''

''I can't wait, Jed.''

''Then you're ready for 'Look Who's Buffed!'''

The two-shot of heads at a phony desk dissolved into the story title, which, in turn, dissolved into Jed walking along Muscle Beach in Venice, California. Jed had no shirt on, and was tanned and well-built, with just a hint of softness above the points of his hips. Dr. Smith noted that Jed was also completely hairless, like a preteenage boy.

''Like most of the people you see around me here on the beach,'' Jed said, ''I work out regularly with a personal trainer. It's the fit-and-healthy life-style here in southern California, where the folks like to show as much skin as the law allows.''

The camera cut to a pair of in-line-skating honeys in thong bikinis as they zipped past Jed on the board-walk. The zoom framed the girls' backsides and held the shot for a good five seconds. Then the entire gratuitous skin sequence was rerun in extreme slo-mo.

''Well,'' Jed went on, ''that trend has finally hit some of the biggest, and I mean that in every sense, movers and shakers in the world. Ladies and gentle-men, I give you Her Royal Highness, Princess Pye....''

The video cut to file footage of the former wife of the heir apparent to the Mossy Throne. She was twenty-three, blond, tall, with a stunningly beautiful face. She was also grossly overweight. The video showed her wearing what appeared to be a pup tent of a pink suit. Its fabric was tortured by her many personal bulges, all of which were on public display. Dr. Smith had heard it rumored that the princess's panty hose lasted only a few hours before the friction between her great shuddering thighs shredded them. On the video, she lifted the veil on her matching pink pillbox hat in order to bring a forkful of food to her lips with a dainty, white-gloved hand.

"This is the princess at a reception in York, England, two months ago," Jed told his viewers. "As you will soon see, the state function quickly escalated into a fruited-scone-and-Devon-cream-eating contest."

Dr. Smith shrank from the sight in disgust.

Jed was seriously overstating the case for a contest. If there was any competition going on, it was strictly between the princess and herself. Like a bulldozer, she plowed across the table of refreshments intended for the crowd of better than two hundred upper-crust well-wishers. The princess slathered on the rich cream even as she raised the half scone to her mouth. And took it down in a single ravenous bite. Smith found her economy of movement mesmerizing. And the pile of baked treats melted away, like the proverbial green cake left out in the rain.

In his cutesy voice-over, Jed scolded the princess for her excess of appetite. "Now, I've heard of a woman eating for two before," he said, "but Her Royal Highness is doing the work of ten. Those of you still wondering how she lost her girlish figure so soon after the wedding the world watched, need wonder no more."

As Smith recalled, the royal separation and divorce, endlessly publicized in the tabloid media, had been granted to the prince because of his wife's eating disorder. Which, according to all accounts, was both a public disgrace and a private nightmare. Apparently the princess didn't stop feeding even during the act of physical love. She always kept a trolley of tea cakes on her side of the marital bed.

"And she isn't the only big-time celebrity with a big-time poundage problem," Jed told his audience. "Consider, if you will, the international rock star, Skizzle..."

The video cut to a hugely fat young man, naked from the waist up, heavily tattooed, barefoot and clad in cutoff Levi's. The superstar Skizzle held a microphone in one hand and a quart bottle of his favorite alcoholic beverage, Black Death Porter, in the other as he cavorted in a spotlight on a stage before tens of thousands of screaming fans. Empty bottles of the super-high-calorie brew littered the stage. Skizzle's grotesque blubber jiggled and shook as he danced to the savage beat of his backup band. He danced and drank, sang and drank. Drank and drank.

Suddenly Skizzle froze. Clutching at his throat, the

rock star pitched facedown on the stage. The six-piece band, which was accustomed to such occurrences, continued to play the vamp with overamplified enthusiasm. They played as an emergency medical team rushed out from the wings of the stage. The paramedic crew quickly voided the hefty headliner of the beer bolus that was blocking his airway.

After a good puke, Skizzle rose from the dead to the tumult of the crowd. Guzzling more Black Death, he picked up the song and dance right where he had left off.

"And last but certainly not least," Jed said, "how about the world's richest man? Ladies and gentlemen, I give you Dewayne Korb, the computer-software billionaire."

The video shifted to a shot of Korbtown, the three-hundred-acre high-rise complex where the thirty-something tycoon's army of fresh-from-college, hand-picked nerds worked, lived, played and earned seven-figure retirement packages by age twenty-six. The shot cut again, this time to Dewayne Korb himself as he walked from the reception center's entrance to his stretch limo, waving and smiling meekly for the assembled paparazzi. His clothes were less a fashion statement than a desperate and fruitless attempt to conceal what lay beneath them. Korb wore loose-fitting, pleated tan cords, a button-down blue shirt under a vast, heather-colored, Shetland V-neck sweater.

From all camera angles, he was round, like the Pillsbury dough boy.

Only with a side part and wearing saddle shoes.

"The way his former associates tell the story," Jed went on, "Dewayne Korb snacked his way to greatness. He kept a Rubbermaid trash can full of high-calorie treats right beside his keyboard. That's how he managed to put in all those twenty-four hour days at the computer. But we all know how quickly brain food turns to butt food...."

The video shot zoomed in on the broad expanse of the billionaire's backside. There was enough wide-wale corduroy there to upholster a large armchair.

"And now the moment you've all been waiting for," Jed announced. "Look at who's buffed!"

Dr. Smith shifted uneasily in his ergonomic chair. Unlike the rest of the show's national audience, the head of CURE had a pretty good inkling of what he was about to see. And despite that, he was not prepared for what came next.

The "Peephole USA" camera caught Princess Pye as she posed for the media outside a Manhattan members-only night spot. Her face was chiseled perfection. Her body no longer a heap of unsightly bulges. Its fat content was near zero. The sleeveless bare-midriff top she wore exposed a sleek stomach that was a perfect gridwork washboard above the small, sexy indent of her navel. She had a waist like a wasp, and though she'd lost a good yard from the girth of her hips, the narrowness of her midsection made it appear that she still had womanly curves. Gone was the shuddering heft of her thighs. Those dimpled columns were just a memory. A dream, fading. The legs the princess's miniskirt revealed were slender and shapely from ankle to hip.

And even more stunning than her fat loss, than her muscle increase, was the overall tone of her body.

Princess Pye absolutely glowed.

One of the reporters present called out a question. "How'd you do it, Princess?"

The blond beauty gave him a dazzling flash of white teeth and baby blue eyes. "Wouldn't you like to know," she teased.

The video then cut to Skizzle, onstage. The rock star had been changed radically, as well. He was no longer the staggering, drunken blimp. He looked like Mr. Universe in cutoff Levi's. The immense size of his chest and arms had stretched his tattoos almost beyond recognition. And there were a couple of new twists to his stage act.

He jumped as he sang and danced.

This was no hidden-trampoline trick. Over and over, Skizzle leaped five or six feet in the air, effortlessly, and completely on his own. This thanks to his hugely developed calves and hams. His high-jumping antics sent his fans into delirium.

And the famous public drunkard had switched from drinking a case of Black Death Porter quarts onstage to drinking a case of Bertolli Olive Oil sixty-eight-ouncers. The plastic bottles with the jug handles.

He also had a new international tour to promote his new CD.

After the concert, the "Peephole USA" camera caught Skizzle toweling off in his dressing room. Amid the crush of bodyguards, music celebs and hangers-on, Jed and his crew fought to get the story.

"Wow, Skizz," Jed gushed, "you look like a million bucks."

"Yeah, that's about right," the rock star said. The answer was vintage Skizzle: purposefully mysterious, apparently unresponsive. A response that, as all his fans knew, had to be jam-packed with hidden, important meaning. The rock star cracked the tamper-proof plastic cap off a chilled bottle of greenish liquid.

"What's your secret?" Jed asked him.

"I want to thank the Bertolli company of Secaucus, New Jersey, for all its support on the Extra Virgin Tour," Skizzle said. As the singer tipped the jug to his mouth, his right biceps bulged far bigger than even Jed's extralarge head—a physical feature that was required for a career in television. The tattoos on Skizzle's enormous arm looked faded and decades old because ink lines were so far apart.

"Cheers, America!" the rock star said. Then he took a long, satisfying chug from the jug.

Skizzle's grinning, unshaved, lantern-jawed face

faded into a long shot of a grassy playing field. Men in T-shirts and shorts ran around with baskets on sticks, chasing a small ball. Behind them, as far as the eye could see, was a sprawling, modern business complex.

Jed's voice over said, "Well, folks, this is just another sunny Saturday afternoon at Korbtown. What you're looking at is a weekend game of the company's intramural lacrosse league. The technical writers are battling the technical editors. It's all part of the nonstop fun-and-games life-style of these young computer whizzes."

The camera closed in on knock-kneed nerds in Nikes trying, in vain, to club each other senseless with their lacrosse sticks. Wild overhead swings ended in clean misses that sent the players staggering, sometimes even spinning to the ground.

"But wait, folks," Jed said. "We have a last-minute substitution on the editors' side...."

The TV audience was treated to a tight shot of a man's bare back. No ordinary back, this. From armpit to armpit, this man's lats were a yard wide. His traps were like great hulking boulders beneath the skin. And all of it shouted density, incredible density, as well as mass.

The man's head, seen from the rear, looked way too small in comparison to the neck width and shoulder spread. Then the head turned.

Dewayne Korb, the new Dewayne Korb, beamed for the "Peephole USA" audience.

The camera retreated to take in the whole picture. The billionaire had traded his extrawide cords for an electric blue Speedo swimsuit. He had ditched his early-eighties hairdo for a slicked-back, super-moussed bullet-head look, with plenty of whitewall over the ears. His bare pectorals were promontories of power, his forearms were tree trunks, his buttocks Rocks of Gibraltar.

With blinding speed, and no word of warning, the computer billionaire snatched up his lacrosse stick and charged into the fray.

Needless to say, it was no contest.

Dewayne Korb not only leveled the opposition, but when he was done with them, he turned on his own team, clobbering them with his stick. Those that tried to escape the field of play, screaming, he ran down.

And summarily cold-cocked from behind.

When he was done, and the grass field of Korbtown was strewed with pale, skinny male bodies, some barely breathing, Dewayne Korb raised his hands over the head and did a Rocky-on-the-steps imitation.

"How could you do that to your own employees?" asked the aghast "Peephole USA" reporter.

"Hey, it's not like they're programmers," the billionaire explained.

Jed nodded as if he understood, eager to move on to his next question. "All of America wants to know about your superhard body," he said. "How about letting us all in on how you did it?"

"With money, Jed," the tycoon said. "Lots and lots of money. Now you'll have to excuse me. The Internet development group is about to throw the first pitch to the hardware guys over on the softball diamond, and I don't want to miss my turn at bat."

The cameraman chased after Korb for a dozen yards. But winded and unable to keep up, he let the muscular figure dwindle in the distance.

"Well, Molly," Jed said as the picture returned to the studio, "what do you think?"

"I'll take whatever they're having," Molly replied.

"You and fifty million other people," Jed said, laughing. "Don't worry, folks. We'll stay on this story...."

Dr. Smith shook his head. Deep in his heart of hearts, he'd been hoping that he'd made a fatal error in his forecast. Not so. Like a train on a track, the doomsday scenario he had predicted was approaching. A mysterious wonder drug gets international publicity. The body-image-crazed public clamors for access to it. And when the product finally arrives on the market, the public gobbles it whole.

Presto!

The end of civilization as we know it.

Dr. Smith had just shut off the TV when his scrambled phone line rang. It was Remo reporting in.

The news wasn't promising.

"Our man is keeping his lip zipped," Remo said. "He doesn't want to go back to being a geezer."

"You've removed his patch?"

"Yeah, but nothing's happened yet. Lud's still buffed."

"Keep on him. Maybe he'll crack when he starts to lose his fountain of youth."

"What about the analysis of the Boomtower patch?" Remo asked. "Has the report come in yet?"

Dr. Smith had arranged for that evidence to be chemically analyzed by a private lab in Los Angeles—an outfit used by the CIA for work they didn't want the FBI to know about. "We had a hit there," Smith said. "The drug-delivery patch was manufactured in Taiwan, part of a job lot purchased by Family Fing Pharmaceuticals, of the same country."

"Never heard of them."

"Up until now, they've mass-produced herbal remedies based on naturopathic and folk recipes. I'm still running down their corporate network, trying to connect names with our list of known users to uncover the pipeline, and hopefully, trace it directly back to Family Fing."

Suddenly, there was an awful scream at the other end of the scrambled line. It was so loud that it made Smith flinch and pull the handset from against his ear.

"It's Lud," Remo said. "Call you back..."

Dr. Smith waited for five interminable minutes, drumming his fingertips on his desktop. He picked up the return call before the first ring had finished. "Yes?"

"Bad news, I'm afraid," Remo said. "Old Lud checked out. He suicided on us."

"What? No one was watching him?"

"We had him securely tied in the next room," Remo defended. "Didn't want him to overhear this conversation. We only left him alone for a couple of minutes. He didn't get loose from his bonds."

"Then how did he manage it?"

"He chewed off his own right foot. I never thought a ninety-year-old could be that limber. Before we could stop it, he bled out on us. Sorry, Smitty. I didn't figure he'd do a thing like that."

Dr. Smith hadn't figured it, either, so he couldn't put all the blame on his assassins. What seemed clear to him was that the negative side effects of the patch were escalating—the longer a person used the drug, the worse things got. It was something that he hadn't included in his forecast, and was a development that kicked the disaster scenario even further over into the danger zone. It meant he had even less time to get the matter under control.

"We've got quite a mess on our hands here," Remo explained.

"Don't worry about it," Smith said with a sigh. "I'll send over a disposal team at once."

After he hung up, the director of CURE pulled up the file of Los Angeles steam cleaners. He had their service rates listed right by their phone numbers. Selecting the least expensive service, he hit the autodialer and waited for Andy the Rug Doctor to pick up the phone.

23

Jimmy Koch-Roche drew himself up to his full height and addressed the biggest box-office couple in movie history. "I'm sorry, but I can't let you drive yourselves home," he said. "It's as simple as that."

"We're not children," Puma Lee protested. She paced the floor of the attorney's walnut-paneled interview room like a caged animal. Four steps to the wall. Turn. Four steps back.

Chiz, who leaned against the front of Koch-Roche's desk, agreed with his wife. "A while back, you said something to me about consequences. Specifically, you said that there wouldn't be any. For your information, I consider being forced to have a baby-sitter a negative outcome."

The little lawyer held up his hands for silence. "I promised you that I could keep any and all charges from sticking, but come on. To do that, I need some cooperation from you both. In the last twenty-four hours, the pair of you have demonstrated a certain, well, let's call it an unevenness of temper. I want to avoid a repetition of similar incidents. I can work miracles in front of a jury, but there's a limit to even what I can do. Understand this, if you pull another grand-scale boner like the SpeeDee Mart debacle, I can no longer assure you of a get-out-of-jail free card.''

"Not good enough, Jimmy boy," Chiz said. "Not good enough by a long shot." He walked over to where the attorney stood and raised his massive fist over the little man's head like the hammer of God.

To his credit, Koch-Roche did not shrink back, even though he'd had ample evidence of what his clients were capable of. His was a world of bluster and bluff, of smoke and mirrors. And five-inch lifts.

Koch-Roche said, "I want you two to allow yourselves to be escorted back to Bel Air by my driver and security team, as per the bail agreement we worked out with the judge." He didn't use the words *house arrest* because they sounded so unpleasant. "I want you to stay there inside your compound under the protection of my men. You'll be safe there and you'll have an unlimited supply of the foods you desire, while I work on your defenses. I'm not asking you to become permanent prisoners on your own estate. We just need some quiet time to sort things out. Some time without further incident."

Chiz let his fist drop to his side.

"Honestly, it doesn't seem like all that much to ask," Koch-Roche said. "Considering the alternative, which is that you both get convicted of first-degree murder.''

''We get restless,'' Puma said.

''Then roam around your own grounds. There'll be no one around to bother you. I've already arranged for your mansion staff to take a holiday. My security people will be taking care of all your needs. Cooking. Cleaning. Grounds. They are there only to help you, so please don't do anything to harm them.''

''You're not going to try and take our patches away, I hope,'' Chiz said. Then he added, ''Because that would be a big mistake.''

''That's the last thing I want to do,'' Koch-Roche replied. ''But I do think it's pretty obvious that you both may be having a little trouble with the dosage that you're currently taking. I've already contacted the manufacturer about correcting that. We should have a solution to the problem from them in the next few days.''

''But if you give us less of the hormone, our bodies might shrink up,'' Puma said.

''Or go back to fat,'' Chiz chimed in.

''Not necessarily,'' the lawyer hedged. ''And anyway, wouldn't it be better to give up a bit of muscle than to have a string of murder charges hanging over your heads?''

Puma and Chiz exchanged dubious looks.

''Isn't there some other way of fixing things?''

Puma asked. "So we don't lose any of what we've got?"

"The manufacturer is looking into that, too," Koch-Roche assured them. "They are as concerned as we are over what's happened. The last thing the manufacturer wants is a drug that nobody will take."

The attorney pushed a button on his desk intercom. "I'll have my people take you home now," he said. "You've both had a long and trying day. You must be exhausted."

After a moment, four large, heavyset men entered the interview room single file. They were dressed head to foot in Threat Level IV body armor, including shiny black helmets, black shin guards, black steel-toed shoes, black gloves and clear, bulletproof shields. They looked like a cross between riot police and ancient samurai. They were armed with assault-style pump shotguns and Taser stun guns, and had headset mikes and earphones. Behind the Plexiglas of their face guards, the security men didn't look happy.

"These are the guys who are going to mow our lawn?" Chiz said incredulously.

"Among other things," Koch-Roche answered.

"Aw, let's just get out of here, Chiz," Puma said. "I'm starting to get hungry again."

ON THE WAY DOWN to the parking garage in the elevator, security man Bob Gabhart was on full red alert. His body was badly bruised from the encounter earlier in the day with the little Oriental. Every time Gabhart breathed, he could feel the contusion above his left kidney. His torso was wrapped with yards of elastic bandage. No way would he hesitate to use deadly force again; from now on, it was shoot on sight.

Amazingly, he hadn't actually felt the blow when it had been delivered. Gabhart was a guy who had been punched plenty of times, given his extensive martial-arts training during his stint in the U.S. Army as a Ranger captain, and during his subsequent, much more lucrative career as a security-systems analyst. Often, in the latter case, he'd been socked by a client while said client was either drunk or stoned, usually trying to make violent contact with someone else, an annoying photographer, a former spouse or business partner. It was part of Gabhart's job to absorb abuse, either directed at or coming from his employer.

The incident at Koch-Roche's mansion earlier in the day had been unusual to say the least. In his professional experience, no matter what happened in the movies, when the odds were seven to two, the side with seven always won. Especially when the side with seven all had guns. That his highly trained team had lost was as surprising as the painless blow that had so thoroughly bruised his back. A blow that had knocked him senseless; like he had been blindsided with a twenty-five-pound feather duster. Only after he had regained consciousness had the pain started. Last time he'd checked, he was still peeing orange. According to the doctors, he was still bleeding a little inside. But no way would Gabhart take the rest of the day off. He had been humiliated in front of his boss. Somehow he had to make it up, to save face.

It was cramped in the elevator car. There were too many big bodies. Too much gear. For Gabhart, the whole situation felt strange and uncomfortable. He'd had no idea that Puma and Chiz were so pumped. They were built like animals. And there was a tension in the car, something electric in the air. Like the pair the security team was supposed baby-sit was about to go berserk. Their muscles kept twitching, twitching, twitching.

The security man had thought that standing less than a foot behind the great Puma Lee would be the thrill of a lifetime. It was, but not in the way he'd expected. It had never occurred to him that he'd feel threatened by a female movie star. Physically threatened.

Even though the actress didn't even look at him, he had a sense that if given the chance, she could and would beat him to a bloody, quivering pulp. Having hit people before, with fists, feet and baton, Gabhart knew what it felt like to make contact with solid muscle. The shock wave shot right up your arm or leg. He had never hit anything as dense as the body Puma Lee displayed. And he had the sinking feeling that nothing he could do with fists, feet or baton would make the slightest impression on her. That he was fully body armored and carried a 10-shot 12-gauge gave him no comfort whatsoever.

When the car opened in the basement, fresh air rushed in. Two of the security men slipped out with shotguns shouldered, and knelt beside the doorway, sweeping the area for hostiles.

A voice in Gabhart's helmet said, "This is Stinger. We are all clear. Let's roll."

A black stretch limo surged from its parking space and came to a squealing stop in front of the elevator. Its black-uniformed driver immediately jumped out and opened the rear passenger door.

As Chiz and Puma got in the limo, a mint green Ford Explorer pulled in behind. It was the troop carrier. Three of the security men got in it. Bob Gabhart opened the limo's front passenger door and climbed into the shotgun seat.

The driver, a blockily built Samoan who looked like he could handle himself, hit the electronic door locks, belted himself in and floored the big Lincoln, sending it screeching away from the elevator.

As they climbed up the concrete ramp to the street, tires squealing as the long vehicle rounded the series of hairpin turns, Gabhart flipped up his Plexiglas face shield but didn't take off the helmet. Behind his head, the soundproof, one-way privacy window that divided the limo's driver and passenger compartments was up. The stars didn't want to be disturbed.

After they'd exited the parking garage and veered

onto the street, a voice in Gabhart's headset said, "Captain Crunch, we are on your bumper."

"Roger that, Stinger," he said. "We'll proceed to base by the prearranged route."

Sticking to the major streets, the limo worked its way to the freeway on-ramp. As the driver merged with the thick evening traffic, Gabhart checked out the view on his side. In the distance were the glittering lights and concrete gridwork of Megalopolis. Just ahead, at the next off-ramp, he could see the sprawling roofline and acres of free parking of the Sepulveda Mall.

Then a knuckle rapped on the other side of the privacy window.

As the window dropped, the familiar face of Puma Lee appeared in the opening. Gabhart saw the tension around her eyes and mouth.

"We need to make a stop," she said.

The driver looked at her in the rearview, then over at Gabhart, who for the purposes of this mission was his boss.

"Sorry, ma'am," Gabhart said, "that's not on our itinerary. My orders are to take you directly to your mansion."

"My husband and I need to pick up a few things at the mall," the movie star insisted. "Take the next off-ramp."

Gabhart steeled himself and looked her straight in the eye. "No need to trouble yourself with that kind of thing, ma'am," he said. "If you'd like to make a list, the security team will be more than happy to pick up whatever you want after we get you settled in at home."

"I told you to take the next off-ramp."

"I'm afraid I can't do that, ma'am. I have strict orders to see that you go straight home. It's for your own protection."

Gabhart saw the actress's fingers tighten on the top of the seat back. Her fingernails dug into the leather. For some reason, he hadn't noticed her nails before. They weren't just red, long and pointed; they were thick, almost like bone. And they sank into the seat cushion like five paring knives into an overripe peach.

Chiz Graham leaned into the window opening beside his wife. "For your protection, son, take the next off-ramp."

"It'll cost me my job, sir...."

Puma Lee reached through the privacy window and touched the driver's wide shoulder. "Turn now," she ordered.

The driver looked at Gabhart, who shook his head.

The movie star responded by sinking her nails into the driver's deltoid. Instantly, the blood drained from his round face, and he swerved the limo for the off-ramp, cutting between a semitruck and a minivan poking along in the slow lane.

Behind the limo, the Explorer's brakes screeched as it attempted maneuver for the off-ramp, but it was cut off by the bumper-to-bumper traffic. The driver swung into the emergency parking lane, locking the brakes again. When the Explorer finally came to a stop, the driver reversed his way back to the ramp, tires smoking.

"This is Captain Crunch," Gabhart said into his headset mike. "Stinger, we've had a sudden change of plans. We're proceeding at once to the Sepulveda Mall."

"Negative, Captain Crunch," said the voice in his ear. "Repeat. Abort that. What is the trouble?"

"Victoria and Albert have the munchies," Gabhart explained. "I'll keep you updated on our position."

When he looked over, he saw the blood dripping down the front of the driver's sleeve and lapel. Puma Lee still had her nails in him.

Gabhart thought about reaching for his side arm. But what then? If he pulled it, would he actually use it? Would he shoot a goddamned movie star he was supposed to be protecting? He didn't know. And the not knowing made him hesitate. He did know that drawing his gun and being unable to use it could put him in an even worse situation, as in being forced to eat it. So he reached for the cellular phone and started punching in the numbers for the Koch-Roche and Associates office.

"Who are you calling?" Puma asked.

"Got to report the change in route, ma'am."

"You don't got to do anything," she said, letting go of the driver and snatching the phone.

Gabhart didn't tussle with her over it. There wasn't time. She took it from him in a single, blindingly fast sweep of her hand, like stealing candy from a small, clumsy and not overbright child.

"I'm really getting tired of this guy, Chiz."

"Ditto," the action star said. "It's like being back in first grade."

"Open the sunroof," Puma told the driver.

As the panel slid back, exposing the rear of the limo to bright sunlight, the movie star seized Gabhart by both shoulders.

"Wait...!" he cried.

But it was already too late. With astounding ease, the woman pulled him through the narrow privacy window. Before the security man could do anything about it, she had thrust him halfway out of the sunroof, headfirst into the streaming wind.

Though he tried desperately to cling to the sunroof's opening, with one hard shove Puma Lee broke the power of his grip and sent him flying up and out of the limo.

Gabhart hit the trunk lid, then the road, bouncing and rolling wildly across the pavement. The driver of the Explorer, in high-speed pursuit of the wayward limo, once again had to slam on the brakes. He swerved the four-by-four into the oncoming lane to keep from running over Gabhart. Despite all the body armor, the impact shattered his right knee and shoulder. He rolled to a stop, facedown in the gutter.

As he lay there, gasping, Gabhart had no idea how lucky he was.

24

When Puma Lee tapped the limo driver on the side of the neck, he flinched, horribly. His eyes full of dread, he glanced up at her in his rearview mirror.

"Stop over there," she said. She pointed across the parking lot, at a side entrance to the mall.

As Chiz opened the door, he warned the driver, "Wait here for us. We'll be back in a minute."

But as soon as the movie-star couple stepped up on the curb, the limo driver put the gas pedal to the floorboard. With a squeal of tires, he shot away, highballing it for the nearest exit.

Chiz started to chase him down, and would have, but Puma caught his arm. "Don't bother," she said. "We'll take a cab home."

The movie stars slipped through the side door and onto the mall's main gallery. The shopping corridor featured marble-veneer floors and three-story-high atrium ceilings. There were full-size tropical trees and jungle plants in strategically positioned beds. Every hundred yards or so, the gallery walls were broken by a waterfall or fountain. Flashing neon lights lined both sides of the main walkway, luring customers into stores aimed at all age and demographic brackets. There was the young-and-baggy look. The old-and-dowdy look. The middle-aged-crazy look.

The stores seemed to be clustered according to the type of merchandise they offered. Chiz and Puma strolled past four jewelry stores in a row. Then four department stores. Shoe stores. Bookstores. It appeared that every business had cloned itself at least twice. The mall was a fertile spawning ground for various mercantile species. And some of them were wheeled. The shopping center had rented out some of the space in the middle of the gallery aisles to arts-and-crafts vendors with display carts. Again, there was strong evidence that some kind of cloning was going on. Witness the multiple outlets for handmade pottery. For watercolor portraits of Labrador retrievers. For potpourri. For wicker baskets. For gnome figurines.

Chiz and Puma Lee never ever shopped in such places. For one thing, they couldn't go out in public without being mobbed. For another, they had no interest in wearing what everybody else was wearing. They were the trendsetters, ahead of the current fashion curve by light-years. Their clothes and accessories were custom-designed, guaranteed one-of-a-kind items. They had appointments with exclusive couturiers and shoemakers. Nothing they put on their backs had ever seen the inside of a plastic bag.

As the movie stars moved purposefully down the gallery, they drew stares and double takes from the regular mall shoppers. People stopped in their tracks, slack jawed, as if witnessing some miracle of Creation. Their eyes were at first puzzled, disbelieving, then brimming with delight. As Chiz and Puma strolled along, they could hear the same words uttered over and over: "Is that really them?"

The mall customers began to follow along behind them like they were pied pipers, dropping whatever it was that they were doing, wherever they were going, whatever they had intended to consume. The gnome and potpourri vendors struggled to keep their carts in place as more and more people surged into the main corridor.

Despite the gathering throng, Chiz and Puma proceeded without incident until they reached the spawning ground of the camera stores. One of the clerks, who happened to be standing outside his shop cleaning a display window, caught sight of the commotion coming toward him. Instinctively, he snatched a loaded camera from the counter and, thinking of posterity, rushed forth into the middle of the aisle to record the moment.

In so doing, he blocked the actors' path.

Chiz didn't react well to the flash going off in his face. It startled and angered him.

The well-scrubbed camera clerk was trying to get both stars in the frame when Chiz took matters into his own hands. He grabbed the camera, which hung around the clerk's neck by a webbed strap, and flung it over his shoulder. The gesture was halfhearted, like he was shooing away an annoying fly.

Halfhearted or not, it jerked the hapless clerk right out of his shoes and sent him hurtling onto the mob forming behind the movie stars, a mob further fueled by people rushing out of the stores for a look at what in the world was going on. Because he landed on the mob and not the marble floor, the camera clerk might well have survived the fall—were it not for the fact he was dead the moment his feet left his shoes, when Chiz's jerk had broken his neck in three places.

The mood in the mall's gallery was so joyous that people didn't seem to notice that someone had just died. The screams of those few who had actually been struck by the corpse were drowned out by the Muzak and the excited rumble of hundreds of other shoppers. Oblivious to what lay beneath their feet, the mob tromped on the camera clerk's body like it was a display dummy or a rolled-up length of carpet.

An obstacle.

Not a victim.

Puma and Chiz were hardly aware of the tumult that surrounded them. They were that focused on aromas, on the myriad delicious smells coming from the direction of the mall's food court.

For its dining area, the mall's developers had created a miniature amphitheater. A sunken oval under huge skylights, with more of the ubiquitous jungle planters, palm trees and ferns, as well as a black tile floor. The semicircular seating area was bordered by individual take-out food shops. The cuisine on offer was a mixture of ethnic and traditional. There was the usual Italian, Mexican and Chinese fast food, but also curious, main-course cross-over items like Moo Shu Chimichangas, Carne Asada Calzones and the like. This, so the businesses could compete with their neighbors on either side. In addition to the full-meal-type of fast food, there were several all-dessert shops, including The Big Cookie, which sold enormous, half-cooked chocolate-chip cookies, and Sin-O-Bun, which sold enormous, half-cooked cinnamon buns.

The tables in the amphitheater were about a third full of shoppers, surrounded by bags full of purchases, by baby carriers, by avalanches of fast-food paper debris. The dull roar of the approaching crowd made them look up from their lasagne stir-fries and deep-dish egg rolls.

It was into this arena that Chiz and Puma strode, with an army of awestruck fans at their heels. Most of these people were under thirty; many of them teen-age mall rats who had been spending time, not money, in the faint hopes of being entertained.

As the juggernaut of humanity rolled onward, some people—the easily baffled—didn't move out of the way quickly enough. Chiz and Puma tossed the living statues left and right, sending them crashing into the plate-glass windows of the lines of shops on either side of them.

As the mob swept into the food court, mall security finally made its presence known. A dozen brown-uniformed men entered the amphitheater from all directions. At the sight of the huge crowd, they also seemed to freeze. There was no question of drawing their side arms; there were too many people for that. They conferred through their walkie-talkies, but it was clear that they didn't have a clue what they should do. Finally, the ranking officer ran to the nearest pay phone to call the LAPD.

Among the people loathe to move out of the way of the throng were the good folks waiting in line at The Big Cookie for a fresh batch hot out of the oven. They had already been waiting ten minutes.

Chiz and Puma weren't really interested in cookies, but the thought that someone else might be eating one right under their noses absolutely infuriated them. If anybody was going to eat cookies, it was them.

And them alone.

They altered their course a few degrees, just enough to put themselves dead center in the middle of the cookie line.

The would-be eaters and the service clerks in blue-gingham paper hats gawked as the movie stars and their entourage bore down on them. They were unsure what it all meant.

Could it be part of a movie that was being filmed?

Were the newcomers trying to cut in line?

The three cookie fans with the mental wherewithal to take a good look into Puma Lee's eyes didn't stick around to find out. They beat feet. The others instantly became HFOs—Human Flying Objects. Chiz and Puma really put some muscle into these tosses, because it was a territorial thing, because there was real anger behind the action. They plucked the cookie fans out of the lineup and, with a single twist of their torsos, sent them into low and tenuous orbits. The cookie eaters' bodies cartwheeled as they arced over into the eating area, crashing limply upon the metal tables and the concrete-and-steel housings of the overflowing trash receptacles.

Mall security looked on in helpless horror.

And the crowd began to chant, "Poo-mah! Poo-mah!"

The confusion in the minds of the shoppers was understandable. Overstimulated by bright neon lights, by loud music, by flashy displays, they weren't really sure what they were witnessing. A music video. A computer game. An infomercial.

On the other hand, Chiz and Puma weren't thinking at all. They were simply reacting to the sights and smells of the food court. Nostrils flared, they moved along the ring of fast-food shops. It wasn't spices they were sniffing at; it was the fat content.

They passed by Veggie Haven with scarcely a sidelong look. At Tex-a-Que, it was a different story. The odors of roasted fatty meat and of steak-fry grease drew the actors like a magnet.

Woe to those fans of down-home barbecue who did not flee.

Practically swallowing his tongue in excitement at the prospect of serving the stars, the Western-shirted, Buddy Holly-spectacled clerk automatically said what he had been programmed to say, "Howdy, folks. What'll you have?"

"We'll take a little of everything," Puma said.

Chiz smashed through the top of the plate-glass counter with his left fist while Puma cleared the queue of Tex-a-Que fans with a single look. After ripping away the remains of the countertop, they plunged their hands into the mounds of heavily sauced beef, smoked chicken and hot links, of potato salad and coleslaw that were ninety-five percent pure mayo, of baked beans swimming in bacon grease.

Behind them, the crowd closed in.

The teenagers continued to chant, "Poo-mah! Poo-mah!"

Some began to make howler-monkey sounds: "Hoo-hoo-hoo-hoo."

The actress picked up a whole pork butt in one hand and a fistful of Louisiana hot links in the other. She alternated bites, gulping and gnawing, until both hands were empty.

Chiz meanwhile concentrated on the coleslaw. He didn't lift his head from the slaw bucket when he heard a megaphone order the mob to clear a path. Only when the amplified voice barked right in his ear did he raise his face.

"Stand back from the counter," the command said.

Of course, that was absolutely the last thing Chiz and Puma were prepared to do. With grease running down their chins, the movie stars stared at the rent-a-cops. All four had their service revolvers drawn.

"We don't want any more trouble," said the head security man. "The LAPD are on their way. Don't make things any worse for yourselves than they already are."

Puma and Chiz shared a look. Trouble? What trouble?

The actress picked up the steel serving tray of barbecue beans and tipped it to her lips. The overflow of beans and sauce spilled all down the front of her cleavage.

"I'm asking you again," the head security guy said, "to please step away from the counter. We need you to follow us to a secure area. For your own safety, please."

The other three rent-a-cops looked mighty nervous, sandwiched as they were between the press of the mob—which was now shouting, "Let 'em eat! Let 'em eat!"—and the huge, animallike, food-covered megastars.

"Mghhmppp!" Chiz said, gesturing with a slab of

baby back ribs, his mouth crammed full of sweet potato pie.

At this point, three of the four bodyguards assigned to the stars by their lawyer finally caught up to them. The private security crew pushed to the front of the crowd.

"Oh, Christ," said Stinger as he viewed the carnage around Tex-a-Que.

"You guys aren't LAPD," said the mall's head security man. "So, who the hell are you?"

"Their court-ordered escort."

"The court isn't going to be real pleased with your service."

"They ditched us. And nearly killed one of our guys who was riding with them."

Above the chaos in the food court came the sound of approaching police sirens.

Lots of sirens.

The mob began to boo. Its size had grown. It looked like everyone in the shopping center, easily four or five thousand people, had migrated to the food-court area. All the shops were deserted, racks of merchandise and cash registers left unguarded, but even the thieves were too fascinated by the little drama to stay on the job.

"We don't want any gunplay here," Stinger told the world-famous couple. "A lot of innocent people could get hurt. The press for you two would be horrible. Before this gets any messier, let's just chill out.''

Stinger moved a little closer to Chiz, with his hands raised. His stubby 12-gauge riot pump hung under his arm on its sling.

The action star lowered the gnawed remnants of the ribs.

Puma stopped licking the trough of beans.

Stinger had unwittingly put himself between them and Señor Chorizo, the next fast-food shop in the row.

He was a red flag; they were bulls.

It wasn't a simple matter of competition, or that he was interfering with the smooth execution of their feeding frenzy. All the fatty meats and bacon drippings they had eaten were already beginning to react with the WHE in their bloodstreams. They had blast furnaces in their biceps, nuclear reactors in their buns. And in their bellies was the glow of power.

Rage seemed so natural, so right.

And the outburst of violence so pleasurable in its release.

Unaccustomed though Chiz and Puma both were to playing before a live audience—neither had ever acted on the stage—they got into the spirit of the thing. The feedback of a crowd was like an energy boost.

Some of the people who cheered and hooted and urged them on were still laboring under the delusion that what was happening was not real.

That bubble quickly burst.

In a movement quicker than the eye could follow, Puma Lee stepped behind Stinger. Before he could react, she took hold of his elbows and lifted, raising and trapping his arms above his head.

Though they hadn't rehearsed this part of the show, Chiz knew exactly what to do. Closing on the bodyguard, he grabbed hold of the top of his armored vest and ripped it down and off. Then he gripped the man's shirt and stripped it down around his waist.

"Jesus, don't..." Stinger pleaded.

They were his last words, if you didn't count the scream.

Chiz snatched hold of his collarbones, and as easily as he had torn off the vest, he ripped the man's muscles from his chest.

The crowd oohed and aahed.

What special-effects treat this?

What high-tech movie magic?

A make-believe torso spurting blood from clusters of broken arteries.

The folks in the front row knew the action was real. The blood that hit them was hot. And the smell that wafted over them, the smell of punctured guts as Chiz continued to root around in the man's body cavity— there was no way to fake that.

Puma slung the corpse aside.

People at the front edge of the mob tried to retreat, but were blocked by those behind them who refused to budge. Likewise, the two security teams found retreat impossible.

And then there was the chorizo.

A Mexican sausage so spicy that it was colored orange from all the chili powder and red peppers it contained. But the main thing about chorizo was the grease. When squeezed out of its casing into a hot skillet, or in this case, on a hot grill, the mound of spiced pork released pungent clouds of steam and a cascade of chili-tinted animal fat. Fat that was scraped off the grill with a spatula and into a gutter that dripped into a five-gallon plastic bucket.

A bucket long overdue for dumping.

The three-person staff of Señor Chorizo, all wearing minisombreros and sequined red felt vests over their aprons, had already jumped ship. As they were all Guatemalan nationals, and not fully Americanized Californians, the sight of brutal murder did not immediately make them think about popcorn and an extralarge soda. It made them think of death squads, which in turn, sent them on their heels, aprons flapping.

This left a half-dozen heaps of deceased sausage oozing on the grill.

If there was perfume of the damned, this was it. Red chili. Cumin. Tumeric. Coriander. Garlic. A hint of clove.

With a higher annual income than the GNP of some island nations, Chiz Graham and Puma Lee could have had literally anything or anyone that their hearts desired. But all they wanted was that slops bucket of chorizo grease.

The security teams tracked Chiz and Puma with their weapons as the movie stars jumped the counter of the Mexican food shop in a single bound, like they had springs on the soles of their shoes.

None of the security guys wanted to shoot. Or rather, they all wanted to shoot, but the consequences of such an act were too unthinkable. Shooting unarmed civilians in the line of duty was one thing; shooting unarmed famous and rich civilians was another. If the first was a no-no, the second was the Empire State Building of no-no's.

Chiz and Puma ignored all the handguns and shotguns pointed at their backs. They were too busy struggling over who would take the first gulp from the chorizo bucket. Both had a firm grip on the container's rim; neither would relent, though the sides of the bucket bowed outward. Neither would relent because he or she knew that to give the other the first taste would mean there would be none left.

With a loud crack, the bucket split down the sides. And the rich orange oil splashed over their bare legs, shoes and the black tile floor.

Chiz flung himself facedown and began lapping at the grease. Puma, now in full control of the slops bucket, took a moment to pour what little remained down her throat. Then she, too, played human rag mop with her tongue.

They had cleaned about half the square footage of the floor when another bullhorn blasted at them from the far side of the counter.

"This is the LAPD SWAT team," said an unfriendly male voice. "Put your hands where we can see them and slowly, I repeat, slowly, rise up from behind the counter."

25

Remo checked the rental car's rearview mirror. At the gated entrance to Chiz and Puma Lee's Bel Air estate, there were still no signs of life. Nothing had moved for better than an hour. That was when the mansion staff was herded off the grounds by three guys in full riot gear. Remo was tired of sitting, tired of looking up in the mirror and seeing zip. It was warm in the car, even with all the windows rolled down. The evening air was dead still.

The only sound was Chiun's snoring.

A low, steady rumble punctuated at irregular intervals by sharp pops. The Master of Sinanju slept sitting up in the front passenger seat, his torso held in place by his shoulder belt.

His napping wasn't a nodding-off every ten minutes, nor was it poor blood circulation to the brain, which one might expect of a normal, semisenile ninety-year-old. One of the benefits of a lifetime of study in mind-and-body control was that the Master was able to sleep anywhere, anytime. To drift off and awake instantly refreshed, ready for action.

Remo checked the clock on the dash. How could it possibly take Puma and Chiz so long to get here? he asked himself. The judge had ordered them to proceed directly from their lawyer's office to the mansion, a journey of no more than fifteen or twenty minutes by surface streets. To disobey the court's order meant both movie stars would go to jail. Which was why Koch-Roche had arranged for them to be escorted to their destination. It didn't figure that the security guys would go along with a side trip to some intermediate destination; what did figure was that something bad had happened. Something real bad.

Remo decided to call Smith. As he reached for the cell phone, it beeped. He knew it had to be Smith calling him, since no one else knew their mobile number.

At the sharp sound, Chiun's eyes snapped open. He gave Remo an irritated look, as if he'd been the one who'd caused the noise.

"Yeah, Smitty," Remo said as he picked up the phone. "What's going on?"

Chiun's expression mellowed and he yawned. The Emperor could do no wrong.

"A change of plans," Smith replied. Because they were talking on a cell phone, which could be monitored without their knowledge, the conversation had to be circumspect. "The job lot you were sent to collect is no longer on the market. It was unexpectedly detoured, and another collector has taken control of the targeted items.''

''Do I know the new owner?'' Remo asked.

''A Mr. Black and Mr. White.''

''No chance of retrieval, then?''

''Not at this time. The situation is fluid. The outcome uncertain.''

''I take it, then,'' Remo said, ''that we have another SpeeDee Mart situation in progress?''

''Yes, only more extreme,'' Smith told him. ''Unfortunately, the matter is out of our hands, perhaps for good. I want you to proceed to the next shop on your list. The item there is definitely in the same league. Once it is under your control, it may open up other profitable areas of search.''

''Got it. Later.'' Remo broke the connection and put the cell phone back in its cradle.

''And?'' Chiun said, stretching like a cat.

''Our movie stars are not coming home anytime soon,'' Remo said. ''The local police have them surrounded somewhere between here and Koch-Roche's office. It sounds like they must've killed again.''

''The wild animal cannot change its spots.''

''An old Korean saying?''

Chiun couldn't hide his disappointment at the feebleness of Remo's memory. It was so poor that he couldn't recall the contributions of one of the greatest men to ever draw breath.

''King Sejong, your fifteenth century,'' the Master

said. He was prepared to go into a lengthy lecture on the scientific and cultural achievements of the Yi Dynasty monarch known as the "Leonardo of Korea." But his one and only pupil was focused on the task immediately at hand.

"No way we can get to Chiz and Puma now," Remo continued. "Smith wants us to pick up the little dipshit attorney instead. Apparently, he's up to his eyeballs in this mess."

Smith was the magic word. It made Chiun forget all about the urgent need to reeducate Remo.

"By all means," the Master said, giving the car's steering wheel an impatient wave of his hand, "let us fly to the dipshit."

26

Jimmy Koch-Roche had to sit on his hands to keep from chewing his nails and ruining a 250-dollar manicure. He was watching the big-screen TV in his private office. A special news bulletin had interrupted regular programming. The live video picture was shot from a helicopter circling over the Sepulveda Mall. It showed an army of black-and-white police cruisers, SWAT vans, paramedic and fire units in the mall parking lot. At the bottom of the screen was the computer-generated headline MegaStars On Mall Kill Rampage.

The TV reporter in the helicopter was rehashing what little information she had while the pilot flew around and around the parking lot. "At about 5:30 p.m.," she said, "Chiz Graham and Puma Lee, both recently arrested for murder, evaded their armed escort and entered the mall at the south entrance. What happened next is still unclear, but authorities believe it precipitated the deaths of at least five more people, shoppers at the mall. The earlier reports we had of automatic-weapons fire inside the mall are all still unconfirmed at this time. The police have sealed off the area and are not answering any questions until the situation on the ground is resolved." The camera cut back to the woman reporter, who was grimacing as she pressed her earphone tighter to her ear. Then she said, "Okay, Jeff, uh, we have located an eyewitness on the ground. I'm breaking to Filberstan Wanajinji. Go ahead, Fil..."

The video switched to a swarthy-looking young man in shirtsleeves standing in front of a gas station. The male reporter turned to a bleached blond, crewcut, nose-ringed youth next to him and said, "You were inside the mall when the incident happened. Can you describe it for our audience?"

"Big movie stars started kicking butt, that's what happened," the boy said. "Royal kick butt, man."

"You saw the violence?"

"Look at my threads, man," he said, lifting the hem of his superbaggy, monochromatic plaid sports shirt. "See that?"

The reporter leaned in for a better look. "Uh, not really..."

"That there's blood. It was flying everywhere. Chiz Graham, man, when he splattered that guy, he ruined my threads."

"What guy?"

"Some dude with a shotgun and strange helmet."

"A police officer?"

"Don't know. Whoever he was, Chiz killed him good."

"We've heard rumors about gunfire inside the mall. Can you tell us anything about that?"

"Oh, man, it was way cool, like a firing squad. Cops lined up on one side, and Puma Lee and Chiz on the other."

"Did Puma and Chiz have guns?" the reporter asked. "Did they do any of the shooting?"

"Nah, they just got the holy crap blown out of them."

"You saw that?"

"Hell, yes. It was like World War III. The cops just cut loose on them. Bullets and guts went everywhere. See this here...?" He held up another part of his shirt. "This is some of Puma, I think."

As the reporter waved the camera in for a close-up, Jimmy Koch-Roche shut off the TV.

To say things weren't going well for the diminutive attorney was a major understatement. First, there was the as-yet-unexplained death of Bradley Boomtower after an attack on the L.A. Riots' training headquarters by two unidentified men claiming to be assassins. Assassins sent by whom, no one knew. But Boomtower had most certainly gone down. Then came the disappearance of Senator Baculum while under the protection of both private and federal security. Despite a three-state manhunt, no trace of him had been found. It was a lucky thing that there had been so many witnesses to the senator's abduction, or Koch-Roche himself might have been suspected in helping the man flee the murder charge.

Again, a two-man team had committed the attack. Probably the same one that had gone after Boomtower. That a pair of men, one of them reportedly Oriental and ancient, could overpower and disarm more than seven trained men was difficult to understand. That one of them could take Boomtower's life without using a weapon of some sort seemed impossible.

The big question was, who sent them? But the huge question was, who was next?

Clearly, someone out there was targeting the high-profile users of WHE. The possibilities gave him cause to sweat. Koch-Roche pulled out a handkerchief and mopped his dripping face. The effort had to be unofficial, as the compound wasn't illegal yet. Perhaps some other drug cartel wanted in on the hormone action, maybe even one of the Golden Triangle gangs. Or some other pharmaceutical house, or a clandestine arm of the U.S. or other government that wanted to nip the new drug in the bud. Whoever they were, they were willing and able to use deadly force, seemingly whenever and against whomever they wanted. It was something that made his twenty percent commission on hormone drug sales seem suddenly way too small.

The intercom on his massive wood desk bleeped. He stabbed the Talk button with a thumb.

"Leon, I told you not to disturb me!"

"Mr. Koch-Roche, I'm sorry," said his executive assistant. "I have Mr. Korb here in the outer office. He would like to see you at once."

The little attorney was not in the mood for the multibillionaire. Like most barristers, he had a low opinion of his clients. An opinion that bordered on contempt. Generally speaking, they were worse liars and thieves than he was. Which is why he always made them pay up front. Before Dewayne Korb had started taking the drug, he'd been an insufferable bore, obsessed with stopping the theft of his intellectual property, and conversely, with defending himself against a mountain of similar claims against him. After taking WHE for a week, he was not only an insufferable bore, but a dangerous one. Though his physique had never been imposing, now all Korb could talk about was the size of his abs, lats and glutes.

Before Koch-Roche could tell his assistant to send the man away, that he'd already gone home for the night, the double oak doors to his office burst off their hinges and came crashing down on the Persian carpet.

Dewayne Korb, the world's richest man, strode over the fallen doors and into the lawyer's private office. "Get rid of your flunky," he said, indicating the male secretary with a jerk of his head, "or I will."

"Go, Leon," Koch-Roche said, shooing him away. "You should have gone home hours ago, anyway."

"I still have a few things to clear up, sir. I'll be outside if you need me for anything."

When the assistant had left, Korb advanced on his attorney's desk. In his case, the change wrought by WHE was particularly spectacular because the original article had been such a complete and total mush ball. Now he was anything but a mush ball. The computer billionaire was easily as wide as Boomtower across the shoulders and back, only he stood seven inches shorter, at a modest five foot ten. Having discarded his trademark cords and loose-fitting crewneck sweater, he wore a kind of turquoise bib-front swimsuit made out of spandex. His bare calves were the size of Smithfield hams.

Korb was no longer the constant butt of computer-nerd jokes.

He was the constant butt kicker.

No matter. Koch-Roche felt secure behind his huge battleship of a desk. The wood it was made of was so hard and so rare, coming as it did from the depths of the endangered tropical rain forest, that it was sold by the ounce. He felt powerful, too, because his desk was on an elevated dais, four steps above the floor of his office. It made Koch-Roche appear to be of slightly taller than normal height.

He loved his dais.

"As you probably know, it's been a rough day for me, Dewayne," the attorney said, holding his ground as the billionaire advanced on him with menace in his eye. "So I'd appreciate your getting to the point."

"The point," Korb said, leaning across the desk, "is that I need some more patches."

Koch-Roche was incredulous. "But I gave you a one-month supply just a week ago."

"I ran out yesterday."

"What's going on, Dewayne? You were given directions about how to use the patches. You've got to level with me."

The billionaire shrugged his massive shoulders. "I figured if one patch was good, then four were four times better. And I was right. Check this out." Korb flexed his right biceps. It was like a huge, oiled piston gliding under Saran Wrap. "Jimmy, I need some more."

"That's gonna be a problem."

"Clarify."

Koch-Roche explained the situation vis-à-vis the sudden deaths and disappearances of the other rich and famous users of WHE. He did not mention anything about the fate of Puma Lee and Chiz, because he didn't want the billionaire freaking out on him. He figured Korb already knew about that anyway—he probably had a goddamned Internet server in his head.

"Bottom line here is," Koch-Roche said, "I'm afraid to go back to my house, and that's where the rest of the patches are. I don't think I'd make it back from there alive."

"I got more security men than you can shake a stick at over in Korbtown. I can round them all up and we can take an M-1 tank over to your place if you want."

"No, I'm not going back there until I know who's behind all this. Tanks can be blown up."

"Not real satisfactory," Korb said. His fingertips were leaving indentations in the tropical hardwood. "I got to tell you, Jimmy, I'm real disappointed in you. I need some more of the hormone and I need it right away. I'm starting to feel funny. Sort of bloated. My fingertips feel swollen. How are we going to fix this problem?"

"It's going to cost you more."

"Am I surprised? Do I care? It's only money. Come on, you greasy little bastard, out with it before I turn your head into a paperweight."

Koch-Roche was thinking fast. He liked his head right where it was. He needed to put a few thousand miles between himself and the pursuers, whoever they were. An entire ocean would do very nicely, thank you.

"The only other supply of the drug is in Taiwan," he said, "at the manufacturer. If we can get over there, you'll have no problem. They've got lots of it in storage at their plant. They'll sell you all you want."

"Taiwan? That's no big deal. I thought this was going to be hard. Grab your passport and let's go."

The attorney patted the breast pocket of his pin-striped suit. "My passport's right here."

When Koch-Roche didn't step down from the dais quickly enough, Korb reached over and picked him up by the scruff of the neck, like a kitten. He gave the attorney a brisk shake, then said, "I've got a private 757 sitting on the runway at LAX, fueled and ready to fly. We're outta here."

27

As Remo and Chiun swept through the glass entry doors to Jimmy Koch-Roche's office suite, they nearly collided with a tall, thin man with an attaché case.

"Can I help you gentlemen?" the thin guy asked. "I'm afraid the office is closed for the day."

"We're looking for Mr. Koch-Roche," Remo said.

"Then you just missed him. Perhaps you could call for an appointment tomorrow? As I said, the office is closed for the day. I've already locked up my desk. I was just on my way out the door."

Remo read the nameplate on the desk. "Leon," he said, "we need to get in touch with your boss at once. It's an emergency."

Leon scrutinized the ancient Oriental, who stood with a placid expression on his wrinkled face and both his hands buried up the sleeves of his silk robe.

"You're not one of Mr. Koch-Roche's current clients," Leon said. "I'm sure I'd remember you if you were. And even if you were, I am under strict instructions not to give out my employer's whereabouts once he leaves the office. I'm sure you can appreciate that. Being such a high-profile attorney, he gets all sorts of unwanted attention, often from well-meaning individuals who are not the least bit insane.''

"This is a matter of life and death," Remo told him.

Leon was thoroughly unimpressed. "In case you never watch TV or pick up a newspaper, the people who come in here are always in trouble."

"No, you don't understand, Leon," Remo said. "We're not the ones in trouble. He is."

"Maybe you'd better identify yourselves and state your business with Mr. Koch-Roche." From the sudden brittleness in his voice, it was evident the executive assistant was losing his patience.

"Of course," Remo said, reaching in his back pocket. He opened the leather ID holder and held it up for Leon to read.

The big blue letters stenciled across the documentation said FBI.

"Remo Reno?" Leon said dubiously. "Who's your friend—Charlie Chan?"

The slender hands slipped out of the baggy cuffs.

Lucky for Leon, the alarm bells were already going off in Remo's head. The name Chan, of course, reflected negatively on the width of nose—and general tendencies toward barbarism, pillage and rape.

"No," Remo said, stepping between the Reigning

Master of Sinanju and the attorney's assistant. "But you're close. It's Charlie Chiun."

"I have to be frank with you," Leon said. "Neither one of you looks like Bureau material to me."

"We left our gray suits at home. Lighten up, Leon. We're here to do your boss a favor."

"First, it's life and death, then it's he's in trouble, now you're offering a helping hand? I think both of you should leave immediately." Leon put his briefcase on top of the desk and picked up the phone. "Leave now or I'm going to call security and have you arrested for trespassing."

"Bad idea," Remo said.

"Oh, really?" Leon hit one of the buttons on the console.

Chiun reached over and jerked the cord connecting the handset to the receiver. It parted with a snap.

Leon looked at the broken cord in astonishment. Then he carefully replaced the handset in its cradle. "If this is a robbery," he said, "you are welcome to everything I have on me. The office keeps no cash except what is in my center drawer."

"Leon, baby, don't blow a gasket on us," Remo told him, "we're not interested in your petty cash or your cuff links. We just want to know where your boss is."

Leon stared at Chiun's long fingernails. "I don't know. He left a few minutes ago."

"Alone?"

"No, he was with a client."

"Don't make us wring the information out of you."

Chiun took a half step toward the executive assistant.

"It was Korb," Leon squeaked. "Dewayne Korb, the computer tycoon. Look, I've had more than enough excitement for one day, thank you. You should see what Korb did to the door. The man's a maniac."

"Where did they go?" Remo asked him.

"I have no idea."

"Why don't you show us Mr. Koch-Roche's office."

Leon obliged reluctantly. And with a little prodding, even opened his boss's wall safe.

"If you tell me what you're looking for," Leon offered, "maybe I could help you find it. Then you wouldn't be leaving me quite such a mess to clean up."

Remo stopped dumping papers from the open safe onto the floor. "We're looking for a list of names of all the clients he's provided drugs to."

"I know nothing about that."

"No, of course not. People come in here one week as ninety-pound weaklings, and the next they look like the Incredible Hulk. Get a bit real, Leon."

"Mr. Koch-Roche has never told me anything about that. I've never seen a list of names."

"Boomtower? Baculum? Chiz Graham?"

"I'm sorry. They are just his legal clients, to my knowledge. If my employer is doing anything against the law, I am not a party to it."

"I can make this one speak," the Master announced.

Chiun backed the tall, thin man into a corner with hand gestures like a snake charmer.

"Don't waste your time, Chiun," Remo said. "He doesn't know anything. I believe him." Then he asked Leon, "Does Koch-Roche keep his passport in the office?"

"Center drawer of his desk."

Remo opened it and looked. "It's not here," he said.

"That's where he keeps it, unless he's using it."

"You've been a big help to us, Leon," Remo said. "Now we're going to need for you to spend some quiet time in a closet."

"I'm claustrophobic," the thin man confessed.

"Is there an office rest room?"

"Yes, of course."

"Then you can wait in there."

After they had locked Leon in the men's bathroom, Remo and Chiun returned to the attorney's private office.

"Time to call Smith," Remo said, picking up the phone.

"Yes," Chiun agreed, "the Emperor in his wisdom will surely guide us."

Remo punched in the code to CURE's scrambled line. He didn't know exactly how the thing worked, but when he dialed the number, his call was somehow rerouted by the Folcroft mainframes, sent through a few hundred thousand other phone numbers from all over the world, making it impossible for anyone to pull up the Koch-Roche phone records and find out whom he'd called.

Smith picked up on the first ring. "What have you got for me, Remo?" he demanded.

"Looks like we just missed our boy Jimmy," Remo said. "Apparently, he's flown the coop with Dewayne Korb, the billionaire nouveau muscle man. We have no idea where he's gone, but his passport isn't here."

"Let me run a quick check through the FAA in Los Angeles," Smith said. "See if Korb's filed a flight plan." After a pause, the director of CURE said, "I'll have that information momentarily. Did you get any break on a list of WHE users?"

"We got nothing there, either."

"That's too bad."

"The hormone heads will turn up eventually, won't they?"

"Yes, but probably only after they've committed some kind of atrocity. We could've saved a lot of innocent people a lot of pain and suffering if we'd isolated the current users.

"The FAA data is scrolling up now," Smith continued. "It shows a Korb-owned Boeing jet at LAX with a flight plan filed to Taiwan, nonstop."

"We'd better get on it, then," Remo said.

"No, it's too late. Their scheduled departure is in ten minutes. You'll never get there in time to stop them from taking off."

"What now?"

"We proceed according to plan. We have to stop the production of the drug at the point of manufacture, which means taking down Family Fing Pharmaceuticals of Formosa. And we have to do it before they have a cheap synthetic version of WHE ready to mass market. Bottom line is, you're going to Taiwan, too."

"So, how're we gonna handle that?"

"Your tickets and documents will be waiting for you at LAX. I'll book you on the next flight out."

"Aisle seat," Remo said.

"What?"

"Chiun likes an aisle seat. He claims it gives him a better view of the in-flight movie."

28

Fosdick Fing touched the LCD screen of his notebook computer, making the densely packed table of five-digit numbers shift to a bar graph. "Now, that's a welcome sight!" he said. An expression of profound relief on his face, Fing showed his American colleague the newly correlated data. "I think Test Subject Three is definitely responding to the change in her diet," he told Carlos Sternovsky.

The American reviewed the computer-generated graph, then looked up at the video monitor bolted to the wall above the patient's locked door. The connection that Fosdick was making seemed tenuous at best to him. Like connecting bad luck with the presence of a black cat, or good luck with the position of the stars. The bar graph was a mathematical construct; it presented facts subject to interpretation. And interpretations were subject to being one hundred percent wrong.

True enough, the game-show hostess turned talk-show hostess turned opera star, known professionally as Okra, seemed to have calmed down. Only minutes before, she had been in the midst of a gibbering, foaming-at-the-mouth rage. Alone in her hospital suite, she had pounded on the walls, kicked at the steel-reinforced door and turned one hundred thousand dollars' worth of medical monitoring equipment into so much twisted wreckage. In her fury, Okra had even de-stuffed her own mattress. The empty ticking lay rumpled on the bed frame like the discarded skin of some enormous, gray-and-white-pin-striped fruit. Ankle-deep drifts of white polyester padding covered the floor of the room.

Since she'd started in on Fosdick's new food regimen, she hadn't moved from her position on the floor. She knelt in front of the jury-rigged feeding tube that had been slipped through a hole the staff had drilled in the wall.

Lips to the clear polyethylene, Okra sucked down a light brown substance, barely pausing for breath.

"I'm positive," Fosdick said, "that the tantrums we've been seeing are related to too low a dietary-fat content. Think about it, Carlos. If the synthetic hormone is making greater and greater demands for fat intake over time, and that additional fat isn't provided, it could cause the test subjects terrible discomfort. And the violence they've exhibited may be directly related to the internal pain they are feeling."

"That may be so," Sternovsky said. "But what you're doing now proves nothing. Except that she likes peanut butter more than she likes tearing the bejesus out of her hospital room.''

"True, it's not a double-blind study," Fosdick admitted, "and the data from this subject isn't fully calibrated yet, but these results certainly give us reason to hope that the negative effects of the drug can be lessened to market-acceptable levels.''

"Without actually going to the trouble of changing the formulation," Sternovsky said.

"My father was adamant. You were there. The future of Family Fing Pharmaceuticals hangs in the balance.''

Sternovsky watched the test subject as Fosdick used the remote control to zoom the camera in on her face. Okra's cheeks hollowed as she nursed on the end of the tube. Her eyes were shut in apparent rapture. She paused in her sucking only for the occasional belch.

Sternovsky had no formal training as a physicist, but he knew that to draw creamy peanut butter through a one-inch tube required an awesome amount of force. And Okra was accomplishing the feat without the aid of a pump. With just a little help from gravity—the five-gallon peanut-butter bucket was elevated about five feet off the floor—Okra was pulling in peanut butter by the foot, all on her own. Based on Fosdick's calculations, she was intaking 3420 calories per yard of suck, and in that yard, 2300 calories came from fat. Roughly estimating Okra's suck rate,

Sternovsky figured she was taking in a human male's recommended daily allowance of calories every ten to twelve minutes. And after more than a half hour of the new regimen, she showed no sign of slowing down on the peanut-butter pipeline.

"I'm not sure we aren't opening an even bigger can of worms here, Fosdick," Sternovsky said.

The youngest Fing waved him off. "Results are what my father wanted, and results are what I'm going to give him."

Fosdick turned to the waiting medical support staff and gave them a crisp order punctuated with jabs of his stubby index finger. "I want you to switch all of the test subjects over to Skippy immediately," he told them. "I think we finally have our answer. Let's use the big containers, people."

Sternovsky scanned the faces of the nurses and attendants. They all looked haggard. Frightened. Like they'd been working in a combat zone or a natural catastrophe. The situation on the ward was that overwhelming. They had seen their fellow workers torn limb from limb, and the bellows and roars of the other less tranquil test subjects were constant reminders that the same thing could happen to them. The staff was still willing to feed the drug-trial lab animals through holes drilled in the walls, but if Fing asked them to confront their patients face-to-face, he was going to have a full-scale rebellion and walkout on his hands.

"The only way we're going to know for sure what

effect the peanut butter is having," Sternovsky said, "is to draw blood samples from her."

"Sure," Fosdick said. "You're the expert on drawing blood. You know where the hypos are. Why don't you do the honors?"

The American scientist shook his head. "I'm serious, Fosdick. Pump some tranquilizer in through the feeding tube, knock her out and let's get a blood-level reading on her."

Fosdick wouldn't hear of it. "A tranquilizer will negate the experiment completely. Think about it. We can't build up people's muscles but in the process turn them into tranked-out zombies who can't get out of bed. Our most recent demographic studies show that eighty-three percent of the fun of having a hard body is showing it off."

"Tails are okay, though," Sternovsky said sarcastically.

"For all we know, the new diet might affect that, too. We could even get a complete reversal."

Sternovsky gawked at the research chemist. For a moment, he was speechless. When he recovered, he asked, "Where did you say you did your graduate work?"

"I didn't."

"You didn't do graduate work?"

"No, I didn't say. Actually, I had a two-year fellowship at Lever Brothers."

Oh, God, Sternovsky thought as a lump the size of

a cantaloupe rose under his breastbone. Now it all
became clear....

"You were in the floor-wax division?" he asked.

"No, I was with the Wisehart Center for Unguent
Development."

Sternovsky was aghast. A balmer! The WHE project was being run by a fucking balmer!

"Fing," he said, barely controlling his understandable anger, "for Pete's sake, open your eyes. Our
subject there has got a real corker of a tail going for
her and, the change in diet notwithstanding, it doesn't
appear to be getting any smaller."

The appendage in question, a stout, furry bit of
baggage with a funny curl at the tip, trailed across the
floor. As Okra nursed on the hose, it twitched and
flipped around as if it had a mind of its own.

"We'd have to measure it to know for sure," Fosdick said. "It looks smaller to me."

Sternovsky had no intention of explaining the basic
theories of biology to his Asian counterpart. "Do you
expect her fur to fall out, too?"

Fosdick shrugged. "We believe that the fur is a
fully manageable side effect. A daily depilatory ap-
plication should handle that."

Sternovsky squinted at the monitor. The nursing
woman had an all-over pelt. It was especially long
and luxuriant on the backs of her legs and the insides
of her arms, like a golden retriever or Irish setter.

"She's going to have to bathe in Nair to get rid of *that* coat," Sternovsky said.

Behind him, the medical-wing staff was already carrying out Fosdick's orders. A couple of female attendants were using cordless drills to bore holes through the walls of the test subjects' rooms. And from the other end of the hallway came a daisy chain of gurneys pushed by nurses and orderlies. Balanced on each hospital cart was a huge drum of peanut butter.

Carlos Sternovsky sagged against the corridor wall and stared at his empty hands. Had it really come down to this? he asked himself. All the dreaming since he was a small boy, all the hard and unrewarded work? Had he suffered the scorn and rejection of his peers for this idiocy? Like a man possessed, he had fled from his own country and sold his soul to the Fings in order to keep his precious line of research alive. And what were they doing with it? They were destroying it. If the Fings released the drug prematurely as they planned, it would undermine everything he had worked for. The drug's future usefulness would be tainted, its scientific and medical reputation ruined.

Somehow, blinded by his own mission, by his own thickheadedness, he had managed to hand the control of a cutting-edge discovery over to a Taiwanese unguentologist, a man whose advanced training was in making a baby's butt softer to the touch.

That Fosdick Fing was a blubbering, father-cowed moron was the icing on the cake.

Sternovsky watched the medical staff thread plastic feeding tubes through the walls of the corridor, thereby connecting the enraged test subjects to the elevated drums of Skippy.

Sure as the nose on his face, he knew.

Things were going to get worse.

29

When Fillmore Fing's bleary-eyed receptionist escorted the firm's U.S. legal counsel and the world's richest man into the boardroom, Fillmore rushed over to greet them. Though it was just past four in the morning, Taiwan time, and though he'd had a sleepless and tension-filled night, the elder Fing was almost painfully chipper.

"Come in, come in," he said, waving them into the nerve center of his global enterprise. Despite the lateness of the hour, he was most pleased to see one of the initial success stories of WHE in person. "Welcome to Taiwan, Mr. Korb," he said. "This is a wonderful surprise. And if I may say so, you are looking tremendously fit."

Dewayne Korb grunted in reply, his eyes narrowed as he searched the boardroom conference desk, the surrounding bookcases, tabletops, work surfaces for a hint of red-and-white foil and plastic pouch—the hermetically sealed packet that contained the drug and its delivery system.

"This is my oldest son, Farnham," Fillmore said,

indicating the casually dressed young man seated on the room's leather couch.

Farnham, who was less of a disappointment to his father than his brother was, nodded politely but didn't offer to shake hands with the computer billionaire. He didn't want to get that close to someone who had been taking the hormone. He and the entire Family Fing medical staff had learned the hard way that impinging on a WHE user's personal space was a good way to lose your head.

Fillmore Fing, a massive smile distorting his round face, gestured for the two Americans to have a seat at the long table. As Dewayne Korb drew back his chair, the patriarch couldn't help but stare at the back of the billionaire's pants. What he was looking for, and so pleased not to discover, was the protruding stub of a tail. There was, however, a certain puffiness to Korb's face, something Fillmore hadn't seen in any of the other subjects—their faces were uniformly lean, just like their bodies.

Jimmy Koch-Roche was dressed for high heat and humidity. In his baggy shorts, his hairless legs looked sickly, spindly, like white toothpicks.

It was Korb who spoke first, his voice gravelly and excessively loud. "I need some patches," he said. "I need them right now. And I'm hungry. I need something to eat, too."

"We ran out of food on the plane over the Marianas," Koch-Roche explained. "And Mr. Korb has been off the hormone medication for ten hours now. His time-release patches are all worn-out."

"How could you let that happen?" Fillmore asked in a tone of disbelief.

On the other side of the long table, from low in his belly, Korb started growling.

"I'll explain that," Koch-Roche said. "But, really, he can't wait any longer. We have to do something...."

"Of course, of course," Fillmore said. "Mr. Korb, we'll go over to the medical wing at once and get you fixed up."

The four of them hurried from the boardroom. In the hall outside the entrance, a pair of electric golf carts was parked. Farnham and Korb got into the first one, and Fillmore and Koch-Roche climbed in the second. Farnham took off with a chirp of tires on the well-waxed tile and zoomed away. His father followed, but at a slower pace, down the otherwise deserted hallway.

Fillmore had waited long enough for an explanation. He turned to his attorney and said, "I thought you had an ample supply of the hormone extract on hand? Have recent sales been that brisk?"

"Sales have been excellent, exceeding even our most optimistic projections," Koch-Roche explained, "but in the last day or so, we've had some unexpected problems."

"I know, I know," Fillmore said. "But my youngest son assures me that he has worked the bugs out of the product. There will be no more unusual behavior from the users of WHE.''

"That's not what I'm talking about," the attorney told him. "The problems aren't directly related to the recent violent public outbursts by my clients and your customers."

Fillmore's brow furrowed. "Go on."

"We've had a string of incidents that make it appear someone does not want WHE to become available, distribution-wise. Someone who is willing to kill in order to keep that from happening."

"You are certain of this?"

"Absolutely," Koch-Roche assured him. "I still have a good supply of patches at my home, but I couldn't retrieve them for fear of being killed myself. There has already been one attack on my residence. A successful attack in which a U.S. senator, the oldest user of the hormone to date, was kidnapped despite the protection of almost a dozen armed guards. He has not been seen again. Another of my clients was brutally murdered on a football field in broad daylight. Presumably by the same pair of hired assassins who kidnapped the senator."

"You may well have led the killers straight to us!" Fillmore exclaimed. "Why didn't you inform me of this before you came?"

The tiny attorney forced a smile. "Because I figured that they had already made the connection between me, the drug and Family Fing. It wouldn't take a rocket scientist, after all. We haven't been too concerned about covering our tracks. Since the drug hasn't been declared illegal yet, there was no need for that kind of secrecy. There was no way you, me or anyone could have anticipated a lethal response to the drug's test-marketing in the States."

"Certainly you don't suspect that this is an official effort of the government?"

"No, I don't think so," Koch-Roche said. "To date, these attacks have targeted individuals using WHE, but there have been no subsequent press releases, no mention of the existence of the drug itself. It seems to me that whoever is behind this campaign doesn't want to give our product any more publicity, positive or negative, but would much prefer to sweep the whole thing under a rug."

"This could be an organized attempt by a competitor to sink our development program, co-opt the discovery and bring out a rival product," the elder Fing speculated.

"That had occurred to me, too."

Fillmore Fing pulled at his silky smooth earlobe. He knew that any one of a half-dozen international rivals in the pharmaceutical trade could be behind the disruption.

And who could blame them?

The profits on global sales of WHE were going to be astronomical. And even if the U.S. FDA refused to approve the drug, even if it was declared illegal and dangerous, it would still turn a huge profit in the Third World, where bureaucrats were not so fussy about what they allowed their people to ingest.

Though he hadn't confided as much to his sons, the patriarch Fing already had a contingency plan in place. To move the heart and soul of the brand-new, state-of-the-art manufacturing plant in New Jersey would cost him a few tens of millions. He had had the entire operation designed so it could be disassembled, placed on a fleet of cargo ships and transferred to some more friendly country—all in a matter of a few weeks. Fillmore Fing had never been one to fail for lack of adequate foresight.

The reason he hadn't told his sons about this fail-safe option was that he wanted to keep the pressure on them. He didn't want to lose so much as a dime on the deal if he could help it. His concern with his boys was that they were, at heart, slackers—especially Fosdick, the mama's boy. He had spared the rod, there, at the urging of the boy's late mother. And now, decades later, he was reaping the bitter reward.

Fillmore would never have reached his elevated position in the world without being an excellent judge of character. He put people into two main categories: the weak or the strong. Both types could be used and manipulated, if you knew how to pull the right strings. For example, this Dewayne Korb, the richest man in the world, wanted physical as well as financial power. He wanted to be able to intimidate others with a look, even if they didn't know who he was or how much money he had. This failing of character, this fatal flaw, led the man straight into the clutches of Family Fing.

Such vulnerabilities were part of the human condition. Fillmore himself was not immune. His own greed had undone him more than once. The difference between the elder Fing and Dewayne Korb was that Fing had mapped his own soft points.

And was ever on guard.

Fillmore pulled the cell phone from inside his suit jacket and, steering with his knees, punched in a number. When the party on the other end answered, he spoke in rapid-fire Chinese. Then he turned to the lawyer and said, "Can you describe the people who did all the damage in Los Angeles?"

Koch-Roche told him what he had been told by his security people. "There were two of them, both male. One was a white American, in his late thirties or early forties, average height and wiry build. The other was an Oriental, origin unknown, well over seventy, with a thin white beard and wearing a brocaded blue robe."

Fing passed this information on to his security force and broke the connection.

Ahead of them, Farnham pulled his golf cart up to the entrance to the wing that housed the plant's hospital facility. A pair of uniformed, armed guards in white steel helmets, white Sam Browne belts, white puttees and camouflage jungle boots, hurried to open the heavy door.

Which looked like it had come from a bank vault.

"This is new," Koch-Roche commented, hooking a thumb at the massive steel barrier.

"I had it installed about a week ago," Fillmore said as he followed his oldest son through the portal. "We've been having difficulty containing some of the synthetic-drug-trial test patients. We don't want to risk their getting loose in the main plant. They'd be a nightmare to subdue and recapture."

On either side of them, floor-to-ceiling glass walls looked in on medical labs tightly packed with technical equipment. As they came to a much smaller window set in a section of cinder-block wall, Fillmore stopped the golf cart so his passenger could look through the glass to the cage enclosure it protected.

In the white tiled cell was a lone wolverine. The number 3271 was branded into its haunch. The top of its skull had been shaved, and from the pale skin a dense cluster of electrodes protruded. The tips of the electrodes were connected to a series of multicolored electrical wires bundled together three feet above the animal's head and disappearing up into the cage ceiling.

"What are you doing to this one?" Koch-Roche asked.

"We're using low-level electrical current to try and

stimulate natural hormone production. It causes a stress reaction, which activates the glandular system."

Even as Koch-Roche looked on, the animal's eyelids began to flutter and it sagged down on its forelegs. The dark lips drew back from four-inch fangs in a grisly predator's smile.

"That looks like it hurts," the attorney said.

"Life hurts," the elder Fing philosophised. Then he punched the cart's accelerator, and with a whir they shot down the hall.

Fing's oldest son had already parked beside the medical station's high counter. As Fillmore pulled up behind him, Farnham said something to the nurse on duty, and she turned at once to a cabinet along the back wall. Beyond Farnham, medical personnel in green scrubs and white lab coats scurried back and forth between opposing, locked doorways.

Overriding the usual antiseptic smell of the hospital was another odor. Unexpected. Mildly sweet, but also earthy and pungent.

"Jesus, is that peanut butter I smell?" Koch-Roche asked.

"My son Fosdick believes it is the solution to our side-effect-management problem."

As the duty nurse turned back from the cabinet, Dewayne Korb bailed out of the cart and snatched the strip of sealed pouches from her hands. After tearing open the front of his shirt, he ripped apart the safety packaging and stuck on four of the patches. That done, he looked down at himself. It was the first time in ten hours that he had examined his own chest. His pectorals sagged. His belly drooped. Though he hadn't been taking WHE during that interval, he had continued to eat as if he had. Korb had lost more than twenty percent of his muscle mass; it had been replaced by solid blubber.

"It looks like we have a lifelong customer there," Fillmore said smugly, giving the lawyer a nudge as they started to walk over to where the billionaire stood. The pharmaceutical baron was not displeased to see that the user was taking considerably more than the recommended dose. If his behavior represented a trend, Family Fing's projected profits might well quadruple.

Before they reached Korb's side, a very distraught Fosdick Fing rushed up to the service counter. He was so distraught, hopping up and down with anger at hio brother, that he spoke in Chinese.

"Family squabble?" Koch-Roche asked.

"No, a technical issue," Fillmore answered.

Actually, the research chemist was having a cow because his playboy sibling had mistakenly told the nurse to give the patient some of the synthetic drug. And also because said patient had immediately overdosed himself by a multiple of four. The "technical issue" under discussion was whether the Fings should have kept Mr. Korb on the natural drug as a one-man control group for the synthetic test subjects.

"Please," Fosdick said, turning to Dewayne Korb, "you've been given the wrong medication. I need to replace those patches with the proper ones."

When the youngest Fing reached out for Korb's stomach to take away the patches, the billionaire slapped his hand away. The sound of contact, flesh on flesh, was like a gunshot. Fosdick slumped to his knees, clutching his shattered wrist, his face suddenly ashen.

Korb advanced on the moaning chemist, but then walked right past him. The other workers gave him plenty of room, flattening themselves against the corridor wall. They had nothing to worry about. It was the massive drums of Skippy that drew the computer billionaire's attention. Tearing the lid off the closest barrel, he grabbed a big, gooey handful and mashed it into his mouth. Groaning with pleasure, he fell upon the brown sticky stuff with both hands. That was too slow, it seemed. Gripping the drum's rim, Korb plunged his head into the top of the barrel.

A tall, skinny, balding man in a white sterile suit rushed around the ostrich-playing billionaire. "You got to make this stop!" Carlos Sternovsky said to Fillmore Fing. He waved a sheaf of computer printouts in the tycoon's face. "What we have here is a disaster, an unmitigated disaster."

Farnham tried to mollify the biochemist. "Easy, Carlos, let's step into an office and talk this over...."

Sternovsky would not be mollified. "Look at these tabulations," he insisted. "Fosdick's whole new diet concept is fatally flawed. I've calculated the potential muscle-mass increase. Its geometric. Don't you get it? The reason the test subjects are placid is because all their available energy is going to produce muscle mass. For Pete's sake, they are semiconscious."

Korb's drum tipped over, fell off its gurney and rolled on the floor. Instead of tipping the barrel back up, as he could have easily done, the billionaire got down on his hands and knees and crawled into it.

At least as far as the breadth of his shoulders would allow.

"And your point?" the patriarch Fing said.

"My figures indicate that the rate of change has already begun to level off," Sternovsky told him. "Very shortly, our test subjects will have maxed out. When the demands of WHE on their bodies to produce muscle begin to slack off, they will wake up. Bigger. Stronger. And even more dangerous."

"Fosdick!" Fillmore barked. "Is this true? You promised me that you had the situation well in hand."

The youngest Fing wanted to reply, to defend himself, but the shock of his injury was such that though he opened his mouth to speak, he couldn't even manage a stutter.

Farnham, sensing that his father was about to turn

on him, diverted attention by attacking the American biochemist and taking up the banner of his fallen brother. "All you're giving us is speculation," he said. "You don't know what's going to happen in the next two minutes, let alone the next half hour. And you certainly can't predict the behavior of our test subjects even if the synthetic's effect does level off as you suggest."

Sternovsky put his hands to his head and pulled at his comb-over, making it stick straight up. "You're not listening!" he cried. "There is no door, no lock on this ward that will hold them."

"I think we've heard enough," Fillmore said.

"No, you haven't," the biochemist countered. "God forgive us for what we've done to them, but these test subjects are no longer human beings. If you don't euthanize them now, and quickly, while they are still in a stuporous state, they will wake up and kill us all."

Fillmore had always figured Sternovsky for a whiner. There was something weak in the eyes and the dark circles that surrounded them. But the expression he now wore clearly declared he had reached his limit. No amount of browbeating would bring him back into line. "I'm canceling your contract, as of this instant," the elder Fing said. "Turn in your security badge at the desk downstairs and be off the grounds in two hours or I'll have you arrested."

"That suits me fine," Sternovsky said. "Just remember I told you so when the shit hits the fan."

The lanky researcher, his hair still alarmingly upright, stormed off and out the bank-vault door.

The Fings and their U.S. attorney watched the man go.

"Could he make trouble for us, patent-wise, somewhere down the line?" Koch-Roche asked.

"A brilliant biochemist," Fillmore said, "but he has absolutely no business sense. The agreement he signed with Family Fing surrendered all commercial rights to the product."

"He actually signed something like that?"

"The contract was written in Chinese."

"Don't tell me," the lawyer said. "He used a translator that you recommended."

Fillmore smiled.

Suddenly, the steady, sloppy sounds of sucking ceased.

"They've stopped eating," one of the orderlies cried. "They've all stopped eating. Look!"

Fillmore half turned to follow the man's pointing finger. The video monitors behind the nurses' station counter all showed movement. The test subjects had dropped their feeding tubes and, one by one, were rising to their feet.

30

Remo had no complaint about the directions he'd been given by the bilingual car-rental clerk at the airport. After an hour and a half of driving on a two-lane road that ran straight as a string through miles of open farmland—pancake flat, diked and about half of it flooded for the cultivation of rice—the lights of Family Fing Pharmaceuticals had come into view. In the distance, he could see the white towers of the plant complex rising up out of the blackness of the plain. The feeling of dread he got every time he looked at them was very intense.

Up until this point, he and Chiun had had the luxury of confronting the hormone-altered killers one at a time. The last one, old Ludlow Baculum, had nearly had Remo's guts for garters, and would have succeeded if Chiun had not intervened at the last second. In the area of sheer physical power, Remo had never encountered foes quite like these. The idea that he would have to confront them en masse, and very soon, sent a chill down the back of his neck.

Chiun sat in the passenger seat, apparently unconcerned about what danger might lurk in the white complex ahead. Under the glow of the map light, he was flipping through the fax Dr. Smith had sent them along with their plane tickets in L.A. As well as the particulars of the layout of the pharmaceutical complex, he'd included photos of all the prime players he'd identified. It was this group of faces that the Master was so intently studying.

"Sheesh, haven't you memorized those stupid mug shots by now?" Remo asked him.

When Chiun looked up from the series of black-and-white pictures, he wore an expression that Remo knew all too well: the mask of Masterly disappointment. Which immediately put the pupil on the defensive.

"What?" Remo said. "What?"

"How do you intend to find our targets?" Chiun asked. "By their noses? Or perhaps their ears?"

"How about the happy confluence of same?" Remo said. "It's called a face. Everybody's got one."

Chiun heaved a sigh before he continued, in lecture mode. "The truly skilled assassin looks deeper than the superficial," he said. "He looks inside, for tendencies, for relationships. Only in this way can he anticipate what the man he hunts will do in a given situation, and use that knowledge to be waiting, ready to strike at exactly the right moment."

"You can tell that from a picture? A bad picture at that?"

"All this can be seen in the position of the brow in relation to the nasal meridian. The circular flow of energy around the eyes. And in other ways..."

"Such as?"

"Take this one," Chiun said, tapping at the top page with the tip of a razor-sharp fingernail. "Here we have a man of about seventy years, who pretends to be much younger. He is willful. He is vain. He is greedy and ruthless. A typical Chinese."

"Did the width of his nose give him away?"

"No," Chiun said. "It was his name—Fing. But that is not important. What is important is what the picture tells me of his true nature. This is a man who will not fight his own battle unless he is cornered. This is a man who cares nothing for the lives of others, not even those of his own flesh and blood. He would sacrifice anyone to keep what he has. What he has is what defines him."

"And how is this going to help us kill him?"

"Are you not listening?" Chiun asked. "This man will hold on with his teeth, if necessary, to keep his possessions. They are the center of his life. His anchor." The Master paused for dramatic effect, then said, "They are his gallows."

"That's all very nice and poetic," Remo said, "but what if your friend Fing has already made liquid most of his assets? What if he can walk away from that white monstrosity over there without ever looking back?"

"You still do not understand, and it pains me deeply," Chiun confessed. "I sometimes think you pretend to be stupid in order to cause me, your teacher, grief. I who have with great patience and care brought you so far from your truly pathetic beginnings—"

"Look, Chiun, you're making about as much sense as mud. The whole idea behind an explanation is that it *explains* something."

"Ah-hah!" the Master said, pouncing on his student's words. "Now we are getting to the basis of your problem."

"That I expect you to be rational?"

"That you expect to be given an answer." Seeing the blank look on his pupil's face, the Master sighed again, this time even more tragically, as if the entire weight of the world were pressing down on his deceptively frail appearing form. That weight took the form of his own, personal Chong-wook.

"Very well," he said, "though I know it is a mistake to coddle you, I will explain my meaning. The Western concept of liquidity, of invisible wealth, of electronic millions, does not compute in this man's mind. Look here, at these shallow lines radiating from the corners of his mouth. They are from many years of sucking on his own tongue. Like this..."

In the greenish glow of the dashlights, Remo could see that Chiun had his lips slightly puckered, and his cheeks drawn in, as if he were nursing on a cough drop.

"I take it that somewhere under your noble beard you're sucking your noble tongue," Remo said.

"This habit denotes a man of a grandiose and pompous type," Chiun told him. "Such a man often builds great monuments to himself. Ugly monuments that he alone finds beautiful."

"And this tongue sucker," Remo said, "you're saying he won't abandon his work of art?"

"Only when all hope is lost."

"So, we must allow him to hope until we have him in our noose," Remo offered. "Happy?"

The Master frowned.

"What's wrong now?"

"The airplane food has filled me with a terrible wind. How could portions so small have such a violent effect?"

"That is a mystery for the ages," Remo said. "I'll roll down my window."

As he did so, the floodlit entrance to the Family Fing complex loomed before them. The plant's grounds, which appeared to stretch on for miles, were ringed by a twelve-foot-high hurricane fence. The fence was topped with steel branches on which were strung garlands of razor wire. The road ended at a counterbalanced steel pole of a gate and a guard hut. Remo slowed as he approached. The barrier was down, barring the way onto the grounds.

When Remo stopped, a white-helmeted guard stepped out of the hut. He took one look at the car's occupants, immediately stepped back into the hut and picked up a phone.

"I don't like this," Remo muttered.

After a very brief conversation, the guard hung up and advanced on the driver's side of the car. He had drawn his service revolver out of its holster, and his finger was on the trigger. He spoke to Remo through the open car window in blindingly fast Chinese.

After a moment or two, Remo raised open palms in the universal gesture of helplessness, then pointed over at Chiun, who waved the guard around to his side of the car. Believing that the ancient Oriental was going to converse with him, the guard walked around the front end of the vehicle, his weapon held along his hip.

As the Master of Sinanju cranked down his window, the guard leaned forward slightly, holding the pistol aimed through the door at the old man. On the other side of the gate, alongside the towering white tanks in the near distance, four men with white helmets were piling into a jeep, and almost instantly the jeep was roaring their way.

When the guard repeated the question he'd asked of Remo—which was "What is your business here?"—Chiun replied with a blow. His hand flicked out through the window like a head of a snake; the fist was closed but soft. So quick, so devastating was the strike that the guard couldn't even pull the trigger by reflex. He dropped to his butt on the asphalt, helmet thunking as his head hit the ground.

Remo jumped out and raised the gate as fast as he could. But by the time he got back in the car, the jeepful of reinforcements was barreling straight for them. And two more jeeps from opposite ends of the complex had joined the party. They were racing across the open courtyard toward the gatehouse.

There was nowhere to go, and no time to get there.

The first jeep screeched to a halt right in front of the rental car. The other two angled in from either side. Four security guards, armed with M-16s, piled out of each vehicle, their weapons leveled at Remo and Chiun through the rental car's windshield.

One of the dozen newcomers, a guy with a pencil mustache and sideburns, immediately started shouting something at them.

"What's he saying?" Remo said. "He's talking too fast for me. I can't make heads or tails of it."

"He says for us to get out with our hands up," Chiun told him.

Remo surveyed the semicircle of autorifle muzzles. "I think we'd better do what he says." He stuck both his hands out the driver's window, opened the car door from the outside, then very slowly exited the car.

Chiun did the same.

The man in charge continued shouting a mile a minute. He seemed very agitated.

Chiun spoke once more, quite distinctly and with great dignity. Remo got the gist of what he said. The Master suggested that the man with the mustache should speak less rapidly so his stupid white companion could understand what he was saying without the necessity and bother of Chiun's making a running English translation of every word.

As if he were talking to a very slow three-year-old, the man in charge told Remo to step to the left. Which he did.

"Do you have any idea what these guys have in mind for us?" Remo asked Chiun.

As the Master also sidestepped, hands raised in the air, he said, "Why would I?"

"I don't know. I thought you might be able to read their energy levels or something. The guy giving the orders sure looks like a teeth grinder to me. Doesn't that tell you something?"

"Only that once again you have failed to grasp a fundamental concept."

The flash suppressors of the twelve M 16s tracked them as they moved past the gatehouse to a stretch of open fence, directly under one of the floodlights. Then the head guy yelled at them to stop.

The other guards lined up on either side of Mr. Mustache, switched their fire-selector switches to full auto and shouldered their weapons.

The man in charge barked a single word.

A Chinese word that Remo understood.

The word was "Ready."

Still in denial, big-time, Remo found himself puzzling over the guy's inflection. Had he heard wrong, or hadn't the end of the word *risen* in pitch? Which would have made it a question, not a statement. If it was a question, it might damned well mean anything. Ready to take a break? Ready to let these guys go? Ready for a little Macarena?

His scant hopes vanished altogether when the mustachioed guard spoke again.

The word this time was "Aim."

31

The Fings, their tiny lawyer and the entire staff of the medical wing stood transfixed by the images on the video monitors.

"They *are* bigger," one of the nurses gasped.

"Hugely bigger," an orderly corrected her.

"You're letting your imagination run away with you," Fillmore told them. "We've all worked practically around the clock. It's just the power of suggestion acting on our tired minds...."

Though Fillmore mouthed the words, he couldn't put any conviction behind them. They were a half-hearted, ill-considered and totally transparent attempt to quiet the panic he could feel building around him.

Obviously, the test subjects were bigger.

In the space of half an hour, while the Fings and their employees had looked on, the patients had increased their muscle mass by fifty percent. And Sternovsky, the deserter, had been right about something else, too. The test subjects no longer looked human.

Even without the shaggy fur or the tails, the density of their muscles made them look like some other, as-yet-unidentified species. There was enough meat on the hooded fan of a single test subject's latissimus dorsi to make ample backs for three normal-sized Homo sapiens. And with the newly added bulk came a return to the insensate fury of their pre-peanut butter time.

The romance writer, her tail curled into a tight spiral behind her back, booted the inside of her door with the sole of her bare foot. The impact shook the walls and sent glassware crashing to the floor all along the corridor.

"Oh, my God," Koch-Roche said, steadying himself against the side of the golf cart.

The noise awakened an army of related devils. The other five test subjects began kicking their doors, too. In the narrow hall, it sounded like volleys of rolling cannon fire. And the force they unleashed against door frames and walls set the floor trembling, rippling as if from an earthquake. Glass walls everywhere shimmied and shattered, sending cascades of fragments whooshing across the hallway floor. The window in front of the wolverine's enclosure likewise dropped away in a spiderwebbed sheet, leaving the test animal stunned, blinking and extremely mad.

"The doors aren't going to hold much longer," Farnham warned. He pointed at the nearest door frame, which was already beginning to splinter away from the wall. The steel door was itself bowing out in the middle from the full-power kicks Toshi Takahara was raining on it.

At the far end of the hallway, the attendants abandoned their posts and started running in the direction of the bank-vault door. As they ran, they yelled at the tops of their lungs.

It was a nightmare come to life.

A horror dream so unthinkable that it froze the Fings, their lawyer and the surrounding medical personnel where they stood.

It did not freeze Dewayne Korb, though. The computer billionaire jerked his head out of the drum of peanut butter, his hair and face smeared with the stuff, his eyes wide with alarm. Thanks to his overdose on synthetic hormone and dietary fat, he had arrived at a new and advanced animal state. Every fiber of his being told him that much bigger dogs than he were about to break loose. It also told him that when these big dogs did free themselves, he stood no more chance against them than the frail, petrified humans. Before anyone else could blink, the billionaire took off, high-kicking. By the time the others regained their wits, he was out the heavy door and gone.

"Don't you think we should go, too?" Jimmy Koch-Roche said.

When no one replied, the lawyer turned around. It was only then that Filmore and Farnham had already come to that same conclusion. And acted on it. Their golf cart was speeding for the exit, with Fillmore driving. They had left poor Fosdick slumped on the hallway floor, broken wrist and all, to fend for himself.

Mixed in with the sounds of the wrecking-ball chorus were the shrieks of lag bolts as they were ripped out of two-by-fours. In their frenzy to escape, the test subjects were pulling the wing down around them. The door closest to Koch-Roche buckled, bowing out so far that a hairy hand was able to thrust through the gap between door and jamb, out into the hall. Ten furry fingers fought to get just the right grip and proper leverage to pop the lock bolt out of its striker plate.

Everyone was running toward Koch-Roche and the exit. Running and falling as the floor shuddered and shifted underfoot. The panicked medical staff crashed down onto the heaps of broken glass, struggled up, only to fall as the floor heaved again.

The attorney had seen more than enough. But before he could climb into the remaining golf cart's driver's seat, the vehicle was commandeered by a pair of burly male nurses. The cart started to scoot away at once. Koch-Roche jumped for the back of the vehicle and managed to get a grip on one of the canopy posts. He hung on like grim death.

Behind him, the doors to the test subjects' rooms began to burst open. Dark, hairy monsters surged out into the hall.

And began to tear the terrified staff to shreds.

"Faster!" the attorney screamed.

As they zipped past the wolverine's open cage, he got a brief glimpse of the experimental animal. It had managed to pull down some slack in the bundled wires and was gnawing through the connections, one by one. The cut electrical wires hung down from its shaved scalp like rainbow-colored strands of shoulder-length hair.

"Faster!" Koch-Roche howled.

But the golf cart was redlined. And to make matters worse, the test subjects seemed to lock on to and pursue anything that was running away. Like giant Airedales, a pair of them dashed down the hall after the cart, their mouths hanging open, their tongues lolling, their bare feet pounding the corridor floor. Behind them down the hall, Koch-Roche could see flying human bodies. The other test subjects were chasing down the fleeing medical personnel and bowling them over. Once the staff members were bowled, some of the beasts stood on their supine torsos and pulled off the limbs. Some just stomped a few times and then ran on. The ruined hallway was thick with huge, dark, darting shapes.

When the attorney looked ahead to try to gauge the distance to the heavy door and safety, he saw that the Fings had stopped their cart on the other side of the barrier.

And they were closing the door!

Realizing what was at stake, the driver of Koch-Roche's cart stomped on the accelerator with both feet, trying to urge a little more speed from the motor. The other nurse knew the only way to go faster was to lighten the load. To this end, he began pounding on Koch-Roche's head and shoulders with his fists, trying to dump him off the back of the vehicle.

But the lawyer would not be moved. He knew that to fall off meant falling into the hands of the beasts that were quickly gaining on them.

His refusal to let go doomed them all.

Forty feet ahead, the bank-vault door slammed shut with an earsplitting clang. The driver of the cart hit the brakes, sending them into a four-wheel, sideways slide. The cart crashed nose-first into the wall and bounced off. Koch-Roche was thrown clear, over the driver's compartment, hood and solidly against the selfsame wall.

For a moment, he was thankfully unconscious. When he awakened, it was to hot wetness splashing over his legs. He opened his eyes and saw the two test subjects—it was no longer possible to tell who they were, or whether they were male or female—tearing the nurses to ribbons with their bare hands.

One of the beasts looked up from its gruesome game and saw Koch-Roche, leaning there against the bottom of the wall, alive. For an instant, their eyes locked. The beast's mind was an open book. It was thinking, More fun.

The attorney didn't think. He reacted. In front of him, the bumper of the golf cart had caved in the metal grate over a ventilation duct. As Koch-Roche scooted for it, he felt a hairy hand graze the back of his knee.

Between the grate and wall was a jagged opening no bigger than twelve inches. The little lawyer squirmed through the gap like he'd been greased and crashed onto his belly inside the square stainless-steel duct.

Ahead of him, the duct made a tight right turn. Behind him, the test subject was ripping at the grate.

When the screen came off, the duct rocked and groaned. But Koch-Roche was already out of reach, moving for the bend. Before he rounded it, he looked back over his shoulder and saw the huge animal face with its dripping fangs, the hairy arm and hand groping to reach his foot.

No way, he thought, his heart thudding high in his throat. The duct opening was too small. The monster could not follow him. To catch him, this beast would have to peel back the sides of the duct, and keep on peeling them back. As strong and as determined as the creature was, such a thing was simply not possible. The ducts ran all through the pharmaceutical complex, miles and miles of them for Koch-Roche's endless retreat.

The attorney belly-crawled around the turn, putting the monster out of sight. Ahead, the way was pitch-dark. Scary, but safe. All he wanted to do was hide.

To hide and stay hidden until someone, somehow, figured out how to kill the big bastards.

He crawled in a straight line for what seemed like a long time. The sounds of bestial rage and terrified screams gradually dwindled behind him, until all he could hear was the bump of his bony knees on the inside of the duct, and the rasp of his own hoarse breathing.

Then he saw a dim light ahead. It appeared to be coming from the floor of the duct. He approached cautiously until he got close enough to see that it was a grated vent. The light was comforting to him after the long crawl in darkness, but he didn't allow himself to linger there. He knew that if one of the test subjects got wind of him, it could and would pull down the ceiling to get at him.

Koch-Roche edged close enough to the grate to peer through the mesh, into the room directly below. He saw nothing, no movement of any kind. He held his breath, straining to pick up a sound over his own pulse pounding in his ears. A shuffle of bare feet. The floor creaking under a tremendous weight. A single sniff of a beast trying to seek him out.

There was nothing.

When he was certain he wasn't being observed, he moved past the vent and started to continue on.

Then he heard it. Not beneath him. But behind him in the duct.

The scraping of powerful claws on steel.

The huffing breath of a predator closing for the kill.

32

It was a moment etched into heightened focus by the adrenaline load coursing through Remo's veins.

A dozen autorifles poised, aimed, waited for the command to fire. Waited while the points of impending bullet impact shifted over Remo's body. He could visualize the track of the bullets' intended flight, feel a warm touch where each would strike.

Here. Here. Here.

Heart. Lungs. Liver.

Brain.

And as the aim of the guards wavered ever so slightly, responding to the intake of breath or the burden of the rifle's weight on the shoulder, the warm touch of death brushed over Remo's skin.

Here, I will strike.

Remo knew there were things beyond even the power of Sinanju. One rifle's sting could be avoided, one man's aim confounded with misdirection, smoke, mirrors. But twelve? Twelve?

In the instant that stretched on and on, Remo studied the faces of the men in the firing squad. Sweating.

Yellow faces. In the eyes of some, there was fear. Others gloried in what they were about to do. In the license to kill that had been granted them.

He could feel the tension build as, in anticipation, their index fingers tightened on the triggers.

Empty, Remo thought. Empty. And he visualized the Nothing. As his minded flushed itself clear of all distraction, his body accepted *chi,* the life force of the universe. Like a sweet cloud entering through his mouth, it coursed down his throat, into his lungs and lower still, to the center of his being, just below the navel. A torrent of energy billowed out from his center to the tips of his fingers and toes, the soles of his feet, the top of his head. It crawled under his scalp like ten thousand ants.

The martial art known as Sinanju was like a dance.

A dance that assassins passed down, from generation to generation.

It was also like a portal, a conduit through which the *chi* power could flow. The amount of transferred power was limited only by the skill and the physiology of the artist. The steps of the Sinanju dance, the various complex motions of the limbs, were an illusion. True, they could be used to kill. But their real intent was to move and focus the spirit-mind, to open the door to the *chi* flow. And after decades of continuous practice, the movements themselves became superfluous. Unnecessary.

For an ascended Master of Sinanju, the door to power was always ajar.

Remo's mind was open, receptive, his body waiting, ready, when the push of air hit him. He didn't have to think about where it came from or what it meant. Like a leaf caught in a gust of wind, he went with it, toes digging into the asphalt, legs driving.

Only moments later, when it was all over and the shooting had stopped, did Remo understand what had happened.

The rush of breeze that had touched his face was from Chiun's left hand. Standing five feet away, the Master had used the air's resistance to the power and speed of his push to launch himself to the right. Somewhere between the push and the rippling roar of autofire, Remo distinctly heard the clack of firing pins. Ragged. Unsynchronized.

Bullets sprayed the spot where he had been standing. Bullets screamed after him, rattling the hurricane fence, kicking up divots of asphalt at his heels. Remo started to turn hard to the right, to force at least some of the guards to hold their fire for fear of hitting the man standing in front of them.

But a volley of bullets cut off that route.

Over his shoulder, he saw the whole line of men crumpling. And he saw why.

The Master had hold of the elbow of the guard at the end of the firing line. With the pressure of thumb and forefinger, Chiun was redirecting the sweep of autofire from the man's M-16, aiming it into the backs of the other guards. He was also controlling the tendons in the man's arm, making it impossible for him to release pressure on the trigger.

When the magazine came up empty, Chiun let the man go. Eleven bodies thrashed on the tarmac, thrashed and then grew still. Astonished and horrified by what he had been made to do, the guard dropped his gun and helmet and ran for the complex's gate.

Remo watched him vanish in the darkness down the road.

Chiun already had the faxes out of the cuff of his robe and, in the light of the flood lamps, was examining the map of the grounds that Smith had provided them.

"Maybe I should have a look at that, too," Remo said. "In case we happen to be separated."

That wasn't why he wanted to see the document. He wanted Chiun not to be in charge of directions.

The Master passed the map over without comment. A combination of body language, facial expression and spiritual aura indicated the Master's displeasure. Remo got a glimpse of lightning bolts behind the old man's eyes.

"It's this way, I think," Remo said.

They crossed the expanse of asphalt and made straight for the main building's entrance. Which, strangely, was unguarded. Remo had figured that a plant this big would have to have more than a dozen guys on its security force. But if there were more guards on the premises, they were nowhere in sight. They'd all either suddenly died or taken a powder. Remo cast his vote for the latter. As he looked along the front of the plant complex, he saw workers by the score pouring out of the various doors and gates of the warehouse and manufacturing areas. They were scooting off as fast as their legs would carry them, like rats leaving the proverbial sinking ship. Instead of running out the main gate, many of the Family Fing employees were taking the shortest possible route off the grounds by dashing straight to and scrambling right over the hurricane fence.

"Something's wrong here," he said.

"Of course," Chiun countered. "And it is our job to fix it."

"That's not what I mean," Remo said. "Those guys climbing the razor wire over there aren't doing it for exercise. They look like they've got the devil after them."

Chiun seemed unconcerned. He opened the door to the lobby, then looked back at Remo. "Do we go this way?" he asked innocently. "I no longer have the luxury of a map...."

"Yeah, yeah," Remo said, "that's the way." He took the lead, heading for the elevator. Once they were inside the car, he glanced at the fax. "We want the tenth floor. That's where the medical wing is."

Remo had to reach around Chiun to press the floor

button. As the Master's hands were up his sleeves, he could not perform the task himself.

The elevator doors opened on a deserted corridor.

Chiun stuck his head out, then wrinkled his nose in disgust. "They are here," he said. "And there are many of them. The stinkers."

Remo looked at the massive, gleaming steel door that completely blocked the hallway at one end. With a carefree tone that was not entirely genuine, he said, "It appears, Little Father, that what we're looking for is behind door numero uno."

The two assassins spread out, each taking a side of the hall as they cautiously advanced on the barrier. Even Remo, whose nasal sensitivity had been compromised years ago by filthy food and a degraded Western life-style, could smell the hormone users now.

"Man, oh man," he groaned. "It's like a convention of skunks in here!"

"It would be best," Chiun told him, "to put that unpleasantness out of your mind. For as we have already seen, these are not skunks...."

Remo nodded. But how does one stop smelling something noxious? By breathing through the mouth, obviously. But Chiun had taught him that mouth-breathing was a big no-no in Sinanju. According to the Master, if you inhaled through the mouth, it made it impossible to correctly position the tongue, which was supposed to lightly touch the roof of the mouth.

Without the tongue in the correct position, the flow of *chi* was impeded. The choice Remo faced was between not smelling the hormone beasts or not being able to fight them. So, it really wasn't a choice at all.

Somewhere, Remo had read that after prolonged exposure, the sensors in the nose become desensitized to aromas. To hurry this end, he breathed in and out rapidly, putting as much stink on his nasal receptors as he could.

"What are you doing?" Chiun asked him. "Why are you making so much noise?"

"Trying to desensitize my nose."

"Why don't you just breathe through your mouth?"

Remembering all the months of working on nothing but proper tongue position, Remo started to complain, but caught himself. After all, what was the use?

The tempered-steel frame of the door filled the hall from side to side and floor to ceiling. Immense bolts tied the tremendously heavy unit into the steel beams that supported the building's exterior walls. The door itself might have been looted from a bank vault. On its front it had a huge lever and three sets of tumblers. It was closed and appeared to be locked.

Remo reached out and ran his fingertips down the millimeter-wide seam between door and frame.

"Definitely locked," he said.

Chiun stepped closer to the door, cocked his head, then pressed his ear to the cold steel.

"What do you hear?" Remo asked him.

The Master waved an impatient hand for silence. "Shh," he said. "Listen."

Remo put his head against the door, too. Through the metal, he heard groaning sounds. Not human. Not animal. The sounds of metal being stressed, over and over.

Then there was a loud crash. Followed by a metallic shriek.

On the other side of the door, something still lived.

Something that had been locked in.

Something that wanted out.

"It's pulling the guts out of the door lock," Remo said as he drew his head back. And even as he spoke, the huge steel lever on the face of the door began to move. A little wiggle at first, then a waggle, then a wide arc.

Both of the assassins took a giant step back.

The lever flipped over, and when it did, the door's many interior bolts slid back.

"We'd better find some cover, and quick," Remo said.

"There is no place to run," Chiun told him. "We must stand and fight right here."

"But we don't know how many are in there!"

The seam between door and frame gaped wider as the door slowly swung out.

"There are too many," Chiun told him. "Does that make you feel any better?"

33

Jimmy Koch-Roche didn't wait to see what the thing that pursued him looked like. By the time it had passed over the duct vent, he was around another turn, crawling as fast as he could go. His bare knees were scraped and bleeding, but that was the least of his problems.

As Koch-Roche fled in panic, somewhere in the back of what remained of his rational mind, it occurred to him that whatever the snuffling, scrabbling thing behind him was, it wasn't a hormone-enlarged human. It was something small enough to get into the duct, something small enough to move quickly and easily through it.

Then, from some hidden juncture along the winding black passage, the air pumps kicked in, blowing hot wind against his sweating back. And along with the heat, an odor swept over him.

Musky, fecal and ever so nasty.

The smell made him whimper and crawl even faster.

If he didn't know what it was, he knew one thing

for sure—it was gaining on him. Over the thunk of his knees on the steel and a rasp of his own breathing, he could hear the clatter of its claws drawing nearer and nearer.

A plan, he thought. He had to have a plan. As the attorney scrambled along, he racked his brain for a solution. He certainly couldn't fight the thing in the closed confines and darkness of the air duct and hope to come out on top. But if he could get to the next vent, if he could through it, get down into a room or a corridor, even if the thing jumped down after him, he would stand a chance of escape. In a room or a corridor, there would be somewhere to hide; if he couldn't lock the thing in a room, he could lock himself in one.

The plan was feasible. The problem was, the duct ahead him was dark as pitch. A long straight stretch with no exit.

Don't look back, Koch-Roche told himself. For Christ's sake, keep on moving. His knees banged harder against the inside of the duct, making echoes boom before him.

In the darkness, he didn't see the T-branch of the tunnel. The top of his head rammed into the unyielding surface, making him see stars. He refused to let himself black out.

To black out was to die.

Shaking off the shock of the impact, the lawyer started frantically stripping off his shirt. He couldn't count on the beast not being able to locate him by smell—although how it could smell anything but itself had to be the eighth wonder of the world. But he could try to confuse it. Koch-Roche tossed his shirt as far as he could down the right arm of the duct. Then he turned the other way and hauled ass.

If his trick slowed the creature down even a few seconds, he told himself, it might be enough.

What had eluded him, due to his fear and the stress of the moment, was that his battered knees were leaving a blood trail everywhere he went. And it was his fresh blood that the creature was tracking.

The attorney's heart leaped when he saw the patch of light filtering up through a grate in the floor just ahead. Reaching it, Koch-Roche hurled himself at the mesh, ripping the grate out of its track and letting it drop through onto the floor of an office below.

At his back, the growling, snarling, scrambling thing was coming his way, fast.

If Koch-Roche hadn't looked up, he might have gotten away. But look up he did. The sight of the experimental-subject wolverine filling the duct, its multicolored electric-wire wig flopping as it bore relentlessly down on him, froze him in place.

For forty-five of his forty-nine years, Jimmy Koch-Roche had had a secret fear that something huge and hairy and powerful would get him. *Get* meaning grab, hurt, stomp, tear, punch, cut, even kill. This nameless thing had taken many forms in the real world. The junior-high-school gym coach. A senior classman at Hami High who used to confiscate his lunch money daily. Various thugs and toughs who, when they saw his size, thought easy pickings. Even as late as law school, he felt at times threatened by those bigger than him. It was only after he'd made his mark on the national legal scene that the terror took a step back into the shadows.

It was not gone, though.

Even though he was rich, a man of influence and authority.

It waited in the wings.

It was a curious irony then, that when James Marvin Koch-Roche finally came face-to-face with the beast that would in fact kill him, it was actually much smaller than he was. He outweighed it by seventy pounds.

What the wolverine in the heating duct lacked in size, it more than made up for in pure, kill-crazed frenzy. Its first vicious bite took him high in the shoulder. The fangs were like red-hot irons piercing his flesh. The bones of his shoulder cracked. As the attorney screamed, his heels drumming on the duct, the wolverine shifted its fangs to the side of his neck. Once its grip was solid, it went to work on his belly with its claws.

34

Fillmore Fing brought the golf cart to a screeching halt outside the ornately carved ebony-and-ivory arch. With Farnham hot on his heels, he ran into the lobby area of his executive suite. The receptionist was long gone; the trail of debris she'd left behind—sheets of bond typing paper, a lipstick tube and a roll of breath mints—led to the door marked Emergency Exit. After father and son had rushed into Fillmore's private office, Farnham slammed and securely bolted the double doors behind them.

"What now, Pop?" he said.

"We've got no choice," Fillmore told him as he snatched up the phone from his desk. He punched the speed dial for the warehouse. While the phone rang at the other end, he said, "We've got to kill all of the human test subjects."

"Yeah, sure, but how?"

"We've got enough cyanide gas stockpiled in our warehouse to wipe out a small city," Fillmore said. "It's simple, really. All we have to do is drill a little hole through the bank-vault door and pump the poison into the medical wing until they're all dead.''

"Uh, Pop, aren't you forgetting that there could be people, people who are still human beings, alive in there?"

The elder Fing scowled at what was, undoubtedly, his only surviving son. "There's nothing we can do for any of them," he said. "Anybody left in the medical wing is in very small pieces by now. We've got to concentrate all our efforts on containing this thing. That's the key here. If we can keep a lid on what's happened in the last twenty-four hours, at the very least we still have a chance of doing a nice piece of business in the Third World. At best, we may be able to proceed according to our original plan. But if we can't black out the news of this disaster, it's all over for Family Fing. We'll never survive the bad publicity. Imposter Herbalistics will go down the drain, too."

Even Farnham was taken aback at this. "Jeez, Pop, you mean we'll go out of business?"

"I mean, we'll go straight to jail, if not the gallows," Fillmore said. He glared at the phone in his hand. No one was answering. He hung up and speed-dialed the number for the plant's technical center.

Something else suddenly occurred to Farnham. Something important. "Uh, Pop, Fosdick is in there, too."

"Goddammit, what's happened to the night shift?"

the patriarch cried. "Has everyone gone home for the day?" He slammed down the phone, then said, "Come on, Farnham, we'll have to do the job ourselves."

Fillmore took the lead, cautiously exiting his private office. Seeing no one in the reception area, he moved quietly to the arched entrance that opened onto the hallway. When Fillmore poked his head around the arch, he saw a hulking dark shape about a hundred feet down the corridor. The elder Fing ducked back so quickly he practically knocked Farnham down.

"Can't go that way," he whispered to his son. "The American computer guy is outside."

"Oh, shit," Farnham groaned softly.

Fillmore was already heading back for his office. When the doors were safely locked once more, he went into his mahogany-paneled private washroom. When he came out a few seconds later, he had an automatic weapon in his hands, and the side pocket of his suit jacket was bulging with extra clips.

"Whoa!" Farnham said, stepping lively to one side and out of the line of fire. "Hey, do you really know how to use that thing?"

The elder Fing gave the M-16's cocking handle a jerk, chambering the first bullet in the 30-round magazine. Then he flipped the fire-selector switch to full auto.

"Now," Fillmore said with a smile, "I'm ready for bear."

"I hope you don't get any of that gun grease on your suit, Pop," Farnham said.

Fillmore took a seat in the throne chair behind his enormous desk. He propped the autoweapon up on the butt of its magazine, with the muzzle aimed between the silver handles of the suite's massive doors.

"First," he told his son, "I'm going to shoot the hell out of Mr. Billionaire, then I'm going to hunt down the skinny white bastard who got us into all this trouble in the first place."

"But Sternovsky tried to warn us what would happen, Pop. Don't you remember? While Fosdick was pushing for us to go ahead with the program, Carlos kept telling us we were in for it. He's been ranting about terminating the human trials for days. Long before any of the real bad stuff started going down. He also said we should kill the test subjects before they woke up, that it was our only chance. Don't you remember? That was right before he walked out."

"He should have made us listen to him instead of taking off like that," Fillmore insisted. "If he had done his job, maybe we wouldn't be in such a god-awful mess now."

"Actually, you had already fired him by then, Pop."

"He doesn't know what fired is," Fillmore said. "But he's sure going to find out."

Farnham Fing knew better than to try to reason with his father when was in this kind of mood, and heavily armed. Instead, the heir apparent to the Family Fing fortune edged himself along the wall, moving as far from the doors as he could get. Out of range of both the hormone-crazed American and his naturally crazed old man.

DEWAYNE KORB, the new and improved Dewayne Korb, was not the least bit alarmed by the sight of dense brown fur sprouting all over his body, nor by the perky little tail that was fast emerging from his backside—he was, in fact, looking forward to his tail growing long enough for him to chase. To make room for its full extension, he had already torn off all his clothes.

The world's richest man, aka Billionaire Blubberboy, had become Korb the Transcendent. Abstractions like software systems, like management flowcharts, like ten-figure mergers, which had featured so large in his daily life, no longer preoccupied him. Korb simply did not have room in his head for such things. In his former existence, he would have categorized the problem as an extreme case of information overload.

Along with the startling increase in his muscle volume over the past ten minutes, he was experiencing changes in the quality of his five senses—particularly in smell, sight and hearing, which suddenly seemed able to pull in staggering amounts of data from the surrounding space. There was so much sensory information coming at him from so many directions that he could hold it all in his mind for no more than a fraction of a second. Then it was gone, displaced by volumes of new data. As detailed as this instant-by-instant picture of his immediate environment was, the former boy genius couldn't remember what he had smelled, tasted, seen or heard even a few seconds before.

Instead of feeling buried under the weight of this constant flow of sensation, Korb was elated by it, profoundly relieved to be fully in the present moment, at one with the all-embracing Now.

Sniffing the air, and finding it lacking, the billionaire hurriedly marked the corridor wall next to the watercooler. For good measure, he sprayed the ornamental broad-leafed plant in a Chinese vase, as well.

That was better.

Dropping to all fours, Korb pressed his nose to the floor. Inhaling, he knew that he'd walked down this hallway before. He could make out the trail of his own footprints. He could smell the footprints of others, too. Those that had intruded upon his territory.

They were not creatures like him.

The billionaire beast took a moment to more fully demarcate his turf, sending a stream halfway up the wall, then set off in pursuit of the intruders.

Though his prey had attempted to mask their secret body odors with flowery perfumes, Korb was not fooled. To him, smells were signposts. They led him past the parked golf cart, which he recognized only as a thing not living. It might as well have been a rock or a pile of dirt—this despite the fact that for six years he had used just such a vehicle to get around his 150-room mansion at the heart of Korbtown. When he entered the reception area, he put his nose flat to the carpet. Amazingly, he could tell which of the scent footprints was the most recent by the intensity of the smell. He could also tell male from female, although in his current state, the distinction between the sexes had no real meaning.

The smell trail led him to a pair of big doors made of highly polished wood. He put his ear to the hairline gap between them. Holding his own breath, he could hear the heartbeats of two living things on the other side. He jammed his wet nose against the crack and sniffed, drawing in a great volume of air, and with it billions upon billions of molecules from inside the room.

Oh, yes, they were there.

Korb the Transcendent didn't think of his quarry as humans anymore. Only as not-Korb. And though the not-Korb were only sometimes eaten, they were always killed.

Wiping the slobber trailing from his chin onto the matted hair of his chest, Dewayne Korb prepared to spring.

35

As the bank-vault door swung out and the rank odor intensified, Remo considered what Chiun had just said. And he decided that knowing that there were "too many" on the other side of the door did actually make him feel better. It defined the rules of engagement in no uncertain terms: every strike had to be perfectly timed and executed, since there would be no second chances. No time to worry about being overmatched physically. Remo's survival depended on concentration, which in turn depended on relaxation.

But he found it very difficult to relax as he watched the door arc back against the wall and saw the space between the doorjambs more than filled by two monumental brutes. The coarse fur on their chests was encrusted with blood; their arms glistened with it, up to the elbow, and so did the shaggy, wet hair that ringed their dripping maws.

Looking at them, Remo guessed their weight at around seven hundred pounds apiece. There was no clue who they might have been before, when they were human. Because they weren't human anymore.

Seeing pupil and Master as new potential victims, the beast who was also the author of more than forty romance novels, including the genre megasellers *Let's Love* and *Let's Love, Love,* tipped back her gore-drenched head and, spewing a gust of foul breath, released an earth-shaking bellow.

Her test-subject companion had a much more luxuriant and remarkable tail, which he lashed back and forth as he leered eagerly at Remo and Chiun. The former sumo wrestler known professionally as Toshi-san sniffed the air like a gourmet about to partake of some rare feast.

Under the layers of blood crust, of fur and underfur, Remo sensed the coiling of vast muscle groups. "They're going to charge," he warned.

And they did.

Both at once.

The two huge bodies hurled themselves at an opening barely large enough for one. The impact of 1400 pounds smashing against the door frame shook the floor and sent a crazy spiderweb of cracks running along the hall's ceiling.

Bouncing off the steel doorjamb, the authoress immediately grabbed the sumo wrestler by the ears and tried to flip him over her shoulder. Because of his tremendous weight and the elasticity of his ears, this proved impossible.

The attempt on her part did, however, make him very, very mad.

Toshi-san threw a wicked elbow into the writer's midsection, then lunged for the doorway and the unmoving, apparently helpless victims. His blow had no effect on his rival. She reached the door frame at the same instant he did.

Remo could not have possibly anticipated what happened next, but because he was centered, grounded and open, he was able to take advantage of the situation.

In their frantic need to be first through the door, and therefore the first to kill, the two beasts thrust themselves through the opening. They hit with enormous force again, this time managing to wedge themselves together in the narrow gap.

The authoress ended up with her head outside the medical wing and her arms trapped inside. The sumo wrestler got one leg and a hip out, while his head and shoulders remained on the other side of the door.

For Remo, it was a green light.

Spinning to build momentum, he hurled himself at the exposed head. As he left the ground, he coiled, drawing his limbs tight to his body. He wasn't thinking about anything as he flew through the air. The only thing on his mind was the target. A place unprotected by dense layers of hormone-enhanced muscle. When the moment of truth came, he combined his forward speed with a front snap-kick.

The blow caught the authoress between the eyes, snapping her head back and into the edge of the steel door frame. The sole of his Italian loafer made solid contact with the front edge of her brainpan. And his follow-through caught the head again as it bounced off the unyielding metal. Which caused yet another impact to the back of the head. Remo's first double-strike broke the animal brain loose from its moorings, while the second turned it into so much mush.

As Remo dropped to the ground, so did his opponent, who fell across the threshold. Which gave the other beast room to operate.

With a roar, it burst through the doorway. And as it did, something light blue seemed to rise and flutter around its head and shoulders. A bright butterfly swooping and diving. But the sounds that accompanied the blur of movement were not the least bit springtime warm and fuzzy. They were the sounds of tremendous blows being landed.

Logs smashing against logs.

Tree limbs snapping.

The sumo beast lunged past Remo, staggered and fell. Only then did the picture come into focus.

Chiun stepped off the monster's neck and dusted off his hands. Though there was not a speck of blood on his blue robe, the beast's head was virtually pulped, reduced to little more than a mass of blood-soaked hair, the skull shattered in a thousand places, like the shell of a hard-boiled egg.

"Now there are two less too many," the Master

said, as they stepped over the threshold and into the wrecked medical wing.

"Actually, there's three less too many," Remo told him. He nodded over at a huge hairy carcass that lay rolled up like an old shag carpet against the foot of the wall. It was what was left of one of the hormone users. The body had been torn inside out, and what had been removed now decorated the back side of the bank-vault door. Remo guessed it was over some kind of territorial dispute between beasts. "That one didn't make the cut," he said.

"Aieee!" Chiun exclaimed, hopping elegantly to one side of the overturned golf cart. "What have I stepped in?"

"'Who,'" Remo corrected. "Who have you stepped in. From what's left of the uniform, it looks like that particular heap once belonged to a nurse."

As they advanced down the corridor, walking over drifts of broken glass without making a sound, Remo could see evidence of the same decorators' hands at work everywhere he looked. Walls. Ceiling. Countertops. Floors. Decorators with an abiding passion for red. Nothing that had once been alive in the Family Fing medical wing was in one piece.

Even the pieces weren't in one piece.

"There are more," Chiun said, on point like an English setter. "And they are close...."

THE BEAST FORMERLY KNOWN as Norton Arthur Grape likewise froze, his dripping brown nose tipped up to sample the faint breeze coming from down the hall.

He smelled not-meat.

In his previous incarnation, he would have further defined the odor as fish, or fishy. Even when served up in a heavy cream-based sauce, he had found the stuff barely palatable and had partaken of it only on those rare occasions when concerns about health and obesity, or career, overcame his lust for well-marbled red meat. Even as a human being, Grape liked his foods hanging with fat he could actually see, and therefore sink his teeth into.

This unpleasant smell—stark, without savor, fat free—was coming from just outside the room in which he crouched. Behind him, in tatters beneath a hospital bed, was what was left of the media personality, cooking-and-decorating guru known as Moira Maillon. In the confines of the Family Fing experimental ward, she was also known as Test Subject One.

While a human being, Maillon had been the perennial Miss Bossy Boots, always telling people how to arrange their lives with her Seven Rules of Baking, of Wallpapering, of Carpet Cleaning, of Upholstery Fabric Selection, etc. As a hormone beast, she had brought some relic of her former control-freak personality along with her. She couldn't seem to leave the others' territories alone. She was always trying to mark inside the lines already drawn, to increase her own turf at the expense of her fellow test subjects. In the human world, such misdemeanors could be overlooked, but not in the medical wing of Family Fing.

For urinary crimes against the body politic, Grape had ripped her a new one.

And a new one was precisely what he intended to give whoever, whatever was creeping so quietly along his section of hallway. As he hunkered down, he caught hold of the end of his tail to keep it from swishing involuntarily and giving him away. He watched as the pair of frail figures moved past his doorway, probing deeper into the wing.

A smile twisted his moist, hair-fringed lips.

Not the capped, perfect smile that had been such an integral part of his network weatherman's song-and-dance act. All those high-priced white caps had been pushed out of his mouth as the shaved tooth stumps beneath them had started to grow. And grow and grow. The teeth that Grape now sported would have not been out of place on a mountain lion.

REMO AND CHIUN had proceeded about twenty more steps down the hall, when at the far end of the corridor, a large, dark figure appeared from a doorway. The figure let out a warbling yell and charged them.

Prepared though Remo was for what he had to face, it was still daunting to watch seven hundred pounds of enraged killer barreling at you, full tilt. The arm span of the thing could almost reach all the way across the width of the hall. As she bore down on them, she spread her arms to make sure they wouldn't get away.

When Chiun moved to the center of the corridor, Remo did the same. They stood shoulder to shoulder.

The beast was coming very fast. Too fast for her to stop or even change course more than a few degrees. And as she came, she snuffled and snorted, her eyes wide with glee. In a second, the thing that had once sung the lead in *Madam Butterfly* would have them.

At the same moment, Master and pupil lowered their heads and dived forward, under the straining fingertips of the onrushing creature. As they tucked and rolled to their feet, the beast tried to put on the brakes, skidded through the broken glass and crashed onto her face.

Okra managed to push up to her knees about the time Remo ran up her back. Before she could throw him off, Remo dropped a meaty forearm in front of her throat and, using the power of his wrists, squeezed shut the creature's airway.

Failing to toss him, the beast stood up and threw her back against the wall. Remo took the shock with knees braced against the creature's spine, and kept on squeezing. He endured two more jarring impacts. The third was noticeably less powerful. And on the fourth both he and the beast slid down the wall. Remo didn't let go until he could no longer feel a pulse in the beast's throat.

As he straightened up, behind him he heard a rush of heavy feet and a shrill cry of surprise, suddenly cut off. When he whirled, he saw yet another monster, but this one had caught Chiun from behind by the neck. The Master's face turned the color of a ripe pomegranate as the beast tried to tear off his venerable head.

Remo leaped forward, intending to come to Chiun's aid. But before he could enter the fray, the tide of battle changed.

The hairy arm that gripped the scrawny neck of the Master of Sinanju became the target for a flurry of too-fast-to-follow blows of fists and feet. Shattered in dozens of places, the arm instantly lost its strength and rigidity, and the hand released its grip on Chiun's neck.

The Master, deeply affronted by the very idea of being touched by such a creature, let alone being almost throttled to death by it, proceeded to break every bone in the beast's body, starting with the toes and working up. And only when this task had been satisfactorily completed did he serve up the killing stroke to the huge shambling thing that, in a former life, was known for putting the best face on a rotten weather forecast.

As Chiun stepped away from the body, he announced, "There are no more creatures here."

"Then it's time for us to find the head man," Remo said as he referred to his map.

As they started back down the corridor, they heard a sustained burst of autofire. It was coming from the other side of the building.

36

Fillmore and Farnham didn't hear the stealthy approach of Korb the Transcendent through the reception area, so when his loud snort came between the gap in the office doors, it made them both jump a mile. Neither father nor son had a moment of doubt whom that snort belonged to, or what it was meant to do.

It was meant to sniff them out.

They also knew what was certain to come next.

Before he had both hands firmly on the M-16, Fillmore pinned back the weapon's trigger. In his eagerness to protect himself, he also badly torqued the point of aim. Once the unintended slide across the desktop was started, the ravening burst of full-auto gunfire kept it moving.

Bullet holes appeared at chest height in the left-hand door and crawled farther and farther left, over the door frame, the paneled wall and the enormous oil painting of the Family Fing founder—a sprig of marjoram in one hand, a foaming test tube in the other. Great splintery rents cut through the front of the mahogany credenza, and choking clouds of cord-ite smoke filled the room.

Fillmore never did get the autorifle under control.

It stopped firing only when it ran out of ammunition.

And when it did that, when the earsplitting burst of gunshots ceased, only then did the elder Fing become aware of another noise.

"Yahh! Yahh!"

It was Farnham. Farnham hollering at the top of his lungs while he tried to hide his head under the legs of an armchair. Failing miserably at that, he sat on the floor, back to the wall, eyes squashed shut, covered his ears with both hands and resumed his bellowing.

That his oldest, and now only, son didn't have so much as a millimeter of spine to his name came as no surprise to Fillmore Fing. What he was witnessing, the stress reaction of a congenital idiot, he had seen too many times before. Farnham looked and dressed like a winner, and he could talk a blue streak if given half a chance—but underneath, the boy's game was all a bluff. And always had been. Of course, the village-idiot genes had come from Farnham's mother's side.

"Shut up!" Fillmore shouted, dumping the empty clip and taking a full one from his suit jacket.

Farnham paid his father no mind. The perpetual infant continued to bawl.

Fillmore cracked in the fresh magazine and jacked a live round into the chamber. "I'm not kidding," he said. "Shut up so I can tell whether I hit the damned thing or not!"

The last statement seemed to have a calming effect on the big-league pharmaceutical salesman. Farnham opened his eyes and bit down hard on his knuckle to keep from crying out.

Fillmore cocked his head in the direction of the door. "I don't hear anything. Do you?"

Farnham shook his head.

"I think I got him," Fillmore said. Then, with more conviction, "I'm sure I must've got him...."

At which point, seven hundred pounds of former computer billionaire came crashing through the bullet-ravaged doors.

The surprise of the sudden entry and the sheer, intimidating size of the creature that faced him gave Fillmore pause. The sights of his assault rifle wavered wide of the intended target.

For his part, Korb the Transcendent seemed torn, as well. There were two not-Korbs in the room. Which to pull apart first? His beady eyes shifted from Fillmore to Farnham, and back again.

Decisions, decisions.

Fillmore, meanwhile, had shouldered the M-16 and was drawing a careful bead on the center of the beast's hairy chest. The smell that Korb had brought into the room with him was enough to gag a maggot; it was making Fillmore's eyes tear.

Farnham blubbered softly on the floor, his eyes unblinking and huge as he took in the creature. He was biting his knuckle so hard he was making blood flow down over his wrist.

"Mr. Korb!" Fillmore cried, cheek to buttstock, his index finger carefully tightening down on the trigger. When he felt resistance to the squeeze, Fillmore held up. "Mr. Korb," he said, "do you know who I am? Can you understand me?"

Fing wasn't playing for time. He was playing for capital. It had occurred to him how grateful the richest man in the world might be if somehow he was saved from this hairy, bad-smelling fate worse than death.

The beast looked at Fillmore with narrowed eyes. He had no idea what the noise coming out of the not-Korb's mouth meant, but it irritated him a great deal.

"We may be able to find a cure," Fillmore told the creature. "If we had suitable funding, I'm sure we could do it. Why don't we work together on this? What do you say?"

Korb the Transcendent smelled the blood on Farnham's finger. Decision made. He darted away from the doorway in a blur.

Fillmore fired a 10-round burst into the reception area, through the space where the beast had been. When he turned to pick up the target again, the thing had hold of Farnham by the arm. Like a cat playing with a mouse, the former billionaire batted the Fing boy against the wall, and when he bounced back, batted him again.

Fillmore took aim, but then changed his mind. He didn't even know if bullets could kill the monster. What if they only made him madder? The prudent thing to do was to take advantage of the golden opportunity that had presented itself.

As the patriarch rounded the front of his desk, it looked like the beast was trying to make a hand puppet out of poor Farnham. Fillmore said nothing. While the creature was thoroughly engrossed, he just lowered his head and hurried out the door.

Korb the Transcendent was far too preoccupied with his new toy to notice that the other not-Korb had left the room. There were so many interesting things to make the toy do. After he tired of playing bouncy-ball, the beast gripped Farnham by the wrist and hurled him like a Frisbee across the room.

Whap! Against the far wall.

With a single bound, Korb the Transcendent crossed the room and retrieved his play toy, then it was Frisbee time again.

Whap went Farnham against the opposite wall.

It was a game that soon bored even a world-class drooler like Korb the Transcendent. There were only so many ways Farnham could go *whap!* And after those ways had been repeated a few dozen times, the beast decided he'd had enough.

With a stiffened claw finger, he poked the unmoving form on the floor. He wanted the toy to get up and run so he could chase it and then bat it down. Maybe even jump up and down on it a few times.

Nothing doing.

So the beast picked the toy up by one foot and gave it a hard shake. The Fing boy's pocket change, money clip and keys went skittering over the floor, but he remained limp as a rag.

If Farnham was *playing* dead, he deserved an Oscar.

Undeterred, Korb the Transcendent felt an urge to take the damned thing apart—not to see what made it tick, but so he could throw the parts around the room. To that end, he put both feet on the toy's chest, grabbed its head under the chin and started to pull.

HEARING THE TREMENDOUS commotion going on inside the private office of Fillmore Fing, Remo and Chiun paused outside the open doors.

The Master pointed through the doorway, then held his nose.

Remo got the picture.

On a silent three-count, they rushed the office entrance.

Inside, they found a monstrous beast beating on the top of a big desk with a man's leg. From the tassle loafer still on the foot, it looked to be a rightie. The rest of the man was scattered around the room, along with a good deal of pocket change.

The beast was having such a great time that he didn't seem to notice he had company. When he saw the newcomers staring at him, however, he stopped what he was doing at once.

"Do you want him or should I take him?" Remo asked, circling purposefully to the left.

The Master shrugged. "It makes no difference to me."

Korb the Transcendent watched both targets, measuring the distance for his leap.

"Okay, then you take him," Remo said.

The beast launched himself at Remo, stretching out full-length in a headfirst dive. Instinctively, Remo spun out of the way, and the beast hurtled on.

Hidden behind the suite's floor-to-ceiling curtain was a floor-to-ceiling window that overlooked the entire complex and grounds. It was an architectural feature that Korb the Transcendent would not have understood even if he'd known it was there. It came as quite a surprise to the seven-hundred-pound beast when he hit the curtain, then the big pane of glass, which shattered outward, allowing him to fall through the empty frame and out into space.

Howling all the way to the ground, the former computer billionaire dropped ten stories to his death.

When Remo and Chiun looked out the window,

they saw a small man in a very expensive suit running across the floodlit tarmac below. He was carrying an automatic rifle.

"That looks like the tongue sucker to me," Chiun said.

They watched as Fillmore Fing jumped the heaped bodies of his guards by the gate, climbed into one of the jeeps parked there and turned the key. The engine turned over but didn't catch.

Fing tried again.

Same result.

"Come on! Before he gets away!" Remo urged, as he sprinted for the door.

37

When Fillmore Fing arrived outside the building's main entrance, he was shocked not to see a jeep waiting there at the security post. For a blinding instant, he thought that all was lost. He could envision the murderous beasts his greed had spawned pursuing him as he raced on foot through the endless rice paddies. Without wheels, he didn't stand a chance.

When he stepped away from the building, he immediately saw the jeeps parked in front of the perimeter fence's main gate. He also saw the men scattered across the ground.

Lots of men.

Had the test subjects already broken loose from the wing? he thought.

Had they wiped out his entire security force?

Fillmore didn't trot over to the still forms because he was that curious to know the answer; he trotted over because that's where the jeeps where. Finding out who killed his men was a bonus, of sorts.

Unpleasant sorts.

Fillmore didn't have to be a medical examiner to

be able to tell how the guards had died. By gunshot. By multiple gunshots at extreme close range. Which pretty much eliminated the test subjects as the murderers. They couldn't tell one end of a gun from another.

As Fillmore moved gingerly through the sprawl of white-putteed corpses, the realization hit him. Just as he had feared, Jimmy Koch-Roche had led the American killers here, to Taiwan. The bodies of his security men were undeniable proof that the assassins were on the grounds, and most likely still alive.

Fing looked over his shoulder, back at the white high-rise monolith of holding tanks, storehouses and office blocks. He had no doubt that whoever had sent the killers here intended the destruction of not only the WHE research program, but of Family Fing Pharmaceuticals itself. And that included its CEO. After all, the assassins had hunted down and killed known users of the drug in the States; they hadn't seized the offending patches and given the users a lecture on substance abuse. Their agenda was annihilation, pure and simple.

Fillmore stepped over the last of the bodies, put the M-16 across the passenger seat and got behind the wheel of the nearest jeep. When he turned the key, the motor growled but didn't start. A cold chill passed down his spine.

This was not the place he was going to die, he

assured himself. When he tried the starter again, he got the same, negative result.

The problem was, he wasn't used to driving the damned thing. In desperation, he gave the gas pedal three hard pumps, then flattened it to the floorboards. When he cranked the starter, the engine caught with a roar.

Fillmore gunned the engine, then popped the clutch, jerking and bucking toward the open gate. He got through the gate and into second gear, winding the engine well into the red zone before shifting into third. The road ahead was black and bleak and straight, and his headlights swept across acres of soggy farmland.

He hadn't actually formulated a plan yet. His main concern was in putting as much distance as possible between himself and the Family Fing complex. He was less than a mile from the gate when something bright flashed in his rearview mirror. He looked up to see a pair of headlights.

And they were gaining on him.

For sure, the other driver wasn't Dewayne Korb.

Which only left the assassins.

Racking his brain, Fing realized that he couldn't let them catch him on the open road. He wouldn't stand a chance there. Not with a single M-16. His security men had had scads of autoweapons, which hadn't done them any good. He needed cover and a diversion, and there was only one place close at hand to get both.

Fillmore Fing swerved left, taking the company road that dead-ended in the wolverine farm.

CARLOS STERNOVSKY SAT in his dark trailer. He'd been sitting there for hours, unable to turn the lights on, unable to start packing his meager belongings. What he faced was nothing less than professional oblivion. He could never go back and work in the States. Not after what he'd done at Purblind. The slaughter of the lab animals and the theft of his research data would hang like an albatross around his neck forever. No institution, reputable or disreputable, would touch a researcher like him, a man who had proved himself a thief and a vandal of university property. He knew that at that very moment his name, picture and biography were circulating on the World Wide Web home page entitled "America's Most-Wanted Academic Criminals." As far as the scientific community was concerned, Carlos Sternovsky and his wolverine hormone extract were dead meat.

So, if he couldn't resume his life's work—which, despite recent setbacks, he still felt had promise— what could he do? Change his name and get a job at some agribusiness giant? Making food preservatives and flavorings? Stay overseas and find a place for himself in some offshore offshoot of one of the major chemical conglomerates? Designing a new, lemon-scented floor wax for the Third World? And when push came to shove, there was always the last resort: unguentology.

Sternovsky hung his head in his hands.

He was in this position when he heard the wild roar of a jeep approaching at high speed. Knuckling aside the wetness on his cheeks, Sternovsky rose to the trailer window and pulled back a corner of the sun-spotted curtain.

In the floodlights that ringed the little hilltop compound, he could see the jeep bouncing down the road. He was relieved to discover that there was a single occupant in the vehicle. His first thought had been that old Fing had sent some of his white-helmeted goons to turn him out. But no. The driver he recognized as Fing himself.

Fing in a major hurry.

The pharmaceutical tycoon drove the jeep past the trailer and brought it to a screeching stop down the slope, at the start of the rows of wolverine pens. Then he took an automatic rifle from the front of the vehicle, quickly lit up a cigar and hurried down one of the aisles between the cages.

Immediately, the wolverines started snarling, snapping and shaking their enclosures. They weren't used to people walking the grounds this early in the morning. And they weren't used to the smell of Fillmore, who never, ever came out for a visit.

Then Sternovsky saw the lights of the second jeep coming from the direction of the plant.

There were two men in this one. Two men that he had never set eyes on before. The driver pulled over the top of the hill and stopped the jeep behind Fillmore's. The pair of strangers, one quite small and dressed in a long blue robe, quickly got out of the vehicle and moved down the hill, after the elder Fing.

Seeing this, Sternovsky had a sudden premonition. If he remained in the trailer, if he remained on Taiwan, he knew that the two men he had just seen would hunt him down and kill him. The research biochemist fumbled in the dark, laying hands on his passport, his small cache of hard currency and three high-capacity data-storage cassettes. With these few possessions, he slipped out the door of the trailer.

In great loping strides, he closed the distance to the rearmost jeep. As he jumped behind the wheel and reached for the ignition key, he checked downslope to see if any of his visitors were coming after him. He saw nothing but rows of cages, and the only movement that registered was inside them.

He gunned the jeep and jammed it in reverse, backing his way up the hill. As he rolled over the crest beside his trailer, he thought he caught a glimpse of something between the aisles below. The glint of electric light on steel mesh.

But that was impossible unless someone was opening a cage door.

Sternovsky shifted into first, cut a hard, wheel-spinning turn and headed for parts unknown.

REMO AND CHIUN MOVED soundlessly down the elevated rows of wolverine cages. The animals on either side of them were restless. Something or someone had already stirred them up. Accordingly, the surrounding air was thick with musk spray. Lucky for Remo and Chiun, the beasts had already spent themselves, musk-wise.

"Smell the tobacco?" Chiun said softly. "He came this way. He will not escape us."

Behind them, the engine of one of the jeeps roared to life. They turned in time to see the vehicle reversing its way up the hill.

"Dammit!" Remo cursed. He started to run for the remaining jeep..

"No," Chiun said, catching him by the arm. "That is not the one we seek. It is not the tongue sucker. He is just ahead."

"You're sure?"

"He waits."

Remo moved out to take the point. In the cages on either side of him, the wolverines suddenly became very agitated. They growled and snapped, throwing themselves at the mesh in an attempt to get at him.

"Boy, am I glad they're all in there and we're out here," he said.

"They're not," Chiun countered. With a long-nailed finger, he pointed at the line of cages ahead. Hundreds of them, with their doors open.

Empty.

Down every aisle, it was the same story, as far as the eye could see. Nobody was home.

Something low and fast zipped behind Remo's back, disappearing under the cages to his right. And as it passed by, he felt a tug at the heel of his shoe. When he lifted his foot to check, he groaned. "Jesus, that little bastard took a chunk out of my loafer."

"Shh," Chiun hissed. "Listen."

Remo shut up. What he noticed first was the silence. The beasties were no longer raising Cain. If it hadn't been for a rustle of wind, it would have been almost too damned quiet.

It took a second or two for him to realize the rustle he heard wasn't wind, after all.

Instead, it was the sound of thousands of recently freed wolverines closing in for the kill.

FILLMORE FING FOUND it difficult not to laugh out loud as he released the last wolverine. With a growl, the creature launched itself out the cage door and shot off down the aisle.

Let the assassins deal with this, he thought, puffing on his cubano. The idea of the hired killers being torn apart by his vicious lab animals gave him such pleasure that he forgot for a moment about the suit those same beasts had ruined with their vile spray.

All he had to do now was work his way around the perimeter, get back in his jeep and drive away.

It sounded almost too easy.

Halfway to the jeep, he began to wonder why he wasn't hearing death screams from the assassins. The wolverines should have circled and attacked the killers en masse by now. He also began to wonder why he kept seeing dark, fast-moving shapes under the cages. Why were they dogging after him?

When one of the little devils scooted out and bit him on the ankle, Fillmore yelped and jumped in the air. He frantically swung the M-16 around and touched off a short burst in the direction the creature had fled.

Then he saw the red glitter of predator eyes beneath the cages, ahead, to the side, behind, and he knew he was surrounded, cut off from the jeep. In panic, he opened fire, emptying the magazine in a half circle around him.

The noise of the gunshots held the wolverines at bay. But only for a moment. Before the last echo died away, they were on him. The scrambling wave of fang and claw drove him to the ground, and there, in a frenzy of greed and gluttony, thousands of wolverines ripped him apart, fighting over the tastiest of the spoils.

FROM INSIDE the wolverine cage where he had taken refuge, Remo listened to the fading sounds of animals doing battle. Then, like a rising tide, down the aisle beside his cage, came wolverines. Tens, then hundreds, all scampering, leaping, deliriously happy to be free, eager to once again be on the hunt. The animals slipped past the farm's perimeter and disappeared, fanning out into the surrounding fields.

"Do you think it's over?" Remo said.

From his own cage, Chiun replied, "They are gone. We have nothing to fear. They will not be back."

The assassins opened the cage doors and climbed out of their temporary shelters.

Near the remaining jeep, they found what was left of Fillmore Fing—hardly more than a scrap of gory gray worsted fabric.

"The tongue sucker is no more," Chiun said. "Emperor Smith will be pleased."

"But there's still the tongue sucker's monument," Remo said, hooking a thumb back in the direction of the Family Fing Pharmaceutical complex.

"We must burn it to the ground," Chiun said.

"It's the least we can do," Remo agreed.

EPILOGUE

Dr. Harold W. Smith peeled back the edges of the green-and-silver plastic pouch, exposing the pale brown end of his midafternoon treat. The no-fat–no-calorie cranberry-maple granola bar was everything he wanted in a snack food. Dry as the Mohave desert, it had twice the dietary fiber of a ten-ounce bag of pitted prunes. The director of CURE nibbled at the top of the brittle bar without taking it out of its plastic pouch. He was concerned about crumbs marring the perfection of his desktop.

As he savored each granule of dried cranberry, the show he had been waiting for finally appeared on the Emerson's screen. The show in question was the weekend edition of "Peephole USA," a summary and general rehash of the week's most exciting stories. Lucky for Smith, the very first story was the one he was interested in.

"Well, Molly," said Jed the talking head, "we've got an update on our 'Look Who's Buffed!' story that ran earlier in the week. Remember Princess Pye with the new body to die for?"

"I sure do, Jed," Molly said. "But let's remind the viewers."

The video cut to pre-aired tape of the princess, WHE buffed, waving to the paparazzi outside a Big Apple nightspot.

"That was the princess then," Jed said, "and this is the princess now...."

At first, Smith couldn't interpret what he was seeing on the screen. There was too much of it and it was all the same color: white. Then something moved, and all the pieces fell into place. The picture was of a queen-size bed. Under a sheet on the bed was the largest person Smith had ever seen. A Mount Everest of flab. With a pair of tiny little arms set high on the opposing slopes. And at the summit, the equally tiny but unmistakable head of Princess Pye. While the video rolled, a uniformed assistant fed her Royal Highness trifle from a bucket with a silver trowel.

"In a related development," Molly went on, "the international rock star Skizzle, who was also featured in our 'Look Who's Buffed!' piece, was fatally injured last night when he fell through the stage at a sold-out concert in Montrose, New York. According to the concert promoter, the stage had been certified as strong enough to bear the full weight of a bull elephant."

Dr. Smith pushed back in his ergonomic chair. What he had just seen and heard had put to rest any lingering fears on his part about the remaining former users of the now extinct drug, WHE. He had been prepared, albeit reluctantly, to send the CURE assassins to track down the rest of the celebrities and bigwigs if they still presented a threat to the social order. It was a relief to know that his concerns were groundless, and that he could avoid such a time-consuming, costly proposition.

As it turned out, without fresh hormone patches the users' bodies quickly lost their inhuman accumulation of muscle, and with it, their homicidal urges. But all was not quite as before. The former drug takers continued to eat at the same prodigious rate as they had while on WHE, with entirely predictable, large-scale consequences.

Dr. Smith popped the last scrumptious shard of granola bar into his mouth. And after fully masticating it to a fine paste, raised a glass of his favorite beverage, lukewarm tap water, in a toast to himself.

"Mission accomplished," he said aloud, "and at no further expense!"

James Axler

OUTLANDERS™

SAVAGE SUN

A reference to ancient mysterious powers sends Kane, Brigid Baptiste and Grant to the wild hinterlands of Ireland, whose stone ruins may function as a gateway for the alien Archons.

But the Emerald Isle's blend of ancient magic and advanced technology, as wielded by a powerful woman, brings them to the very brink of oblivion.

Available December 1997,
wherever Gold Eagle books are sold.

Take
4 explosive books
plus a
mystery bonus
FREE

**A violent struggle for survival
in a post-holocaust world**

JAMES AXLER

DEATH
LANDS®

Watersleep

In the altered reality of the Deathlands, America's coastal waters
haven't escaped the ravages of the nukecaust, but the awesome
power of the oceans still rules there. It's a power that will let
Ryan Cawdor, first among post-holocaust survivors, ride the crest
of victory—or consign his woman to the raging depths.

Don't miss out on the action in these titles!